THIRD MAN BOOKS

MOON SONGS

THE SELECTED STORIES OF

CAROL EMSHWILLER

Edited by Matthew Cheney
Foreword by Kelly Link

"Emshwiller's readers know her to be a major fabulist, a marvelous magical realist, one of the strongest, most complex, most consistently feminist voices in fiction."
—URSULA K. LE GUIN

"Carol Emshwiller's imagination is fierce and funny, never mean. She creates people, situations, and combinations of words that make me read her sentences and paragraphs again and again for the sheer pleasure of reading."
—GRACE PALEY

"Carol Emshwiller's stories are wonder-filled, necessary, and beautifully crafted."
—SAMUEL R. DELANY

"I have always thought that Carol had the most inventive mind in science fiction. It is not possible to summarize her work as a whole nor describe it satisfactorily piece by piece, but it does all have a particularly tough kind of femininity that appeals to me very much. … Other writers can be funny one moment and heart-breaking the next, but Carol is routinely both at once and she makes it look effortless or accidental."
—KAREN JOY FOWLER

Published by
Third Man Books, LLC
623 7th Ave S
Nashville, Tennessee 37203

Art direction: Jordan Williams, Amin Qutteineh
Cover/book design: Amin Qutteineh

Cover image from Ed Emshwiller's 1970 short film "Carol"

ISBN: 979-89-89908-93-6

THIRD MAN BOOKS

thirdmanbooks.com

CONTENTS

FOREWORD

BY KELLY LINK

"It is important and salutary to speak of incomprehensible things," they said, and so we did till dawn.
—"The Start of the End of It All"

I first met Carol Emshwiller at a workshop on the campus of Bryn Mawr. There were other writers present, whom I knew from their fiction—Jonathan Lethem, Bruce Sterling, John Kessel, Maureen McHugh—but I had not yet read Carol's work, though in graduate school, a friend had said, "Have you ever read the novel *Carmen Dog*? I really think you ought to read it."

The workshop was housed in a very grand manor, much too elegant for a bunch of science fiction writers, though upstairs our sleeping quarters were bare-bed dormitory rooms. We ate fabulous meals prepared by writers like Gregory Frost and Maureen McHugh (why are so many science fiction writers marvelous cooks?) but after dinner it was mostly the women writers who did the dishes. There was croquet on the lawn, moderate drinking, lots of industry gossip, but mostly we talked about the unpublished stories we had each brought with us, a condition of attending.

I don't remember what story Carol brought that year (she may, in fact, have brought the start of her novel *The Mount*), but I do know that as soon as I got home I tracked down a copy of *Carmen Dog*, her comic masterpiece in which women begin turning into animals while animals become women—a dog named Pooch, upon finding herself a young human woman, sets out to fulfill her dream of becoming an opera singer.

And I remember the critique she gave to my story, that critique a story itself of how, when she had first begun to write short stories, an editor had said to her, "These are quite good, but they are too much like Donald Barthelme's stories."

Emshwiller had not, in fact, read any Barthelme, but after this conversation, she sat down with his work and then set out to deliberately write something quite different. And, of course, what she hoped I would take away was that my story was, perhaps, too Emshwillerian, and I should carve out another corner. And what I have always thought, once I began to read her work, was: if only! If only I knew how to do what Emshwiller does!

It was either the same year or the next that at the same workshop Emshwiller gave a galvanizing critique to another writer. When it was her turn, she said, emphatically, a little triumphantly, and with great passion, "I can't believe no one else here has pointed this out, but you have used the word 'penis' every time you ought to have used 'phallus' and 'phallus' every time you ought to have said 'penis.'"

Later on, when that critique session was over, it became clear no one else in the workshop understood what she meant by this, but I have never forgotten it.

In person, Carol Emshwiller was lively; lovely; somewhat

birdlike. She had a habit of cocking her head to one side while she listened to someone speak. She wore extraordinarily thick-lensed glasses, which gave her an owlish aspect. She had a remarkable laugh and she laughed easily. Well into her eighties, she walked up and down the dozen flights to her New York apartment near Union Square rather than take the elevator. She carried a walking cane, usually wore a backpack and sensible shoes, and at all times gave the impression she was setting off, well prepared, on some kind of marvelous but possibly fearsome adventure. She spent part of each year in the Sierra mountains of California after the death of her husband, the artist Emsh, and much of her fiction draws strongly on place, on wildness and wilderness, on the spaces where the human and the inhuman encounter each other, though I only ever saw her in cities.

She had been a model for many of Emsh's pulp magazine covers—I still remember a particular reference photo of Carol, wide eyed, beautiful in the manner of a Rockwell Kent pen and ink illustration, dressed in a kind of singlet. She's standing on a sofa in a kind of martial pose, wielding a mop, the mop no doubt to be translated into a ray gun or something like that. I hold this in conjunction with a story she told, many times, about how as a mother she would sometimes climb into a play-crib with her typewriter so that she could write, for a space, out of the reach of her young children.

Sometimes, looking at collections of *The Magazine of Fantasy and Science Fiction*, I take in the covers and think "Here's Carol. And here's Carol, too!" How many people have ever been both the subject of an illustrative cover of a magazine (not themselves at all but rather translated into something quite improbable) and inside the magazine, too (as the author of a story)?

When my husband and I founded Small Beer Press, we began with my own debut collection, *Stranger Things Happen*, and *Meet Me in the Moon Room*, a collection by the writer Ray Vukcevich. When these first two books found some success, I asked Carol if she had enough material for a collection. She did, and she had the novel *The Mount* as well, and *The Mount* and *Report to the Men's Club* became the second year of Small Beer's publishing work. At the same time, we were moving from Brooklyn to Northampton, Massachusetts, in part so we would have more space in which to run a small press. I drove back down, however, on several occasions, in order to meet with Carol in a diner near her apartment so we could go over the commas in her manuscript. This was one of my first and most useful lesson as an editor: Carol detested being copy-edited, and would call us, outraged, over queries in the manuscript, all of them punctuation related. I would then drive down and we would sit in the diner together, going over every single comma. In person, she was cheerfully combative and seemed to enjoy the process a great deal, while on the phone, on the subject of commas—of all things—I found her ferocious and, frankly, terrifying. But the process of editing is never the same, writer to writer, and Carol taught me that to be a good editor I needed to discover the method which a particular writer would find most helpful.

In the end all of us were happy, including, I believe, our long-suffering copyeditor. And I still find it incredible that Ray and Carol—Carol Emshwiller!—were willing to take a chance with Small Beer. Carol's publishing career is virtually a tour of small presses. *Joy in Our Cause* was published in 1974 by Harper & Row—after that her books were published by Mercury House, The Women's Press, Coffee House, Small Beer, and Tachyon. We published, later on, a new edition of *Carmen Dog*, using a scanner to capture the text of the novel and it seems worth mentioning that we then discovered that the scanner had, through some interaction of device and font, somehow turned every "he said" to "lied."

Back to punctuation—this may seem like a small thing, but I have always been fascinated by Carol's use of commas, m-dashes, exclamation points, and especially ellipses. Often her stories are first person, present tense, and her use of ellipses works as a kind of translation of the thought processes of the busy, investigative perspective of her protagonists. There's a kind of exuberance to the point of view she often chooses: willful, trusting, sometimes fumbling, curious and easily spooked. Punctuation in an Emshwiller story feels like choreography marks: there's a lively, vigorous almost visual quality of movement, whether it's intellectual, emotional, or anchored in the body. But then, the intellect and the emotions are, of course, anchored in the body. Carol, more than any writer, seemed able to convey that.

She wrote about men—she said, often, that what nobody understood was that she adored men—and women, she wrote swooningly, achingly, about love and loneliness, she wrote about children and sasquatch and sea dwellers. She wrote about predators and prey, and the complex dynamics inherent in being human, which is to belong to both categories. Her alien invasion stories are comic masterpieces, sympathetic to both invaders and humans. She made the monstrous both ridiculous and sublime. She wrote, more often as she grew older, about war: she'd been a Red Cross volunteer in World War II (perhaps an ambulance driver?), and her war stories are often about the periphery: about the confusion and aftermath and unintended effects of large actions on the small and the powerless.

Her writing is ebullient, clear-eyed, her premises often startling or absurd, but treated with utmost seriousness, which I suppose is the only way to approach the absurd. And while her narrative territory may overlap, yes, with Barthelme, it has a great deal in common with Grace Paley's short stories, too. She knew Paley—it pleases me a great deal to know these two great chroniclers of that absurd creature, the human, both found joy as well as tragedy, and dealt with both conditions so briskly.

I can't think of a writer so intertwined with the history of fantasy and science fiction— married to the artist and film-maker Emsh, a cover model many times over for the pulps, published in *Dangerous Visions* and most of the notable magazines, large and small, writer of the novel (*Carmen Dog*) that inspired Karen Joy Fowler and Pat Murphy to start the Tiptree Award (now the Otherwise Award), teacher at many workshops, friend of writers like Le Guin. (When we asked Le Guin if she would blurb Carol's novel, she wrote back, "I can't! Because I've just asked Carol if she will blurb me!)

Her writing career spanned from the fifties through the first decade of this century. When we published *Report to the Men's Club*, we said over and over again that she was "a writer's writer"—someone whose name perhaps you, a reader browsing in a bookstore, might not know. But it was more than likely that the writers whose name you do know—the writers you loved—knew Carol's work and adored it. The problem was always that her vision was so singular, so peculiarly wonderful, that publishing never quite knew how to reach the audience she ought to have had. She remains a discovery, the center of a cult of writers and readers who fell under her spell and have stayed there ever since.

Rereading her now, her work still feels brand new, inventive and rigorous, experimental and slapstick and astonishing. Her novels, too, remain marvelously fresh. If this is your first experience with Emshwiller's work, I envy you more than I can say. And I hope that you will pick up her novels, too: *Ledoyt*, a Western, which belongs in the same camp as *True Grit*, is a particular favorite, as is *Carmen Dog*, but really, you can't go wrong with Emshwiller.

When I sat down to write this, I pulled my Emshwiller collections off the shelf in order to reread them. In my battered paperback copy of *The Start of the End of It All*, with its ridiculous Renee Flower illustration, looking straight out of the late 80s with its wavy, excitable lines, bright colors, rounded cat, leaping fish, and smiling coffee pot, I turned to the title page where Carol had signed it. She wrote, "Dear Kelly, Well, just love—isn't that good enough. Carol Emshwiller." And so I'm ending this with love: the enduring love I have for these stories, the love I have, still, for Carol, and with love to Matt and Third Man for bringing out this new selection of stories— and, finally, much love to you the reader, holding this book in your hands. I hope you love it, too.

EDITOR'S PREFACE

BY MATTHEW CHENEY

MOON SONGS GATHERS SOME OF THE BEST SHORT STORIES of Carol Emshwiller together in one book, providing, for the first time, a selection from her entire body of work. In selecting stories, I have not sought to be comprehensive (for that, we have the two volumes of *Collected Stories* published by Nonstop Press) but rather to offer readers a sample of excellent short fiction from across the whole length of a career that began with "Built for Pleasure" in the *Long Island Suburban* in November 1954 and ended, just about 150 stories later, with "All I Know of Freedom" in the anthology *After*, released in October 2012.

The challenge for this book was how to represent such a rich oeuvre in only a few stories. I began the selection with the stories that won or were nominated for major awards, a group worth listing on its own:

- Pushcart Prize: "Yukon"
- Nebula Award: "Creature" (winner), "I Live with You and You Don't Know It" (winner), "Grandma" (nominee)
- James Tiptree, Jr. Memorial Award short list: "All of Us Can Almost…", "Boys"
- *Asimov's Science Fiction* Readers' Award: "The Lovely Ugly" (1st place), "The Bird Painter in a Time of War" (3rd place)

Next, I looked for additional stories reprinted in anthologies of note, such as *SF: The Best of the Best* (ed. Judith Merril), *The Best of Orbit* (ed. Damon Knight), *The Norton Book of Science Fiction* (ed. Ursula K. Le Guin & Brian Attebery), *The Big Book of Science Fiction* (ed. Ann & Jeff VanderMeer), and *The Future Is Female* (ed. Lisa Yaszek): "Day at the Beach", "Pelt", "Sex and/or Mr. Morrison", "Al", "The Start of the End of It All", "Moon Songs".

"Baby" had to be included, I thought, because Carol Emshwiller frequently spoke of it as the story in which she found her voice. Additionally, ending the book with the last Emshwiller story to be published seemed right (particularly so given that story's mix of sweetness and sadness at the end of the world). Finally, I made a list of stories recommended by friends and acquaintances as well as personal favorites that I would miss if they weren't here ("If Not Forever, When?", "Desert Child").

Some favorites did get cut. It was inevitable. This book could be twice the length and still be filled with gems. From the beginning, however, we did not want this to be an intimidatingly big book — though ultimately it exceeded my original plan for its size … because how could I leave any of these stories out?

Stories from the twenty-first century fill just over half the length of this book. Carol Emshwiller was an excellent writer from the beginning (as "Baby", "Pelt," and "Day at the Beach" prove), but she had an extraordinary late career flowering. The second volume of the *Collected Stories* fills over 600 dense pages almost exclusively with stories published between 2002 and 2012. Nonetheless, another editor might have chosen more stories from Emshwiller's 1960s and '70s avant-garde style.

She herself was mostly dismissive of these stories, few of them have ever been reprinted, none won awards, and while they were important to her development as a writer, they seem to me more products of the literary taste of their time than work that speaks across the eras.

The organization of *Moon Songs* is primarily associational rather than chronological. Readers who want to get some sense of Emshwiller's growth and change as a writer can consult the publication history for dates of first publication. Readers who like to read a story collection in order can do so with, I hope, pleasure, as I have put stories together that seem to me to speak well alongside each other, exploring similar themes and settings in different ways. But this is also a Greatest Hits collection, and you won't go wrong just picking a story randomly and reading it. Every reader will have particular favorites here, but I hope you agree that each of these stories is in some way or another impressive, affecting, and surprising.

The texts are based on those in collections from *Joy in Our Cause* (1974) to the 2011 double collection from PS Publishing *In the Time of War and Other Stories of Conflict / Master of the Road to Nowhere and Other Tales of the Fantastic*. These were books Emshwiller herself had at least some input into proofreading. For uncollected stories, I used the first publication and/or first book publication. For every story, I was able to compare multiple texts, including some of Carol Emshwiller's own computer files. In the frequent case of discrepancies in punctuation and the less frequent case of discrepancies in words or sentences, I privileged Emshwiller's own collections over other publications. Her punctuation could be nonstandard, especially with her frequent use of three or four dots/

periods, and I have not attempted to standardize her most distinctive stylistic features any more than I would try to standardize Emily Dickinson's dashes. Carol Emshwiller's style and punctuation privileged rhythm and surprise over standard rules of usage, so you will find throughout this book passages that another writer would have put more commas or hyphens in, or phrases that require us to slow down and consider them in the way we might a phrase from Gertrude Stein. I learned long ago that often it is best to approach Carol Emshwiller's writing as a species of poetry.

I am among a group of writers who started publishing in the first years of this century and who would proudly admit we are, in the words of Karen Joy Fowler in a 2011 essay for *Strange Horizons*, Emshwillerians. When I was a young teenager, I got hold of a copy of Harlan Ellison's anthology *Dangerous Visions*, where "Sex and/or Mr. Morrison" first appeared, and I remember being struck and puzzled by Ellison's characterization of Emshwiller as "the first writer I ever encountered who said she wrote to please herself whom I believed." I wondered what this meant. I read the story and did not understand it very well. I decided to strive to become the kind of reader who might be able to understand better both that story and what it meant to be a writer who sought to please herself first. A couple years later, I bought a paperback of *The Start of the End of It All* at the legendary Avenue Victor Hugo bookstore in Boston. The title story reconfigured my entire sense of what a short story might be and do. Later, I met Carol Emshwiller a few times, and had the honor of interviewing her at a bookstore event for her 90th birthday in Brooklyn. She was always sharp, smart, funny, and beguiling — just like her stories.

In describing the Emshwillerians, Karen Joy Fowler said, "She made me see that the things you could do in and with stories were more varied and vaster than I'd thought. She made me want to work at the outermost limits of my imagination rather than in the nearer spaces. She made me worry less about the scaffolding that might or might not be holding me up." This is true for all of us who have been influenced by Carol Emshwiller's work. We do not write like her, because nobody who is not Carol Emshwiller could write like Carol Emshwiller, but we continue to be inspired by her. This book seeks to honor that inspiration and to extend it.

Welcome, Emshwillerians!

I wrote these stories because I'm a writer, and I like to write, and I'm always sitting down at the typewriter. I hardly ever start out with a preconceived idea of what I'm going to write about. I write to find out what I want to write. I like to surprise myself. I'd never write if I knew too much about what I was going to do. These stories (mostly) turned up as I was improvising. They grew out of first sentences and first paragraphs that looked promising. They seemed to come out of my fingers, not my mind. My mind, it has always seemed to me, isn't very clever — is too pedestrian. My fingers and my typewriter seem much smarter.

—CAROL EMSHWILLER, 1991

MOON SONGS

A TINY THING THAT SANG. NOTHING LIKE IT MENTIONED in any of my nature books, and I had many. At first no name we gave it stuck. Sometimes we called it Harriet, or Alice, or Jim. Names of kids at school. All ironies. More often we just called it Bug. This mere mite — well, not really that small, more the size of a bee — pulled itself up by its front legs, the back ones having been somehow bent. Or so it seemed to us. Perhaps it happened when we caught it.

How can such a tiny thing have such a voice? Clear. Ringing out. Echoing as though in the mountains or in some great resonating hall. Such a wonderful other-worldly sound. We felt it tingling along our backbones and on down into the soles of our feet.

My sister kept it in a cricket cage. Fed it lettuce, grains of rice, grapes, but never anything of milk or butter, "in order to keep down the phlegm," she said, even though we didn't know how it made its sounds. We asked ourselves that first day, "Is it by the wings? Is it the back legs? Is it, after all, the mouth?" We looked at it through a magnifying glass, but still we couldn't tell. Actually we didn't look at it long that time, for (then) we didn't like the look of it at all. There were hairs or barbels hanging down from its mouth and greenish fur at the corners of its eyes. We didn't mind the yellow fur on its body as that seemed cuddly and beelike to us. "Does it have a stinger?" my sister asked, but I couldn't say yes or no for sure, except that it hadn't stung us yet … me yet, for that first day I was the one that held it.

"I would suppose not," I told my sister. "Maybe it has its voice to keep it safe, and besides, if it had a stinger it would have used it by now." I did look carefully, though, but could see no sign of one.

To make it sing you had to prick it with a pin. It would sing for ten or fifteen minutes and then would need another prick. We knew enough to be gentle. We wanted it to last a long time.

How we discovered the singing was by the pricking, actually. The thing lay as though dead after we first caught it and we wanted to know for sure was it or wasn't it, so we pricked it. One prick got a little motion. Two, and it sat up, struggling to pull its poor back legs under itself. Three, and it began to sing and we knew we had something startling and worthwhile — a little jewel — better than a jewel, a jewel that sang.

My sister insisted she had seen it first and that, therefore, it was hers alone. She always did like tiny things, so I supposed it was right that she should have it, but I saw it first, and I caught it, and it was my hand first held it for she was frightened of it … thought it ugly before she heard it sing. But she had always been able to convince me that what I knew was true, wasn't.

She was very beautiful and it was not just I who thought so. Heads turned. She had pale skin and dark eyes and looked at everything with great concentration. Her hair was black and hung out from her head in a sort of fan shape. She wore a beaded headband she'd made herself with threads and tiny beads.

We were in the same school, she, a full-blown woman about to graduate, and I in the ninth grade, still a boy … still in my chubby phase before I started to grow tall. I felt awkward and ugly. I *was* awkward and, if not exactly ugly, certainly not attractive. Her skin was utter purity, while I was beginning to get pimples. For that reason alone, I believed that everything she said was right and everything I said was wrong. It had to be so because of the pimples.

Beautiful as she was, my sister wasn't popular, yet popularity or something akin to it … something that looked like it, was what she wanted more than anything, and if that were impossible, then fame. She wanted to make a big splash in school. She wanted to sing, and dance, and act, but she had a small, reedy voice and, although graceful as she went about her life, she was awkward when on stage. Something came over her that made her like a puppet — a self-conscious stiffness. She was aware of this and she had gone from the desire to be on stage to the desire not to expose herself there because she knew how, as she said, ridiculous she looked — how, as she said, everyone would laugh at her, though I knew they wouldn't dare laugh at her any more than I dared. People were afraid of her just as I was. They called her "The Queen," and they joked that she had taken vows of chastity. They called me "Twinkie." Sometimes that was expanded to "Twinkle Toes," for no reason I could tell except that the words went together. I certainly wasn't light on my feet, though perhaps I did twinkle a bit. I was so anxious to please. I smiled and agreed with everyone as though they were all my sister and I always agreed with her. It was safer to do so. I don't remember when I first figured that out. It was as though I'd always known it as soon as I began to realize anything at all.

"I wish it would have beginnings and ends to its singing instead of being all middles, middles, middles," my sister said and she tried hard to teach it to have them. Once she left it all day with the radio tuned to a rock and roll station while she was at school. It was so exhausted — even we could tell — by the end of the day that she didn't do anything like that again. Besides, it had learned nothing. It still began in the middle and ended in the middle, almost as though it sang to itself continuously and only switched to a louder mode when it was pricked and then, when let alone again, lapsed back into its silent music.

I wouldn't have known the first time my sister took the mite to school, had I not sat near her in the cafeteria. She never wanted me to get close to her at school and I never particularly wanted to. Her twelfth graders were nothing like my ninth graders. She and I never nodded to each other in the halls though she always flashed me a look. I wasn't sure if it was a greeting or warning.

But this time I sat fairly close to her at lunch and I noticed she was wearing the antique pearl hat pin we'd found in the attic. She had it pinned to her collar, which was also antique yellowed lace, as though we'd found that in the attic, too. She could laugh a tense, self-conscious wide-mouthed laugh. (She was never relaxed, not even with me. Probably not even with herself, though, now that I think about it. Sometimes when we lay back, she on her bed and I in her chair, and listened to the mite sing ... sometimes then she was, I'm sure, relaxed.) She was laughing that laugh then, which was why I looked at her more closely than I usually allowed myself to do when in school. I was wondering what had brought on that great, white-toothed derision, when I saw the hat pin and knew what it was for, and then I saw the tiny thread attached to her earring. No, actually attached to her earlobe along with the earring, right through the hole of her pierced ear, and I saw a little flash of yellow in the shadow under her hair, and I thought, no, our mite (for I still thought of it as "ours" though it seemed hers now), our mite should stay safely at home and it should be a secret. Anything might happen to it (or her) here. There were boys who would rip it right out of her ear if they knew what it could do, or perhaps even if they didn't know. And the hat pin made it clear that she was thinking of making it sing. I wondered what would happen if she did.

Also I worried that it wouldn't be easy for her to control her pricking there by her ear. She'd have to hold the mite in one hand and try to feel where it was and prick it with the other, and she couldn't be sure where she would be pricking it — in the eye for all she knew.

I wanted to object, but instead, when we were home again and alone, to let her know I knew, I asked her if she was hearing it sing to her all through school? If, tethered that close to her ear, she could hear its continuous song, but she said, no, that sometimes she heard a slight buzzing, and she wasn't even sure it came from it. It was more like a ringing in her ear. Still, she said, she did like the bug being there, close by. It made her feel more comfortable in school than she'd ever felt before. "It's my real friend," she said.

"What about if it stings? What if it *does* have a stinger? We don't know for sure it doesn't."

"It would have stung already, wouldn't it? Why would it wait? *I'd* have stung if *I* had a stinger."

And I thought, she's right. It hadn't been so well treated that it wouldn't have thought to sting if it could have.

So we lay back then and listened to it. We could feel the throbbing of its song down along our bodies. We shut our eyes and we saw pictures … landscapes where we floated or flew as though we were nothing but a pair of eyes. Sometimes everything was sunny and yellow and sometimes everything was foggy and a shiny kind of gray.

It was strange, she and the mite. More and more she'd had only male names for it: George, Teddy, Jerry — names of boys at school — but now Matt. Matt all the time though there was no Matt that I knew of. I began to feel that she was falling in love with it. We would sit together in her room and she'd let it out of the cage … let it hobble around on her desk, flutter its torn wings, scatter its fairy dust. She was no longer squeamish about studying it in the magnifying glass. She watched it often, though not when it sang. Then she and I would always lie back and shut our eyes to see the Visions.

And then she actually said it. "Oh, I love you, love you. I love you so much."

It had just sung and we were as though waking up from the music.

"Don't," I said. And I felt a different kind of shiver down my spine, not the vibrations of the song, but the beat of fear.

"What do you mean, don't. Don't tell *me* don't. You know nothing. Nothing of love and nothing of anything. You're too young, And what's so bad about having barbels? You don't even shave yet."

I was beneath contempt though I was her only companion — not counting the mite, of course. She had no friend but me and yet I was always beneath contempt. I did feel, though, that should I be in danger, she'd come to my aid … come to help me against whatever odds. She'd not hesitate.

She wore the mite to school every day after that first day. As far as I could tell she told no one, for if she'd told even one person it surely would have gotten back to me. Such things always did in our school. I began to relax. Why not take it to school if it gave her such pleasure to do so? It wasn't until I saw the list of finalists in the talent show that I understood what she was up to. She'd already used it in the tryouts. She (not she and her mite), *she* was listed as one of the seven finalists.

She was a sensation. She left her mouth open all the time as though in a sort of open-mouthed humming. She moved just as awkwardly as always, as though deciding to hold out one arm and then the other, alternating them, and deciding to smile now and then as she pretended to sing, but she looked beautiful anyway. The music made it so … made it flowing. Also she was dressed in gray (with yellow earrings and beads) as though to make herself a part of that landscape we often saw as we listened. I knew nobody would make fun of her, whisper about her afterward, or imitate her behind her back.

She was accompanied on the piano by the leader of the chorus, who was pretty good at improvising around what the mite was doing. I thought it was a good thing she had the accompaniment, for it made the music a little less strange and that seemed safer. There was less chance of the mite's being discovered.

Everybody sat back, just as the two of us always did, feeling the vibrations of it and no doubt seeing those landscapes. After ten or so minutes of it they clapped and shouted for more and my sister pricked the mite once again and pretended to sing for ten more minutes and then said that was all she could do. Afterward everybody crowded around and asked her how she had learned to do it. Of course she got first prize.

After that she didn't exactly have friends, but she had people who followed her around, asked her all sorts of questions about her singing, interviewed her for the school paper. Some people wanted her to teach them how to do it, but she told them she had a special kind of throat, something that would be considered a defect by most, but that she had learned to make use of it.

Because of her I became known at school, too. I became the singer's brother. I became the one with the knowledge of secrets, for they did sense a secret. There was something mysterious about us both. You could see it in their eyes. Even I, Twinkle Toes, became mysterious. Talented because close to talent.

After that she was asked to sing a lot though she always said she couldn't do it often. "Keep them wanting more," she told me, "and keep them guessing." Sometimes she would come down with a phony cold just when she'd said she would sing and the auditorium was already filled with people who'd come just to hear her.

But something stranger than love … more than love began to happen between my sister and the mite. Or, rather, the mite was the same, but my sister's relationship with it changed. That first performance she'd pricked it too hard. A whitish fluid had come out of it, dripped down one side and dried there, making the yellow fur matted … less attractive. She felt guilty about that and said so. "I'm such a butcher," she said, and she seemed to be trying to make up for it by finding special foods that it might like. She even brought it caviar, which it wouldn't touch. And she *wanted* punishment. Sometimes she would ask it to sting her. "Go ahead," she'd say. "I deserve it. And you have a right to do it and I don't care if you do, I'll love you just the same. Matt, Matt, Matt, Matty," she said, and it occurred to me perhaps it was a name she'd made out of mite. She had called it sometimes Mite, Mite, and now had made it clearly male with Matt. "My Matt," she said, "all mine." I was out of it completely except as watcher and listener. Its song had not suffered from the wounding. It just had more difficulty moving itself about. My sister had tried to wash the white stuff off, but that had only smeared it around even more, so that the mite was now an ugly, dull creature with, here and there, one or two yellow hairs that stuck out. "Sting me," my sister said, "bite me. I deserve it."

Now she would lie on her bed with her blouse pulled up and let it crawl on her stomach. It moved with difficulty, but it always moved, except now and then when it seemed to sit contentedly on her belly button. "I don't deserve you," she'd say. "I don't deserve one like you." And sometimes she'd say, "Take me. I'm yours," spread-eagled on her bed and laughing as though it were a joke, but it wasn't a joke. Sometimes she'd say, "You love me. Do you really? Don't you? Do you?" or, "Tell me what love is. Is it always small things that once could fly? Is it small things that sting?"

I sat there watching. She hardly seemed to notice me but I knew it was important that I be there. Even though beneath contempt, I was the observer she needed. I saw how she let it crawl up under her blouse or down her neck and inside her bra, how she giggled at its tickle or lay, serious, looking at the ceiling.

In the cricket cage she'd placed a velvet cushion and she'd hung the cage over her bed by a golden-yellow cord.

"I'm your only friend," she'd say. "I'm your keeper, I'm your jailer, I'm your everything, I'm your nothing," and then she'd carefully place the mite in its cage and I would know it was time for me to leave.

At school she became known as an artist with a great future and she walked around as though it were true, that she *was* an artist, that she could dress differently from anyone else, that she was privileged and perhaps a little mad. "I live for my art," she'd say, "and only for that." She stopped doing her homework and said it was because she practiced her music for hours every day.

I told her she might be found out. "Can you live with this secret forever?"

"Not to sing is to die," she said and it was as though she had forgotten it wasn't she who sang. "I will die," she said, "if I can't sing."

"What if *it* dies or stops singing? It might. It's not that healthy by the looks of it."

"Why are you asking this? Why do you want to hurt me?"

"I'm scared of what's happening."

"Love always scares people who don't know anything about it, and art does too. I'l always be this ... in the middle of the song in the middle of my life. In the middle. No end and no beginning. I had a dream of such a shining rain, such silver, such glow, as if I were on the moon, or I were a moon myself. Do you know what it's like to be a moon? I was a moon."

But I knew that she was frightened too ... of herself and of her love, and I thought that if I weren't there she'd not be this way, that I was the audience she played to, that without me she'd not believe in her drama. Without me there'd be no truth to it. That night … the night I thought of this, I stayed away from our evening of music. I went back to my nature books and, it was true, she did need me. She brought me back with a bribe of chocolate. I even think her sexual dreams, as she ignored me and stared at the ceiling, were of no pleasure to her without me there to be ignored. I did come back, but I wasn't sure how long I would keep doing it.

And she was, in her way, nice to me then. To show her gratefulness, she bought me a little book on bees. The next night she threw it at me while I sat, again, in her chair and she lay on her bed. "It's nothing," she said, "but *you* might like it."

"I do," I said, "I really do," because I knew she needed me to say it and I did like it.

"I'm going to give a program all my own," she told me then. "It's at school, but it's for everybody in town and they're charging for it and I'm to get a hundred dollars even though it's a benefit for band uniforms. It's already beginning and I haven't even tried. I just sat here and didn't do my homework and everything's beginning to come true just as I've always wanted it to."

I began to feel even more frightened thinking of her giving a whole program. We'd never had the mite sing more than about forty minutes at a time at the very most. "Well, I won't be there" I said. I had never challenged her directly before, but now I said, "And I won't let you do this, but if I can't stop you, I won't be there."

"Give me back that book," she said.

I was sorry to lose it, but I gave it back. I would be sorrier to lose her. It was odd, but the higher she went with this artist business, and the higher she got in her own estimation, the more she, herself, seemed to me like the mite: torn wings, broken legs, sick, matted fur …

"It's just like you," she said. "This is my first really big moment and you want to take my pleasure in it from me." But I knew that she knew it wasn't at all ike me. "You're jealous," she said, and I wondered, then, if that were true. I didn't think I was but how can you judge yourself?

The mite inched along her desk as we spoke and I had in mind that I should squash it right then. Couldn't she see the thing was in pain? And then I saw that clearly for the first time. It *was* in pain. Maybe the singing was all a pain song. I couldn't stand it any longer, but she must have seen something in my face for she jumped up and pushed me out the door before I hardly knew myself what I was about to do … pushed me out the door and locked it.

I thought about it but there was no way that I could see how to stop her. I could tell everybody about the mite, but would they believe me? And wouldn't they just go and have the concert anyway even if they knew it was the mite that sang? Maybe that would be an even greater draw. I had lost my chance to put the creature out of its misery. My sister wouldn't let me near it again. Besides, I wasn't sure if what she said wasn't true, that she'd die if she couldn't sing … if she couldn't, that is, be the artist she pretended to be.

She was going to call her program MOON SONGS. There would be two songs with a ten-minute intermission between them. I decided I would be there, but that she wouldn't know it. I would stand in a dark corner in the wings after she had already stepped on stage.

The concert began as usual, but this time I was changed and I could hear the pain. It *was* a pain song. Or perhaps the pain in the song had gotten worse so that I could finally understand it. I didn't see how my sister could bear it. I didn't see how anyone in the audience could bear it, and yet there they sat, eyes closed already, mouths open, heads tipped up like blind people. As I listened, standing there, I, too, tipped my head up and shut my eyes. The beauty of pain caught me up. Tears came to my eyes. They never had before, but now they did. I dreamed that once everything was sun, but now everything was moon. And then I forced my eyes to open. I was there to keep watch on things, not to get caught up in the song.

We … she never made it to the intermission. After a half hour, the song became more insistent. It was louder and higher pitched and I could see my sister vibrating as though from a vibrato in her own throat that, then, began to shake her whole body. Nobody else saw it. Though a few had their eyes open, they were looking at the ceiling. The song rose and rose and I knew I had to stop it. My sister sank to her knees. I don't think she pricked the mite at all any longer. I think it sang on of its own accord. I came out on the stage then and no one noticed. I wanted to kill the mite before it shook my sister to pieces, before it deafened her with its shrieking, but I saw that the string that held it to her earlobe was turned and led inside her ear. I pulled on it and the string came out with nothing tied to it. The mite was still inside. My sister was gasping and then she, too, began to make the same sound of pain. The song was coming from her own mouth. I saw the ululations of it in her throat. And I saw blood coming from her nose. Not a lot. Just one small trickle from the left nostril, the same side, where the mite had been tied to the left ear.

I slapped her hard, then, on both cheeks. I was yelling, but I don't think anybody heard me, least of all my sister. I shook her. I hit her. I dragged her from the stage into the wings and yet still the song went on and the people sat in their own dream, whatever it was. Certainly not the same dream we'd always seen before. It couldn't be with this awful sound. Then I hit my sister on the nose directly and the song faltered, became hesitant, though it was still coming from her own mouth and nowhere else. Her eyes flickered open. I saw that she saw me. "Let me go," she said. "Let *us* go. Let us both go." And the song became a sigh of a song. Suddenly no pain in it. I laid her down gently. The song sighed on, at peace with itself and then it stopped. Alive, then dead. With no transition to it … both of them, my sister and the mite, stopped in the middle.

I never told. I let them diagnose it as some kind of hemorrhage.

In many ways my life changed for the better after that. I lived for myself, or tried to, and, the year after, I became tall, and thin, and pale, and dark like my sister and nobody called me Twinkie ever again.

DAY AT THE BEACH

"IT'S SATURDAY," THE ABSOLUTELY HAIRLESS WOMAN SAID, and she pulled at her frayed, green kerchief to make sure it covered her head. "I sometimes forget to keep track of the days, but I marked three more off on the calendar because I think that's how many I forgot, so this *must* be Saturday."

Her name was Myra and she had neither eyebrows nor lashes nor even a faint, transparent down along her cheeks. Once she had had long black hair, but now, looking at her pink, bare face, one would guess she had been a redhead.

Her equally hairless husband, Ben, sprawled at the kitchen table waiting for breakfast. He wore red plaid Bermuda shorts, rather faded, and a T-shirt with a large hole under the arm. His skull curved above his staring eyes more naked-seeming than hers because he wore no kerchief or hat.

"We used to always go out on Saturdays," she said, and she put a bowl of oatmeal at the side of the table in front of a youth chair.

Then she put the biggest bowl between her husband's elbows.

"I have to mow the lawn this morning," he said. "All the more so if it's Saturday."

She went on as if she hadn't heard. "A day like today we'd go to the beach. I forget a lot of things, but I remember that."

"If I were you, I just wouldn't think about it." Ben's empty eyes finally focused on the youth chair and he turned then to the open window behind him and yelled, "Littleboy, Littleboy," making the sound run together all L's and Y. "Hey, it's breakfast, Boy," and under his breath he said, "He won't come."

"But I *do* think about it. I remember hot dogs and clam chowder and how cool it was days like this. I don't suppose I even have a bathing suit around anymore."

"It wouldn't be like it used to be."

"Oh, the sea's the same. That's one thing sure. I wonder if the boardwalk's still there."

"Hah," he said. "I don't have to see it to know it's all gone for firewood. It's been four winters now."

She sat down, put her elbows on the table and stared at her bowl. "Oatmeal," she said, putting in that one word everything she felt about the beach and wanting to go there.

"It's not that I don't want to do better for you," Ben said. He touched her arm with the tips of his fingers for just a moment. "I wish I could. And I wish I could have hung on to that corned beef hash last time, but it was heavy and I had to run and there was a fight on the train and I lost the sugar too. I wonder which bastard has it now."

"I know how hard you try, Ben. I do. It's just sometimes everything comes on you at once, especially when it's a Saturday like this. Having to get water way down the block and that only when there's electricity to run the pump, and this oatmeal; sometimes it's just once too often, and then, most of all, you commuting in all that danger to get food."

"I make out. I'm not the smallest one on that train."

"God, I think that every day. Thank God, I say to myself, or where would we be now. Dead of starvation that's where."

She watched him leaning low over his bowl, pushing his lips out and making a sucking sound. Even now she was still surprised to see how long and naked his skull arched, and she had an impulse, seeing it there so bare and ugly and thinking of the commuting, to cover it gently with her two hands, to cup it and make her hands do for his hair; but she only smoothed at her kerchief again to make sure it covered her own baldness.

"Is it living, though? Is it living, staying home all the time, hiding like, in this house? Maybe it's the rest of them, the dead ones, that are lucky. It's pretty sad when a person can't even go to the beach on a Saturday."

She was thinking the one thing she didn't want to do most of all was to hurt him. No, she told herself inside, sternly. Stop it right now. Be silent for once and eat, and, like Ben says, don't think; but she was caught up in it somehow and she said, "You know, Littleboy never did go to the beach yet, not even once, and it's only nine miles down," and she knew it would hurt him.

"Where is Littleboy?" he said and yelled again out the window. "He just roams."

"It isn't as if there were cars to worry about any more, and have you seen how fast he is and how he climbs so good for three and a half? Besides, what can you do when he gets up so early?"

He was finished eating now and he got up and dipped a cup of water from the large pan on the stove and drank it. "I'll take a look," he said. "He won't come when you call."

She began to eat finally, watching him out the kitchen

window and listening to him calling. Seeing him hunched forward and squinting because he had worn glasses before and his last pair had been broken a year ago. Not in a fight, because he was careful not to wear them commuting even then, when it wasn't quite so bad. It was Littleboy who had done it, climbed up and got them himself from the very top drawer, and he was a whole year younger. Next thing she knew they were on the floor, broken.

Ben disappeared out of range of the window and Littleboy came darting in as though he had been huddling by the door behind the arbor vitae all the time.

He was the opposite of his big, pink, and hairless parents, with thick and fine black hair growing low over his forehead and extending down the back of his neck so far that she always wondered if it ended where hair used to end before, or whether it grew too far down. He was thin and small for his age, but strong-looking and wiry with long arms and legs. He had a pale, olive skin, wide, blunt features and a wary stare, and he looked at her now, waiting to see what she would do.

She only sighed, lifted him and put him in his youth chair and kissed his firm, warm cheek, thinking, what beautiful hair, and wishing she knew how to cut it better so he would look neat.

"We don't have any more sugar," she said, "but I saved you some raisins," and she took down a box and sprinkled some on his cereal.

Then she went to the door and called, "He's here, Ben. He's here." And in a softer voice she said, "The pixy." She heard Ben answer with a whistle and she turned back to the kitchen to find Littleboy's oatmeal on the floor in a lopsided oval lump, and him, still looking at her with wise and wary brown eyes.

She knelt down first, and spooned most of it back into the bowl. Then she picked him up rather roughly, but there was gentleness to the roughness, too. She pulled at the elastic-topped jeans and gave him two hard, satisfying slaps on bare buttocks. "It isn't as if we had food to waste," she said, noticing the down that grew along his backbone and wondering if that was the way the three-year-olds had been before.

He made an *Aaa, Aaa,* sound, but didn't cry, and after that she picked him up and held him so that he nuzzled into her neck in the way she liked. "Aaa," he said again, more softly, and bit her just above the collar bone.

She dropped him down, letting him kind of slide with her arms still around him. It hurt and she could see there was a shallow, half-inch piece bitten right out. "He bit me again," she shouted, hearing Ben at the door. "He bit me. A real piece out even, and look, he has it in his mouth still!"

"God, what a … "

"Don't hurt him. I already slapped him good for the floor and three is a hard age." She pulled at Ben's arm. "It says so in the books. Three is hard, it says." But she remembered it really said that three was a beginning-to-be-cooperative age.

He let go and Littleboy ran out of the kitchen back toward the bedrooms.

She took a deep breath. "I've just got to get out of this house. I mean really away."

She sat down and let him wash the place and cross two bandaids over it. "Do you think we could go? Do you think we could go just one more time with a blanket and a picnic lunch? I've just got to do *something.*"

"All right. All right. You wear the wrench in your belt and I'll wear the hammer, and we'll risk taking the car."

● ◑ ○ ◐ ●

She spent twenty minutes looking for bathing suits and not finding them, and then she stopped because she knew it didn't really matter, there probably wouldn't be anyone there.

The picnic was simple enough. She gathered it together in five minutes, a precious can of tuna fish and hard, homemade biscuits baked the evening before when the electricity had come on for a while, and shriveled, worm-eaten apples, picked from neighboring trees and hoarded all winter in another house that had a cellar.

She heard Ben banging about in the garage, measuring out gas from his cache of cans, ten miles' worth to put in the car and ten miles' worth in a can to carry along and hide someplace for the trip back.

Now that he had decided they would go, her mind began to be full of what-ifs. Still, she thought, she would not change her mind. Surely once in four years was not too often to risk going to the beach. She had thought about it all last year too, and now she was going and she would enjoy it.

She gave Littleboy an apple to keep him busy and she packed the lunch in the basket, all the time pressing her lips tight together, and she said to herself that she was not going to think of any more what-ifs, and she was going to have a good time.

Ben had switched after the war from the big-finned Dodge to a small and rattly European car. They fitted into it cozily, the lunch in back with the army blanket and a pail and shovel for playing in the sand, and Littleboy in front on her lap, his hair brushing her cheek as he turned, looking out.

They started out on the empty road. "Remember how it was before on a weekend?" she said, and laughed. "Bumper to bumper, they called it. We didn't like it then."

A little way down they passed an old person on a bicycle, in jeans and a bright shirt with the tail out. They couldn't tell if it was a man or a woman, but the person smiled and they waved and called, "Aaa."

The sun was hot, but as they neared the beach there began to be a breeze and she could smell the sea. She began to feel as she had the very first time she had seen it. She had been born in Ohio and she was twelve before she had taken a trip and come out on the wide, flat, sunny sands and smelled this smell.

She held Littleboy tight though it made him squirm, and she leaned against Ben's shoulder. "Oh, its going to be fun!" she said. "Littleboy, you're going to see the sea. Look, darling, keep watching, and smell. It's delicious." And Littleboy squirmed until she let go again.

Then, at last, there was the sea, and it was exactly as it had always been, huge and sparkling and making a sound like ... no, *drowning out* the noises of wars. Like the black sky with stars, or the cold and stolid moon, it dwarfed even what had happened.

They passed the long, brick bathhouses, looking about as they always had, but the boardwalks between were gone, as Ben had said, not a stick left of them.

"Let's stop at the main bathhouse."

"No," Ben said. "We better keep away from those places. You can't tell who's in there. I'm going way down beyond."

She was glad, really, especially because at the last bathhouse she thought she saw a dark figure duck behind the wall.

They went down another mile or so, then drove the car off behind some stunted trees and bushes.

"Nothing's going to spoil this Saturday," she said, pulling out the picnic things, "just nothing. Come, Littleboy." She kicked off her shoes and started running for the beach, the basket bouncing against her knee.

Littleboy slipped out of his roomy sneakers easily and scampered after her. "You can take your clothes off," she told him. "There's nobody here at all."

When Ben came, later, after hiding the gas, she was settled, flat on the blanket in old red shorts and a halter, and still the same green kerchief, and Littleboy, brown and naked, splashed with his pail in the shallow water, the wetness bringing out the hairs along his back.

"Look," she said, "nobody as far as you can see and you can see so far. It gives you a different feeling from home. You know there are people here and there in the houses, but here, it's like we were the only ones, and here it doesn't even matter. Like Adam and Eve, we are, just you and me and our baby."

He lay on his stomach next to her. "Nice breeze," he said.

Shoulder to shoulder they watched the waves and the gulls and Littleboy and later they splashed in the surf and then ate the lunch and lay watching again, lazy, on their stomachs. And after a while she turned on her back to see his face. "With the sea it doesn't matter at all," she said and she put her arm across his shoulder. "And we're just part of everything, the wind and the earth and the sea too, my Adam."

"Eve," he said and smiled and kissed her and it was a longer kiss than they had meant. "Myra. Myra."

"There's nobody but us."

She sat up.

"I don't even know a doctor since Press Smith was killed by those robbing kids and I'd be scared."

"We'll find one. Besides, you didn't have any trouble. It's been so damn long." She pulled away from his arm. "And I love you. And Littleboy, he'll be way over four by the time we'd have another one."

She stood up and stretched and then looked down the beach and Ben put a hand around her ankle. She looked down the other way. "Somebody's coming," she said, and then he got up too.

Far down, walking in a business-like way on the hard, damp part of the sand, three men were coming toward them.

"You got your wrench?" Ben asked. "Put it just under the blanket and sit down by it, but keep your knees under you."

He put his T-shirt back on, leaving it hanging out, and he hooked the hammer under his belt in back, the top covered by the shirt. Then he stood and waited for them to come.

They were all three bald and shirtless. Two wore jeans cut off at the knees and thick belts, and the other had checked shorts and a red leather cap and a pistol stuck in his belt in the middle of the front at the buckle. He was older. The others looked like kids and they held back as they neared and let the older one come up alone. He was a small man, but looked tough. "You got gas," he said, a flat-voiced statement of fact.

"Just enough to get home."

"I don't mean right here. You got gas at home is what I mean."

Myra sat stiffly, her hand on the blanket on top of where the wrench was. Ben was a little in front of her and she could see his curving, forward-sloping shoulders and the lump of the hammer-head at the small of his back. If he stood up straight, she thought, and held his shoulders like they ought to be, he would look broad and even taller and he would show that little man, but the other had the pistol. Her eyes kept coming back to its shining black.

Ben took a step forward. "Don't move," the little man said. He shifted his weight to one leg, looking relaxed, and put his hand on his hip near the pistol. "Where you got the gas to get you home? Maybe we'll come with you and you might lend us a little of that gas you got there at your house. Where'd you hide the stuff to get you back, or I'll let my boys play a bit with your little one and you might not like it."

Littleboy. she saw, had edged down, away from them, and he crouched now, watching with his wide-eyed stare. She could see the tense, stringy muscles along his arms and legs and he reminded her of gibbons she had seen at the zoo long go. His poor little face looks old, she thought, too old for three years. Her fingers closed over the blanket-covered wrench. They'd better not hurt Littleboy.

She heard her husband say, "I don't know."

"Oh, Ben," she said, "oh, Ben."

The man made a motion and the two youths started out, but Littleboy had started first, she saw. She pulled at her wrench and then had to stop and fumble with the blanket, and it took a long time because she kept her eyes on Littleboy and the two others chasing.

She heard a shout and a grunt beside her. "Oh, Ben," she said again, and turned, but it was Ben on top attacking the other, and the small man was trying to use his pistol as a club but he had hold of the wrong end for that, and Ben had the hammer and he was much bigger.

He was finished in a minute. She watched, empty-eyed, the whole of it, holding the wrench in a white-knuckled hand in case he needed her.

Afterward, he moved from the body into a crouching run, hammer in one hand and pistol, by the barrel, in the other. "You stay here," he shouted back.

She looked at the sea a few minutes, and listened to it, but her own feelings seemed more important than the stoic sea now. She turned and followed, walking along the marks where the feet had swept at the soft sand.

Where the bushes began she saw him loping back. "What happened?"

"They ran off when they saw me after them with the other guy's gun. No bullets though. You'll have to help look now."

"He's lost!"

"He won't come when you call. We'll just have to look. He could be way out. I'll try that and you stay close and look here. The gas is buried under that bush there, if you need it."

"We've got to find him, Ben. He doesn't know his way home from here."

He came to her and kissed her and held her firmly across the shoulders with one arm. She could feel his muscles bunch into her neck as hard almost as the head of his hammer that pressed against her arm. She remembered a time four years ago when his embrace had been soft and comfortable. He had had hair then, but he had been quite fat, and now he was hard and bald, having gained something and lost something.

He turned and started off, but looked back and she smiled

and nodded to show him she felt better from his arm around her and the kiss.

I would die if anything happened and we would lose Littleboy, she thought, but mostly I would hate to lose Ben. Then the world would really be lost altogether, and everything would be ended.

She looked, calling in a whisper, knowing she had to peer under each bush and watch behind and ahead for scampering things. He's so small when he huddles into a ball and he can sit so still. Sometimes I wish there was another three-year-old around to judge him by. I forget so much about how it used to be, before. Sometimes I just wonder about him.

"Littleboy, Littleboy. Mommy wants you," she called softly. "Come. There's still time to play in the sand and there are apples left." She leaned forward, and her hand reached to touch the bushes.

Later the breeze began to cool and a few clouds gathered. She shivered in just her shorts and halter, but it was mostly an inner coldness. She felt she had circled, hunting, for well over an hour, but she had no watch, and at a time like this she wasn't sure of her judgment. Still, the sun seemed low. They should go home soon. She kept watching now, too, for silhouettes of people who might not be Ben or Littleboy, and she probed the bushes with her wrench with less care. Every now and then she went back to look at the blanket and the basket and the pail and shovel, lying alone and far from the water, and the body there, with the red leather cap beside it.

And then, when she came back another time to see if all the things were still there, undisturbed, she saw a tall, two-headed seeming monster walking briskly down the beach, and one head, bouncing directly over the other one, had hair and was Littleboy's.

The sunset was just beginning. The rosy glow deepened as they neared her and changed the colors of everything. The red plaid of Ben's shorts seemed more emphatic. The sand turned orangeish. She ran to meet them, laughing and splashing her feet in the shallow water, and she came up and held Ben tight around the waist and Littleboy said, "Aaa."

"We'll be home before dark," she said. "There's even time for one last splash."

They packed up finally while Littleboy circled the body by the blanket, touching it sometimes until Ben slapped him for it and he went off and sat down and made little cat sounds to himself.

He fell asleep in her lap on the way home, lying forward against her with his head at her neck the way she liked. The sunset was deep, with reds and purples.

She leaned against Ben. "The beach always makes you tired," she said. "I remember that from before too. I'll be able to sleep tonight." They drove silently along the wide empty parkway. The car had no lights, but that didn't matter. "We did have a good day after all," she said. "I feel renewed."

"Good," he said.

It was just dark as they drove up to the house. Ben stopped the car and they sat a moment and held hands before moving to get the things out.

"We had a good day," she said again. "And Littleboy saw the sea." She put her hand on the sleeping boy's hair, gently so as not to disturb him and then she yawned. "I wonder if it really *was* Saturday."

THE START OF THE END OF IT ALL

FIRST THE DISTANT SOUND OF LAUGHTER. I THOUGHT IT was laughter. Kind of chuckling … choking maybe … or spasms of some sort. Can't explain it. Scary laughter coming closer. Then they came in in a scary way, pale, with shiny raincoats and fogged glasses, sat down, and waited out the storm here. Asked only for warm water to sip. Crossed their legs with refined grace and watched late-night TV. They spoke of not wanting to end up in a museum … neither them, nor their talismans, nor their flags, their dripping flags. They looked so vulnerable and sad … chuckling, choking sad that I lost all fear of them. They left in the morning, most of them. All but three left. Klimp, their regional director, and two others stayed.

"It is important and salutary to speak of incomprehensible things," they said, and so we did till dawn. They also said that their love for this planet, "this splendid planet," knows no bounds and that they could take over with just a tiny smidgen of violence, especially as we had been softening up the people ourselves as though in preparation for them. I believed them. I saw their love for this place in their eyes.

"But am I" — and I asked them this directly — "am I, a woman, and a woman of should I say, a certain age, am I really to be included in the master plan?" They implied, yes, chuckling (choking), but then everyone has always tried to give me that impression (former husband especially) and it never was true before. It's nice, though, that they said they couldn't do it without me and others like me.

What they also say is, "As sun to earth, so kitchen is to house, and so house is to the rest of the world. Politics," they say, "begins at home, and most especially in the kitchen, place of warmth, chemistry, and changes, means toward ends. Grandiose plans cooked up here. A house," they say, "hardly need be more than a kitchen and a few good chairs." Where they come from that's the way it is. And I agree that, if somebody wanted to take over the earth, it's true: they could do worse than to do it from the kitchen.

They also say that it will be necessary to let the world lie fallow and recoup for fifteen years. That's about step number three of their plan. "But first," they say (step number one), it will be necessary to get rid of the cats."

● ◑ ○ ◐ ●

Klimp! His kind did not, absolutely not, descend from apelike creatures, but from higher beings. Sky folk. We can't understand that, he said. Their sex organs are, he told me, pure and unconnected to excretory organs in any way. Body hair in different patterns. None, and this is significant, under the arms, and, actually what's on their head really isn't hair either. Just looks like it. They're a manifestation in living form of a kind of purity not to be achieved by any of us except by artificial means. They also say that, because of what they are, they will do a lot better with this world than we do. Klimp promises me that and I believe him. They're simply crazy about this world. "It's a treasure," Klimp keeps saying.

I ask, "How much time is there, actually, till doomsday, or whatever you call it?"

No special name, though Restoration Day or (even better) Resurrection Day might serve. No special time either. ("Might take a lifetime. Might not.") They live like that but without confusion.

● ◑ ○ ◐ ●

But first, as they say, it is necessary to get rid of the cats, though I am trying to see both sides: (a) Klimp's and his friends' and (b) trying to come to terms with three hyperactive cats that I've had since the divorce. The white one is throwing up on the rug. Turns out to be a rubber band and a long piece of string.

● ◑ ○ ◐ ●

Of the three, Klimp is clearly mine. He likes to pass his cool hands … his always-cold hands through my hair, but if I try to sit on his lap to confirm our relationship, he can't bear that. We've known each other almost two weeks now, shuffled along in the park (I name the trees), the shady side of streets, examined the different kinds of grasses. (I never noticed how many kinds there were.) He looks all right from every angle but one, and he always wears his raincoat so we don't have any trouble.

"I accept," I say, when he asks me a few days later, anthropomorphizing as usual, and tired of falling in love with TV stars and newsmen or the equivalent. I put on my old wedding ring and start, then, to keep a record of the takeover, kitchen by kitchen by kitchen …

Klimp says, "Let's get in bed and see what happens."

Something does, but I won't say what.

I haven't seen any of them, even Klimp, totally naked, though a couple of times I saw him wearing nothing but a teacup.

(They read our sex manuals before beginning their takeover.)

But willing servants (women are) of almost anything that looks or feels like male or has a raspy voice, regardless of the real sex whatever that may be, or if sex at all. And sometimes one has to make do (we older women do, anyway) with the peculiar, the alien or the partly alien, the egocentric, the disgruntled, the dissipated … But also, and especially, willing servants of things that can fly, or things, rather, that may have descended from things that could fly once or things that could almost fly (though lots of things can *almost* fly). But I heard some woman say that someone told her that one had been seen actually vibrating himself into the sky, arched back, hands in pockets … had also, this person said, been seen throwing money off the Ambassador Bridge. The ultimate subversion.

Also I heard they may have already infiltrated the mayonnaise company. A great deal of harm can be done simply by loosening all the jar lids. Is this without violence! And when one of them comes up behind you on the street, grabs your arm with long, strong thumb and forefinger, quietly asking for money, and your watch, and promising not to hurt you … especially not to hurt you, then you give them. Afterward I hear they sometimes crumple the bills into their big, white pipes and smoke them on the spot. They flush the watches down toilets. This last I've seen myself.

But is all this without violence! Klimp takes the time to explain it to me. We're using the same word with two somewhat different meanings, as happens with people from different places. But then there's never any need to justify the already righteous. Sure of his own kindnesses, as look at him right now, Klimp, kiss to earlobe and one finger drawing tickly circles in the palm of my hand. He sees, he says, the Eastern Seaboard as it could be were it the kind of perfection that it should be. He says it will be splendid and these are means toward that end.

Random pats, now, in the region of the belly button. (His pats. My belly button.) Asks me if I ever saw a cat fly. It's important. "Not exactly," I say, "but I saw one fall six stories once and not get hurt, if that counts."

As we sit here, the white cat eats a twenty-dollar bill.

●　◓　○　◑　◐

I was divorced, as I mentioned. We were, all of us women who are in this thing with them, all divorced. DIVORCE. A tearing word. I was divorced in the abdomen and in the chest. In those days I sometimes telephoned just to hear "Hello." I was divorced at and against sunsets, hills, fall leaves, and, later on in the spring, I was divorced from spring. But now, suddenly I have not failed everything. None of us has failed. And we want nothing for ourselves. Never have. We want to do what's best for the planet. Sometimes lately, when the afternoon is perfect … a pale, humid day, the kind they like the most … cool … white sky … and Klimp or one of the others (it's hard to tell them apart sometimes, though Klimp usually wears the largest cap … yellow plastic cap) … when the one I think is Klimp is on the lawn chair figuring how to get rid of all the bees by too much spraying of fruit trees or how best to distribute guns to the quick-tempered or some such problem, then I think that life has turned perfect already, though they keep telling me that comes later … but perfect right now, at least as far as I'm concerned. I like it with the takeover only half begun. Doing the job, it's been said, is half the fun. To me it's all the fun. And I especially like the importance of the kitchen for things other than mere food. Yesterday, for instance, I destroyed (at the self-cleaning setting) a bushel of important medical records plus several reference works and dictionaries, also textbooks, and a bin of brand-new maps. When I see Klimp, then, on the lawn, or all three sometimes, and all three gauzy, pale blue flags unfurled, and they're chuckling, and whispering, and chok- ing together, I feel as though the kitchen itself, by its several motors, will take off into the air … hum itself into the sunset, riding smoothly on a warm updraft, all its engines turned to low. I want to tell them how I feel. "Perfect," I say. "Everything's perfect except for these three things: wet sand tracked into the vestibule, stepping on the tails of cats, and please don't look at me with such a steady, fishlike gaze, because when you do, I can't read the recipes you gave me for things that make people feel good, rot the brain, and cost a lot."

But I shouldn't have reminded them of the cats. They are saying again that I have to choose between the cats or them. They say their talismans are getting lost under the furniture, that some of their wafers have been found chewed on and spat out. They say I don't realize the politics of the situation and I suppose I don't. I never did pay much attention to politics. "You have to realize everything is political," they say, "even cats."

I'm thinking perhaps I'll take them to the state park outside of town. They'll do all right. Cats do. Get rid of them in some nice place I'd like to be in myself, by a river, near some hills … Leave them with full stomachs. Be up there and back by evening. Klimp will be pleased.

● ◑ ○ ◐ ●

But look what's coming true now! Dead cats … drowned cats washed up on the beaches. I saw the pictures on the news. Great flocks of cats, as though they had been caught at sea in a storm, or as though they had flown too far rom shore and fallen into the ocean from exhaustion. Perhaps I understand even less about politics than I thought.

I decide to please my cats with a big dish of fresh fish. (Klimp tonight turning up amplifiers in order to impair hearing, while the others are out pulling the hands off clocks.)

The house has a sort of air space above the attic. If the little vent were removed, a cat could live up there quite comfortably, climbing up and down by way of the roof of the garage and a tree near it. A cat could be fed secretly outside and might not be recognized as one who lived here. It isn't that I don't dedicate myself to Klimp and the others. I do, but, as for the cats, I also dedicate myself to them.

● ◑ ○ ◐ ●

Klimp and the others come back at dawn, flags furled, tired but happy. "Job's well done," they say. I fill the bathtub, boil water for them to dip their wafers in. They chuckle, pat me. (They're so demonstrative. Not at all like my husband used to be.) They move their hands in cryptic signals, or perhaps it's nervousness. They blink at each other. They even blink at me. I'm thinking this is pure joy. Must never end. And now I have the cats and them also. I love. I love. Luff … loove … loofe … they can't pronounce it, but they use the word all the time. Sometimes I wonder exactly what they mean by it, it comes so easily to their lips.

At least I know what *I* mean by "love," and I know I've gone from having nothing and nobody (I had the cats, of course, but I have people now) to having all the best things in life: love, and a kind of family and meaningful work to do … world-shaking work … All of us useless women, now part of a vast international kitchen network and I'm wondering if we can go even further. Get to be sort of a world-watching crew while the earth lies fallow. "Listen, what about us in all this?" I ask, my arm across Klimp's barrel chest. "We're no harm. We're all over childbearing age. What about if we watch over things for you during the time the earth rests up?"

He answers, "Is as does. Does as is." (If he really loves me, he'll do it.)

"Listen, we could see to it that no smart ape would start leveling out hills."

"What we need," he says, "are a lot of little, warm, wet places." He tells me he's glad the cats are no longer here. He says, "I know you love ('luff') me now," and wants me to eat a big pink wafer. I try to get out of it politely. Who knows what's in it? And the ones they always eat are white. But what has made me worthy of this honor, just that the cats are no longer in view?

"All right," I say, "but just one tiny bite." Tastes dry and chalky and sweet … too sweet. Klimp … but I see it's not Klimp this time … one of the others … urges another bite. "Where's Klimp?"

"I also love ('luff') you," he says and, "Time to find lots of little dark, wet places. We told you already."

I'm wondering what sort of misunderstanding is happening right now.

● ◑ ○ ◐ ●

I have a vision of a skyful of minnows … silver schools of minnows … the buzz of air … the tinkling … the glitter … *my* minnows flashing by. Why not? And then more and more, until the sky is bursting with them and I can't tell any more which are mine. Somewhere a group of thirty-six … more than that … eighty-four … I'm not sure. One hundred and eight? Yes, my group among the others. They, my own, swim back to me, then swirl up and away. Forever. And forever mine. Why not?

I wake to the sounds of sheep. I have a backyard full of them. Ewes, it turns out. They are contented. As I am. I watch the setting moon, eat the oranges and onions Klimp brings me, sip mint tea, feel slightly nauseous, get a call from a friend. Seems she's had sheep for a couple of weeks now. Took her cats up to the state park just as I'd thought of doing and had sheep the next day, though she wishes now she had put those cats in the attic as I've done, but she's wondering will I get away with it? She wants me to come over, secretly if I can. She says it's important. But there's a lot of work to be done here. Klimp is talking, even now, about important projects such as opening the wild animal cages at the zoo and the best way to drop water into mailboxes and how about digging potholes in the roads? How about handing out free cartons of cigarettes? He hangs up the phone for me and brings me another onion. I don't need any other friends.

She calls me again a few days later. She says she thinks she's pregnant, but we both know that can't be true. I say to see a doctor. It's probably a tumor. She says they don't want her to, that they drove her car away somewhere. She thinks they pushed it off the pier along with a lot of others. I say I thought they were doing just the opposite. Switching road signs and such to get people to drive around wasting gas. Anyway, she says, they won't let her out of the house. Well, I can't be bothered with the delusions of every old lady around. I have enough troubles of my own and I haven't been feeling so well lately either, tired all the time and a little sick. Irritable. Too irritable to talk to her.

The ewes in the backyard are all obviously pregnant. They swell up fast. The bitch dog next door seems pregnant, too, which is funny because I thought she was a spay. It makes you stop and think. I wonder, what if *I* wanted to go out? And is my old car still in the garage? They've been watching me all the time lately. I can't even go to the bathroom without one of them listening outside the door. I haven't been able to feed the cats. I used to hate it when they killed birds, but now I hope there are some winter birds around. I think I will put up a bird feeder I think spring is coming. I've lost track, but I'm sure we're well into March now. Klimp says, "I luff, I luff," and wants to rub my back, but I won't let him … not any more … or not right now. Why won't they all three go out at the same time as they used to?

What's wrong with me lately? Can't sleep … itch all over … angry at nothing … . They're not so bad, Klimp and the others. Actually better than most. Always squeeze the toothpaste from the bottom, leave the toilet seat down … they don't cut their toenails and leave them in little piles on the night table, use their own towels usually, listen to me when I talk. Why be so angry?

I must try harder. I will tell Klimp that he can rub my back later. I'll apologize for being angry and I'll try to do it in a nice way. Then I'll go into the bedroom, shut the door, brace it with a chair and be really alone for a while. Lie down and relax. I know I'll miss cooking up some important concoctions, but missed a lot of things lately.

● ◑ ○ ◐ ●

Next thing I know I wake up and it's dark outside. I have a terrible stomach ache as if a lot of gas is rolling around inside. I feel strange. I have to get out of here.

I can hear one of them moving outside my door. I hear him brush against it … a chitinous scraping. "Let me in. I loofe you." Then there's that kind of giggle. He can't help it, I know, but it's getting on my nerves. "Is as does," he says. "Now you see that." I put on my sneakers and grab my old sweatshirt.

"Just a minute, dear" — I try to say it sweetly — "I just woke up. I'll let you in in a minute. I need a cup of tea. I'd love it if you'd get one for me." (I really do need one, but I'm not going to wait around for it.) I open the window and step out on the garage roof, cross to the tree, and climb down. Not hard. I'm a chubby old woman, but I'm in pretty good shape. The cats follow me. All three.

As I trot by, I see all the ewes in the backyard lying down and panting. God! I have to get out of here. I run, holding my stomach. I know of an empty lot with an old Norway spruce tree that comes down to the ground all around. I think I can make that. I see cats all around me, more than just my own. Maybe six or eight. Maybe more. Hard to see because, and thank God, Klimp has broken all the streetlights. I cross vacant lots, tear through brambles, finally crawl under the spruce branches and lie down panting … panting. It feels right to pant. I saw my cat do that under similar circumstances.

I have them. I give birth to them, the little silvery ones squeaking … sparkling. I'll surprise Klimp with eighty-four … ninety-six together! But it wasn't Klimp and I. Suddenly I realize it. It was Klimp and that other. Through me. And all those ewes … fourteen ewes and one bitch dog times eighty-four or one hundred and eight. That's well over a thousand of them that I know about already.

My little ones cough and flutter, try to swim into the air, but only raise themselves an inch or so … hardly that. They smell of fish. They slither over one another as though looking for a stream. They are covered with a shiny, clear kind of slime. Do I love them or hate them?

So that's the way it is. As with us humans, it takes two, only I wasn't one of them. I might just as well have been a bitch or a ewe … better, in fact, to have been some dumb animal. "Lots of little warm, wet places!" It must have been a big night, that night. Some sacred sort of higher beings they turned out to be. That's not love … nor luff, nor loove. Whatever they mean by those words, this can't be it.

But look what all those hungry cats are doing. Eating up my minnows. I try to gather the little things up, but they're too slippery. I can't even get one. I try to push the cats away, but there are too many of them and they all seem very hungry. And then, suddenly, Klimp is there helping me, kicking out at the cats in a fury and gathering up minnows at the same time. For him it's easy. They stick to him wherever he touches them. He's up to his elbows in them. They cluster on his ankles like barnacles, but I'm afraid lots are eaten up already. And now he's kicking out at me. Hits me hard on the cheek and shoulder. Stamps on my hand.

"I'm confused," I say, getting up, thinking he can explain all this in a fatherly way, but now he stamps on my foot and knocks me down with his elbow. Then I see him give a kind of hop step, the standard dance way of getting from one foot to the other. He's going to lift. I don't know how I know, but I do. He has that look on his face, too, eyes half closed … ecstasy. I see it now — flying, or almost flying, is their ultimate orgasm … their true love (or loofe) … this *is* flying. Yes, he's up, but only inches, and struggling … pulling at my fingers. This is *not* flying.

"You call this flying!" I yell. "And you call this whole thing being a pure aerial being! I say, cloaca … cloaca, I say, is your only orifice." I have, by now, one leg hooked around his neck and both hands grabbing his elbow, and he's not really more than one foot off the ground at the very highest, if that, and struggling for every inch. "Cloaca! You and your 'luff'!" The slime and minnows are all over him. He seems dressed in them … sparkling like sequins. He's too slippery with them. I can't hang on. I slip off and drop lightly into the brambles.

Klimp slides away at a diagonal, right shoulder leading, and glides, luminous with slime, just off the ground. Disappears in a few seconds behind the trees. "Cloaca!" I shout after him. It's the worst I've ever said to anyone. "Filthy fish thing! Call that flying!"

● ◑ ○ ◐ ●

Everything is going wrong. It always does, I should know that by now. I'm thinking that my former husband slipped away in almost exactly the same way. He was slippery too, sneaked out first with younger women and then left me for one of them later on. I tried to grab at him the same way I grabbed at Klimp. Tried to hold him back. I even tried to change my ways to suit him. I know I've got faults. I talk too much. I worry about things that never happen (though they did finally happen, almost all of them, and *now* look).

I hobble back (with cats), too angry to feel the pain of my bruises. No sign of the ewes or the dog, but the backyard looks all silvery. No minnows left there, though, just slime. I have to admit it's lovely. Makes me feel romantic feelings for Klimp in spite of myself. I wonder if he saw it. They're so sensitive to beautiful things and they love glitter. I can see why.

The house is dark. I open the door cautiously. I let in all eight … no, nine … maybe ten cats. I call. No answer. I lock all the windows and the doors. I check under the beds and in the closets. Nobody. I go into the bathroom and lock that door too. Fill tub. Take off my clothes. Find two minnows stuck inside my sweatshirt. One is dead. The other very weak. I put him in the tub and he seems to revive a little. He has big eyes, four fins where legs and arms would be, a minnow's tail … actually big blue eyes … pale blue, like Klimp's. He looks at me with such pleading. He comes to the surface to breathe and squeaks now and then. I keep making reassuring sounds as if I were talking to the cats. Then I decide to get in the tub with him myself. Carefully, though. With me in the tub, the creature seems happier. Swims around making a kind of humming sound and blowing bubbles. Follows my hand. Lets me pick it up. I'm thinking it's a clear case of bonding, perhaps for both of us.

Now that I'm relaxing in the water, I'm feeling a lot better. And nothing like a helpless little blue-eyed creature of some sort to care for to bring brightness into life. The thing needs me. And so do all those cats.

I lie quietly, cats meowing outside the door, but I just lie here and Charles (Charles was my father's name) … Charles? Howard? Henry? He falls asleep in the shallows between my breasts. I don't dare move. The phone rings and there's the thunk of something knocked over by the cats. I don't move. I don't care.

●　◑　○　◐　●

So what about ecology? What about our favorite planet, Klimp's and mine? How best save it? And who for? Make it safe for this thing on my chest? (Charles Bird? Henry Fishman?) Quietly breathing. Blue eyes shut. And what about all those thousands of others? Department of fisheries? Department of lakes and streams? Gelatin factory? Or the damp basements of those housing developments built in former swamps?

● ◗ ○ ◑ ●

I blame myself. I really do. Perhaps if I'd been more understanding of their problems … accepted them as they are. Not criticized all that sand tracked in. And so what if they did step on the tails of cats? I've been so irritable these last few days. No wonder Klimp kicked out at me. If only I had controlled myself and thought about what they were going through. It was a crucial time for them too. But all I thought about was myself and my blowing-up stomach. Me, me, me! No wonder my former husband walked out. And now the same old pattern. Another breakup, another identity crisis. It shows I haven't learned a thing.

● ◑ ○ ◑ ●

I almost fall asleep lying here, but when the water begins to get cold we both wake up, Charles and I. I rig up a system, then, with the electric frying pan on the lowest setting and two inches of water on top of a piece of flannel. Put Charles … Henry? … inside, sprinkle in crumbs of wafer. Lid on. Vent open. Lock the whole business in my bedroom on top of the knick-knack shelves. Then I check out their room, Klimp's and the others'. It's a mess, wafers scattered around … several pink ones, bed not made. If they were, all three, men, I'd understand it, but that can't be. I wonder if they used servants where they come from … or slaves? Well, Charles will be brought up differently. Learn to pick up his underwear and help out around the house, cook something besides telephone books and such. I find a talisman under the bed. I shut my eyes, squeeze hard, wondering can I lift with it? Maybe, on the other hand, it's some sort of anchor to stop with or to be let down by. Something thrown out to keep from flying. I'll save it for Charles.

I sit down to rest with a cup of tea, two cats on my lap and one across my shoulders. All the cats seem fat and happy, and I really feel pretty happy too … considering.

The telephone rings again and this time I answer it. It's a love call. I think I recognize Klimp's voice, but he won't say if it's him and they do all sound a lot alike, sort of muffed and slurred. Anyway, he says he wants to do all those things with me, things, actually, he already did. I suppose this call is part of a new campaign. I don't think much of it and I tell him so. "How about breaking school windows and stealing library books?" I say. But whose side am I on now? "Listen," I say, "I know of a nice wet place devoid of cats. It's called the Love Canal and you'll love it. Lots of empty houses. And there's another place in New Jersey that I know of. Call me back and I'll have the exact address for you." I think he believes me. (Evidently they haven't read all the books about women.)

● ◑ ○ ◐ ●

Political appointees. I'll bet that's what they are. Makes a lot of sense. I could do as well myself. And did, actually. Who was it sent them out with spray-paint cans? Who told them how to cause static on TV? Who had thousands of stickers made up reading: NO DANGER, NONTOXIC, and GENERALLY REGARDED AS SAFE?

We can do all this by ourselves. Let's see: number 1, daycare-aquarium centers; number 2, separate cat-breeding facilities; number 3, the takeover proper; number 4, the lying fallow period. And we have time … plenty of time. Our numbers keep increasing, too, though slowly … the rejected, the divorced, the growing older, the left out … Maybe they've already started it. I can't be the only one thinking this way. Maybe they're out there just waiting for my call, kitchens all warmed up. I'll dial my old friend. "Include me in," I'll say.

Everything will be perfect, and I even have Charles. We don't need them. Bunch of bureaucrats. *That* wasn't flying.

YUKON

HE'S A DRAGON. HE'S A WOLF. HE'S CARIBOU. SHE TRIES TO please him. She tries to keep out of his way and, at the same time, tries to get him to notice her by doing little things for him when he's gone or asleep. She needs him for warmth so they can cuddle up and he can warm her. She's afraid to leave because that's all the warmth she has. But she's afraid to stay. Is it possible to rush away when you live this far north? These high valleys never get warm. Mountain water coming down from glaciers is bright turquoise.

He's always looking at the sky or the ground or the horizon, not at her. But bits of red wool is all she has to look good in and then she never was a popular girl. If had big fur boots and hat, then maybe make a move. Make a run for it.

As valley to mountain top … might as well be ship-to-shore, sending signals. How live that way. How love?

He's a rattlesnake, but no immediate threat (that she can tell). Comes home when he feels like it, bringing dead things to eat. Holds conventional views. Passes judgments on. Everything that needs to be said, he says, already said, and she thinks he's probably right, or almost. Make him chopped liver. Make him hasenpfeffer. Make him big mugs of glogg, but might not be home till three AM anyway. Wait up. And always those

Englemann spruce. A couple of hundred years old — even more — but still skinny. Nothing to them. She loves them, though what else is there to love? It's the only tree around.

He's a giant. He's a dwarf. She has to help him climb up onto his throne. For the love of the spruce trees, she nuzzles into his furry chest, thinking that to love him you have to love horses, spiders, and raw oysters, thinking how now she's going to have a baby. Should she tell him? She's already fairly big-with-child, but he hasn't noticed. She decides not to tell him. She decides, boy or girl, she will name it Englemann as though they were Mr. and Mrs. Spruce.

Their mansion is unfinished still. Only the vestibule built (but it's a big one, even as mansion vestibules go) and one tower (small) from which to view the mountains above the tops of trees. Both vestibule and tower are made out of the local rocks, so on the walls are the faint etchings of trilobites and prints of the leaves of ancient, ginkgo-like trees. In the fireplace they stand out clear, outline by the smoke. Once upon a time it was warm here, and covered with water. The land has shifted, quake by quake, away from some southern latitude and it's still going. North by northwest. Also rising straight up. On land such as this, it's easy to go astray.

And now she's going just a little bit crazy. She wants and wants. Stands at window as if caged. Plastic that's in front of the glass to keep the heat in, makes things fuzzy. Snow outside begins to look soft and warm. Just right. So she leaves. She's not so crazy she doesn't take cheese sandwiches, peanuts, raisins, carrots .... Also takes his big fur boots and hat and now she's out in those nice adolescent-looking spruce trees that are older … much, much older than they look. She hugs some (though not much to hug). Touches them as she goes by. Wants to soak up the stolid way they are and also wants them to know how she feels: that even though they're stunted because of their hardships, she loves them all the more for it. She stops to drink glacier milk along the way. She's following, at first, browse trails that go no special place. It's cold. She just goes on. Easy to go astray. Thinks: years of going astray … was always astray, so if now astray, it's no different from before.

Meanwhile he's home — just woke up and sitting by the fire she'd laid before she left, asking himself ultimate questions, or, rather, penultimate questions as, What about the influence of theory on action? What about negative ends versus positive means and vice versa? He doesn't notice she's gone, slipping around out there in his too-big-for-her boots. She had not meant to be going in a northerly direction. She had not meant to be climbing on up higher into the cold. She thought for a while she'd maybe creep back after he'd gone to sleep with no supper, but she's too far now for that. (He'll miss his boots before he'll miss her.) She was thinking: South and warm and down, down, into the lower valleys, but she's been going up because it's the hardest and she's always done whatever was the hardest. The spruce get older and smaller the higher she goes until there's — all at once — no more of them. Meanwhile he keeps putting on another log until the whole vestibule dances with the fire and he pulls off sweater after sweater, watches his giant shadow writhe along the walls, falls asleep in his chair.

If there had been flowers blooming up there on the mountains, she would have known the names of every single one. If birds had called out, she'd have known which birds and would have whistled back.

Since she'd started in the morning after a sleepless night (though all her nights have been sleepless for a long time. She can hardly remember the times when she used to sleep well) …. Since she'd started early she gets almost all the way to the top before its too dark to go on. She finds a kind of cairn built by summer climbers. There's a slit at the bottom big enough to slither into. She does. Sleeps, not well, but better than she's slept in a long time, dreaming: Loves me? Loves me not? And: Who (or what!) is number one in his heart? It's his boots, and his hat keeps her warm enough (or almost warm enough) all night, so in the morning she's (as usual) full of grateful love for him and wondering: Why hasn't he followed no matter how hard? Why hasn't he come for her by now with something nice and warm to drink? He's never done anything remotely like that, but still she wonders why he's not already there, maybe having climbed all night just for her.

She squirms out and, first thing, she sees she's almost to the top so goes on up. What she thought was five minutes' worth of climbing turns out to take a half an hour. At top she sits on fossils and looks out — little shivers of pleasure or of cold — eating raisins and soaking up comfort and courage from the view, this side, too: Englemann, Englemann, everywhere Englemann below her, first in the sheltered hollows and then, lower down, nothing but. Thinks: Nothing like them, and nothing like being up this high, and nothing like what it took to get this far, nothing like the cold, clear air. She even forgets she's pregnant.

Now, down in the big stone vestibule, he is shouting, "Bacon, bacon!" Searches what few crooks and crannies there are to search, groans and spits, hisses into the corner under the king-sized bed, makes his own black coffee, spends the morning writing out new rules while she walks the col, too exhilarated to feel fear of heights. One last bit of glacier still sits in the steep pocket below her. She can tell by the old blue ice showing where the pure white snow's been blown off. She follows the ridge above and then past, and then starts down, but she's being too courageous … too sure of herself now, falls, slides the whole bare slope till stopped … saved by one thin old Englemann, her knee twisted back behind. Hurts. Probably nothing broken though she's not sure. Waits, lying there clutching tree because of pain. She's looking straight up through the narrow, scraggly circle of branches to the sky that's clouding over, thinking: Tree, tree, *this* tree and sky. Ties her scarf tight around her leg. That helps. It's getting windier. Big black clouds off over next mountain. She must get lower and to some sheltered spot. Can't stop now. Gets up. Goes from tree to tree to tree (she's *depending* on them) steeply down. Thinks: If not for Englemann spruce to hang on to! … .

By late afternoon finds bear's cave still warm from that big body. She knows it's a bear's cave. She can smell it. She can see the footprints in the snow, people-like prints but wider, leading out. She needs the shelter now and the warmth of it. Can't go on. And she's more cold than scared. Also it's beginning to snow. She creeps in. Wedges herself among the tree roots along the left-hand side away from the more open part of the cave. She knows the bear will come back, but she thinks she already knows how to keep away from something big (or small) and dangerous. She falls asleep, a dreamless sleep, not so full of unanswered questions about love or the lack of it.

The bear comes back at three AM. She hears him sniffing

around outside and giving little warning growls. Also he's got the hiccups. Nothing here she hasn't heard already, and many times. She's only half awake. Before she realizes it she's told him she loves him. She's talking soft and low. He grunts, then hunkers on in, rolls to far side, back turned. (She thinks: As usual.) He lets her be. Snores. Storm goes on outside. Later (as usual) she moves close, snug against his back.

They sleep two days and nights, or so she guesses. When she wakes up later as he's leaving, she finds he's eaten all her cheese sandwiches, carrots, peanuts and raisins, and she thinks: As usual.

She hurries to the entrance of the cave and calls out to him before he goes. Her knee hurts and maybe she's a little feverish. She speaks without thinking. That's not her usual way, but he seems a little bit safer than her own male, even though he's the biggest and most masculine thing she's ever been this close to (dangerous, too). No doubt about it. She does like his looks, though: his hump, his shoulders, his yellow-brown fur .... Now he hangs his head low, almost to the snow, and looks back at her suspiciously, and it isn't as if she hasn't seen that same look a thousand times before. But what is there to lose? She talks to him of things she'd never dared to talk about before. "HOW can love last," she says, "if this goes on? How can love even begin? How can it go on and on, and we all," she says, "want undying love. Even you, though you may not think so. It's normal. And, by the way," she says, "food is love, you know. Love is food. It's how we live. It's what we live by, and you've eaten it all up."

Needless to say she'd never said any such thing to her own overbearing, legal, lord and master, though she'd wanted to for a long time.

The bear watches her as she speaks, as though too polite to interrupt or move even. His little beady black eyes take everything in, that's clear. There's a dull, sleepy, intelligent look about him. He waits patiently until she's finished, then humps off in powdery snow.

She sucks ice from the cave entrance. Finds a piece of root to make a splint for her knee. After that makes a broom from root ends and tidies up, all the while chewing root hairs from the cave ceiling. When everything is spic-and-span she sleeps again. At three AM or thereabouts he comes back with a small black bass for her. It seems as if he's taken what she said to heart. She lets him have half though she knows he's already eaten (not only all her food, but lots more, too). He licks up the fish scales she leaves. He eats the head (she gets the cheeks and also swallows down the eyes, though that's not easy to do). While they eat she talks and talks like she never talked before. She tells him all she knows about bears and that she hopes to learn lots more. Later she rubs the back of his neck and behind his ears. Top of his head. She likes the feel of him, and he's so warm. It's like the fireplace is lit when he comes in. She sings and he hums back a tune of his own she learns by heart. (She loves the sound of his voice.) They sleep again, she can't tell how long. Next time he leaves, they kiss, and not just cheeks. When he comes back, he brings another fish. And it goes on like this except they're kissing more and sleeping longer and longer periods, breathing slowly into each other's faces and not even getting up to pee, he, not turning his back to her except now and then and, when he does, giving her a bear hug first. It's a whole other rhythm she'd never known about before. And not bad, she thinks, to let the storms go on by themselves and forget about everything and just be warm and cuddled and cuddling all the time. It's what she's always wanted: arms around her that hardly ever let go. It's what she didn't get when she was little.

They don't even feel the earthquake, though it shakes a little dirt and pebbles down on them. She dreams it, though, and in the dream the quake is her husband's big feet shaking the mountain as he comes to get her to tear her away from her embrace. Before that she'd sometimes dreamt that the storms are him, too, tearing at the cave to pull her out. When those dreams come, she hugs tighter to her bear and he embraces her yet more snugly. Then she knows she's safe and thinks she finally has all one needs of real love and that it will last forever though maybe that's too much to hope for.

Meanwhile, back at the vestibule, the earthquake has caused quite a bit of damage. Some walls have crumbled and part of the roof come down. The fireplace is still ok though. He can squat in front of it mooing for his woman, and he still has most of his tower from which to growl out at the moon or stars or sun. Now he'll have to clean up the debris by himself as well as cook, cut his own firewood, skin his own marmots. If she knew this she could feel some sweet revenge, or maybe, I-told-you-so, except she never had.

One starry winter night when her knee is better, though not completely, she limps out with her bear and it's so nice the bear stands up and does a little soft-shoe while she throws snowballs at the sky. She limps, but she can shuffle and wobble from tree to tree, kissing them and him. They're singing all the songs they know, but by now she's forgotten most of the words. Knows only rhyme and alliteration though she remembers the oxymorons, especially since "the brightness of midnight" is all around them right now. It's sharply cold, but even so they both know spring is in the air. After this night, they begin to sleep less and then she has the baby. He's so small and thin she hardly knows she's birthed him except she hears the peeping. The bear helps by licking it clean and then eats the placenta. By then it's not a question of naming it. She can't even remember what names are for.

It gets warmer and the bear's gone more and more and brings back less and less. The baby might as well be a little bird. Besides her own milk, she feeds it worms and grubs. She tweets at it and it tweets back. When the bear stays out six days in a row, she suspects she's made the same old mistake … same kind of destructive relationship she's always had before. He'll go for good. He'll forget about her. Or if he comes back, turn savage on her. Maybe push her out along with her robin, sparrow, little tufted titmouse.

Then, when he doesn't come back at all anymore, thinks: Yes, yes, she knew it would happen and now she'll have to go, too. Be out on her own. Find the next meal herself. It's a bright spring day, wild flowers coming out, but she no sooner starts down, baby perched on her shoulder, pecking at her ear, than it flies away and she has no name to call it back by. She tries to caw him down. She whistles all the bird calls she knows, but none work. He circles for a few minutes while she finds the words to tell him he can't fly, or anyway, not yet. It only wobbles him a little. He utters one harsh quack she'd never heard him make before, then soars away, out over the valley. She thinks she hears soft coos and cuckoos even after he disappears into the trees below.

Well, she'll just go down by herself. And south. But this other valley, not towards home. This time maybe not take the hard way, though she's wondering, as usual, Where is the creature with which she can live happily ever after?

Then she sees a figure climbing up. First it's just a greenish-brown slowly moving spot, but then it becomes green *and* brown … tweeds and corduroys. Thin, small, wiry. Has a greenish-gray beard. Alpine hat with little red feathers in it. Black-button bearish eyes. She sees them as he comes closer. Though she's never seen him before, she knows who it is. Knickers, hiking boots — the old-fashioned kind. "Englemann," she says, "Englemann, Englemann." It's one of the few words she's not forgotten … never would forget though she is, by then, almost free of words. She will have to start over now from the beginning with wah, bah, and boo.

He comes up the last switchback. They look at each other and smile. He has a little tuft of fragrant mountain misery in his buttonhole. He takes it out, sniffs it once, then gives it to her.

"Oh, Englemann," she says and, "wah" and "bah" and "boo."

MRS. JONES

Cora is a morning person. Her sister, Janice, hardly feels conscious till late afternoon. Janice nibbles fruit and berries and complains of her stomach. Cora eats potatoes with butter and sour cream. She likes being fat. It makes her feel powerful and hides her wrinkles. Janice thinks being thin and willowy makes her look young, though she would admit that — and even though Cora spends more time outside doing the yard and farm work — Cora's skin does look smoother. Janice has a slight stutter. Normally she speaks rapidly and in a kind of shorthand so as not to take up anyone's precious time, but with her stutter, she can hold people's attention for a moment longer than she would otherwise dare. Cora, on the other hand, speaks slowly and if she had ever stuttered would have seen to it that she learned not to.

Cora bought a genuine Kilim rug to offset, she said, the bad taste of the flowery chintz covers Janice got for the couch and chairs. The rug and chairs look terrible in the same room, but Cora insists that her rug be there. Janice retaliated by pawning Mother's silver candelabras. Cora had never liked them, but she made a fuss anyway, and she left Janice's favorite silver spoon in the mayonnaise jar until, polish as she would, Janice could never get rid of the blackish look. Janice punched a hole in each of Father's rubber boots. Cora wears them anyway. She hasn't said a single word about it, but she hangs her wet socks up conspicuously in the kitchen.

They wish they'd gotten married and moved away from their parent's old farm house. They wish, desperately, that they'd had children — or husbands for that matter. As girls they worked hard at domestic things: canning, baking bread and pies, sewing … waiting to be good wives to almost anybody, but nobody came to claim them.

Janice is the one who worries. She's worried right now because she saw a light out in the far corner of the orchard — a tiny, flickering light. She can just barely make it out through the misty rain. Cora says, "Nonsense." (She's angry because it's just the sort of thing Janice would notice first.) Cora laughs as Janice goes around checking and rechecking all the windows and doors to see that they're securely locked. When Janice has finished, and stands staring out at the rain, she has a change of heart. "Whoever's out there must be cold and wet. Maybe hungry."

"Nonsense," Cora says again. "Besides, whoever's out there probably deserves it."

Later, as Cora watches the light from her bedroom window, she thinks whoever it is who's camping out down there is probably eating her apples and making a mess. Cora likes to sleep with the windows open a crack even in weather like this, and she prides herself on her courage, but — quietly, so that Janice, in the next room, won't hear — she eases her windows shut and locks them.

In the morning the rain has stopped, though it's foggy. Cora goes out (with Father's walking stick, and wearing Father's boots and battered canvas hat) to the far end of the orchard. Something has certainly been there. It had pulled down perfectly good, live apple branches to make the nests. Cora doesn't like the way it ate apples, either, one or two bites out of lots of them, and then it looks as if it had made itself sick and threw up not far from the fire. Cora cleans everything so it looks like no one has been there. She doesn't want Janice to have the satisfaction of knowing anything about it.

That afternoon, when Cora has gone off to have their pickup truck greased, Janice goes out to take a look. She also takes Father's walking stick, but she wears Mother's floppy pink hat. She can see where the fire's been by the black smudge, and she can tell somebody's been up in the tree. She notices things Cora hadn't: little claw marks on a branch, a couple of apples that had been bitten into still hanging on the tree near the nesting place. There's a tiny piece of leathery stuff stuck to one sharp twig. It's incredibly soft and downy and has a wet-dog smell. Janice takes it, thinking it might be an important clue. Also she wants to have something to show that she's been down there and seen more than Cora has.

Cora comes back while Janice is upstairs taking her nap. She sits down in the front room and reads an article in the *Reader's Digest* about how to help your husband communicate. When she hears Janice come down the stairs, Cora goes up for her nap. While Cora naps, Janice sets out grapes and a tangerine, strawberries, and one hard-boiled egg. As she eats her early supper, she reads the same article Cora has just read. She feels sorry for Cora who seems to have nothing more exciting than this sort of thing to read (along with her one hundred great books) whereas Janice has been reading: *How Famous Couples Get the Most Out of Their Sex Lives*. Just one of many such books that she keeps locked in her bedside cabinet. When she finishes eating, she cleans up the kitchen so it looks as if she hadn't been there.

Cora comes down when Janice is in the front parlor (sliding doors shut) listening to music. She has it turned so low Cora can hardly make it out. Might be Vivaldi. It's as if Janice doesn't want Cora to hear it in case she might enjoy it. At least that's how Cora takes it. Cora opens a can of spaghetti. For dessert she takes a couple of apples from the "special" tree. She eats on the closed-in porch, watching the clouds. It looks as if it'll rain again tonight.

About eight-thirty they each look out their different windows and see that the flickering light is there again. Cora says, "Damn it to hell," so loud that Janice hears from two rooms away. At that moment Janice begins to like the little light. Thinks it looks inviting. Homey. She forgets that she found that funny piece of leather and those claw marks. Thinks most likely there's a young couple in love out there. Their parents disapprove and they have no place else to go but her orchard. Or perhaps it's a young person. Teenager, maybe, cold and wet. She has a hard time sleeping, worrying and wondering about whoever it is, though she's still glad she locked the house up tight.

● ◑ ○ ◐ ●

The next day begins almost exactly like the one before, with Cora going out to the orchard first and cleaning up — trying to — all the signs of anything having been there, and with Janice coming out later to pick up the clues that are left. Janice finds that the same branch is scratched up even more than it was before, and this time Cora had left the vomit (full of bits of apple peel) behind the tree. Perhaps she hadn't noticed it. Apples — or at least so many apples — aren't agreeing with the lovers. (In spite of the clues, Janice prefers to think that it's lovers.) She feels sorry about the all-night rain. There's no sign that they had a tent or shelter of any kind, poor things.

By the third night, though, the weather finally clears. Stars are out and a tiny moon. Cora and Janice stand in the front room, each at a different window, looking out towards where the light had been. An old seventy-eight record is on: Fritz Kreisler playing the Bach Chaconne. Janice says, "You'd think, especially since it's not raining … ."

Cora says, "Good riddance," though she, too, feels a sense of regret. At least something unusual had been happening. "Don't forget," Cora says, "the state prison's only ninety miles away."

Little light or no little light, they both check the windows and doors and then recheck the ones the other had already checked, or, at least Cora rechecks all the ones Janice had seen to. Janice sees her do it and Cora sees her noticing, so Cora says, "With what they're doing in genetic engineering, it could be anything at all out there. They make mistakes and peculiar things escape. You don't hear about it because it's classified. People disapprove so they don't let the news get out." Ever since she was six years old, Cora has been trying to scare her younger sister, though, as usual, she ends up scaring herself.

But then, just as they are about to give up and go off to bed, there's the light again. "Ah." Janice breathes out as though she had been holding her breath. "There it is, finally."

"You've got a lot to learn," Cora says. She'd heard the relief in Janice's big sigh. "Anyway, I'm off to bed, and you'd better come soon, too, if you know what's good for you."

"I know what's good for me," Janice says. She would have stayed up too late just for spite, but now she has another, secret reason for doing it. She sits reading an article in *Cosmopolitan* about how to be more sexually attractive to your husband. Around midnight, even downstairs, she can hear Cora snoring. Janice goes out to the kitchen. Moves around it like a little mouse. She's good at that. Gets out Mother's teakwood tray, takes big slices of rye bread from Cora's stash, takes a can of Cora's tunafish. (Janice knows she'll notice. Cora has them all counted up.) Takes butter and mayonnaise from Cora's side of the refrigerator. Makes three tunafish sandwiches. Places them on three of Mother's gold-rimmed plates along with some of her own celery, radishes, and grapes. Then she sits down and eats one plateful herself. She hasn't let herself have a tunafish sandwich, especially not one with mayonnaise and butter and rye bread, in quite some time.

It's only when Janice is halfway out in the orchard that she remembers what Cora said about the prison and thinks maybe there's some sort of escaped criminal out there — a rapist or a murderer, and here she is, wearing only her bathrobe and nightgown, in her slippers, and without even Father's walking stick. (Though the walking stick would probably just have been a handy thing for the criminal to attack *her* with.) She stops, puts the tray down, then moves forward. She's had a lot of practice creeping. She's been creeping up on Cora ever since they were little. Used to yell, "Boo," but nowadays creeping up and standing very close and suddenly whispering right by her ear can make Cora jump as much as a loud noise. Janice sneaks along slowly. Has to step over where whoever it is has already thrown up. Something is huddling in front of the fire, wrapped in what at first seems to be an army blanket. Why it *is* a child. Poor thing. She'd known it all the time. But then the creature moves, stretches, makes a squeaky sound, and she sees it's either the largest bat, or the smallest little old man she's ever seen. She's wondering if this is what Cora meant by genetic engineering.

Then the creature stands up and Janice is shocked. He has such a large penis that Janice thinks back to the horses and bulls they used to have. It's a Pan-type penis, more or less permanently erect and hooked up tight against his stomach, though Janice doesn't know this about a Pan's penis, and, anyway, this is definitely not some sort of Pan.

The article in *Cosmopolitan* comes instantly to her mind, plus the other, sexier books that she has locked in her bedside cabinet. Isn't there, in all this, some way to permanently outdo Cora? Whether she ever finds out about it or not? Slowly Janice backs up, turns, goes right past her tray (the gleam of silverware helps her know where it is), goes to the house and down into the basement.

They'd always had dogs. Big ones. For safety. But Mr. Jones (called Jonesy) had died a few months ago and Cora is still grieving, or so she keeps saying. Since the dog had become blind, diabetic, and incontinent in his last years, Janice is relieved that he's gone. Besides, she has her heart set on something small and more tractable, some sort of terrier, but now she's glad Jonesy was large and difficult to manage. His metal choke collar and chain leash are still in the cellar. She wraps them in a cloth bag to keep them from making any clanking noises and heads back out, picking up the tray of food on the way.

As she comes close to the fire, she begins to hum. This time she wants him to know she's coming. The creature sits in the tree now and watches her with red glinting eyes. She puts the tray down and begins to talk softly as though she were trying to calm old Jonesy. She even calls the thing Mr. Jones. At first by mistake and then on purpose. He watches. Moves nothing but his eyes and big ears. His wings, dangling along his arms, are olive drab like that piece she found, but his body is a little lighter, especially along his stomach. She can tell that even in the moonlight.

Now that she's closer and less startled than before, she can see that there's something terribly wrong. One leathery wing is torn and twisted. He's helpless. Or almost. Probably in pain. Janice feels a rush of joy.

She breaks off a bit of tunafish sandwich and slowly, talking softly all the time, she holds it towards his little clawed hand. Equally slowly, he reaches out to take it. She keeps this up until almost all of one plateful is eaten. But suddenly the creature jumps out of the tree, turns around, and throws up.

Janice knows a vulnerable moment when she sees one. As he leans back on his heels between spasms, she fastens the choke collar around his neck, and twists the other end of the chain leash around her wrist.

He only makes two attempts to escape: tries to flap himself into the air, but it's obviously painful for him; then he tries to run. His legs are bowed, his gait rocking and clumsy. After these two attempts at getting away, he seems to realize it's hopeless. Janice can see in his eyes that he's given up — too sick and tired to care. Probably happy to be captured and looked after at last.

She leads him back to the house and down into the basement. Her own quiet creeping makes him quiet, too. He seems to sense that he's to be a secret and that perhaps his life depends on it. It was hard for him to walk all the way across the orchard. He doesn't seem to be built for anything but flying.

There is an old coal room, not used since they got oil heat. Janice makes a nest for him there, first chaining him to one of the pipes. She gets him blankets, water, an empty pail with lid. She makes him put on a pair of her underpants. She has to use a cord around his waist to make them stay up. She wonders what she should leave him to eat that would stay down. Then brings him chamomile tea, dry toast, one small potato. That's all. She doesn't want to be cleaning up a lot of vomit.

He's so tractable through all this that she loses all fear of him. Pats his head as if he were old Jonesy. Strokes the wonderful softness of his wings. Thinks: If those were cut off, he'd look like a small old man with long, hard fingernails — misshapen, but not much more so than other people. And clothes can hide things. Without the dark wings, he'd look lighter. His body is that color that's always described as *café au lait*. She would have preferred it if he'd been clearly a white person, but, who knows, maybe a little while in the cellar will make him paler.

After a last rubbing of his head behind his too-large ears, Janice padlocks the coal room and goes up to her bedroom, but she's too excited to sleep. She reads a chapter in *Are You Happy with Your Sex Life?*, the one on "How to Turn Your Man into a Lusting Animal." ("The feet of both sexes are exquisitely sensitive." And, "Let your eyes speak, but first make sure he's looking at you." "Surrender. When he thinks he's leading, your man feels strong in *every* way.") Janice thinks she will have to be the one to take the initiative, though she'll try to make him feel that he's the boss — even though he'll be wearing the choke collar.

● ◑ ○ ◐ ●

For a change, Janice wakes up just as early as Cora does. Earlier, in fact, and she lies in bed making plans. She gets a lot of good ideas. She comes downstairs whistling Vivaldi — off-key, as usual, but she's not doing it to make Cora angry this time. She really can't whistle on key. Cora knows that Janice knows Cora hates the way she whistles. Cora thinks that if Janice really tried, she could be just as in tune as Cora always is. Cora thinks Janice got up early just so she could spoil Cora's breakfast by sitting across from her and looking just like Mother used to look when she disapproved of Father's table manners. And Cora notices, even before she makes her omelet, that one can of tunafish is missing, and that her loaf of rye bread has gone down by several slices. She takes a quart of strawberries from Janice's side of the refrigerator and eats them all, not even bothering to wash them.

Janice doesn't say a word, or even do anything. She doesn't care, except that Jonesy might have wanted some. Janice is feeling magnanimous and powerful. She feels so good she even offers Cora some of her herb tea. Cora takes the offer as ironic, especially since she knows that Janice knows she never drinks herb tea. She retaliates by saying that, since they're both up so early, they should take advantage of it and go out to the beach to get more lakeweed for the garden.

Janice knows that Cora decided this just to make her pay for the tunafish and mayonnaise and such, but she still feels magnanimous — kindly to the whole world. She doesn't even say that they'd already done that twice in the spring, and that what they needed now were hay bales to put around the foundations of the house for the winter. All she says is, "No!"

It's never been their way to shirk their duties no matter how angry they might be with each other. When it comes to work, they've always made a good team. But now Janice is adamant. She says she has something important to do. She's not ever said this before, nor has she ever had something important to do. Cora has always been the one who did important things. This time Cora can't persuade Janice to change her mind, nor can she persuade her that there's nothing important to be done — at least nothing more important than lakeweed.

Finally Cora gives up and goes off alone. She hadn't meant to go. She's never gone off to get lakeweed by herself, but she goes anyway, hoping to make Janice feel guilty. Except Cora knows something is going on. She's not sure what, but she's going to be on her guard.

As soon as Janice hears the old pickup crunch away on the gravel drive, she goes down in the basement, bringing along Father's old straight razor (freshly sharpened), rubbing alcohol, and bandages. Also, to make it easier on him, a bottle of sherry.

Cora comes back, tired and sandy, around six-thirty. Her face is red and she has big, dried sweat marks on her blue farmer's shirt, across the back and under the arms. She smells fishy. She's so tired she staggers as she climbs the porch steps. Even before she gets inside, she knows odd things are still going on. There's the smells … of beef stew or some such, onions, maybe a mince pie, and there, on the hall table, a glass of sherry is set out for her. Or seems to be for her. Or looks like sherry. Though the day was hot, these fall evenings are cool, and Janice has laid a fire in the fireplace, and not badly done. Cora always knew Janice could do it properly if she really tried. Cora takes the sherry and sits on the footstool of Father's big chair. It's one of the ones Janice had covered in a flowery pattern — looks like pinkish-blue hydrangea. Cora turns away from it and looks at the fire. Thinks: All this has got to be because of something else. Or maybe it's going to be a practical joke. If she lets down her guard she'll be in for big trouble. But even if it's a joke, might as well take advantage of it for as long as she can. The sherry relaxes her. She'll go up and shower — if, that is, Janice has left her any hot water.

● ◑ ○ ◐ ●

For several days, Mr. Jones is in pain. Janice is glad of it. She knows how a wild thing — or even a not-so-wild thing — appreciates being nursed back to health. (As soon as he's better, she hopes to bond him to her in a different way.) She hopes Mr. Jones was too drunk to remember about the … removal … amputation … whatever you'd call it. (Funny, he only has four fingers on each hand. She'd not noticed that at first.)

Cora is still suspicious, but doesn't know what to be suspicious about. The good food is going on and on. After supper Janice cleans up and doesn't ask Cora for help even though Janice has done all the cooking. And Janice disappears for hours at a time. Goes up to take her nap — or so she says — but Cora knows for a fact that she's not in her room. After the dishes are cleaned up in the evenings, Janice sews or knits. It's not hard to see that she's knitting a child-sized sweater and sewing a child-sized pair of trousers. At the same time, she's working on a white dress, lacy and low-necked. Cora thinks much too low-necked for someone Janice's age. But perhaps its not for Janice. Maybe Janice has some news she's keeping from Cora. That would be just like her. Someone is getting married or coming for a visit. Or maybe both.

● ◐ ○ ◑ ●

Mr. Jones is getting better, eating soups, nuts, and seeds and keeping everything down, finally. Janice is happy to see that his skin has faded some. He might pass for a gnarled, little Mexican, or maybe a fairly light India Indian. And he's beginning to understand some words. She's been talking to him a lot, more or less as she used to talk to old Jonesy. He knows: good boy and bad boy, and sit, lie down, be quiet … . She thinks he even has the concept of, "I love you." She'd never said that to any other creature ever before, not even to the pony they'd had when they were little. She's been doing a lot of patting, back rubbing, scratching under the chin and behind the ears. Though he's always wearing a pair of her underpants tied up around his waist, and though she hasn't even tried the stroking of the "exquisitely sensitive" feet, every now and then she notices his penis swelling up even larger than it already is.

One night, after reading over again the chapter "How to Turn Your Man into a Lusting Animal," she puts on her flowery summer nightgown (even though the nights are colder than ever and they haven't started up the furnace yet). She puts on lipstick, eyeshadow, perfume, combs her hair out and lets it hang over her shoulders .... (She's only graying a little bit at the temples. Thank God, not like Cora; she's almost completely gray.) She goes down into the cellar with a glass of sherry for each of them. Not too much, though. She's read about alcohol and sex.

She tells him she loves him several times, kisses him on the cheeks and then on the neck, just below the choke collar. Finally she kisses his lips. They are thin and closed tight. She can feel the teeth behind them. Then she rolls her nightgown up to her chin. She hopes he likes what he sees even though she's not young anymore. (If anything, he looks surprised.) But no sooner has she lain herself down beside him than it's over. She's even wondering, did it really happen? Except, yes, there's blood and it did hurt. But this isn't at all like the books said it would be or should be. She's read about premature ejaculation. This must be it. Maybe later, when he knows more words, they can go for sex therapy. But — oops — there he goes again, and just as fast as before. After that he falls asleep. She not only didn't get any real foreplay, but no afterplay either. She's wondering, where's the romance in all this?

Well, at least she's a real woman now. She hasn't missed all of life. She may have missed a lot, but no one can say she's missed all, which is more than Cora can say about herself.

Janice thinks she is, and probably permanently — at least she hopes so — one up on Cora. She has joined the human race in a way Cora probably never will, poor thing. Janice will be kind.

● ◑ ○ ◐ ●

Janice hardly ever drives. She has always left that to Cora. She knows how, but she's out of practice. Now she has several errands to do. She wants a nice pin-striped suit, though she wonders if they come in boys' sizes — a suit like her father never would have worn. She wants a good suitcase. Not one from the five-and-ten. Shiny shoes big enough for rough claws, though she's cut those claws as short as she could, using old Jonesy's nail clippers. Since Mr. Jones looks sort of Mexican, she'll get him a south-of-the-border Panama hat and dark glasses.

● ◑ ○ ◐ ●

It only takes a couple of days for Janice to get her errands done and then a couple more to get the guest room ready: aired out, curtains washed, bed made. (Good it's a double bed.) She whistles all the time and doesn't even remember that it always bothers Cora.

Cora watches the preparation of the guest room, but refuses to give Janice the satisfaction of asking her any questions. It's easy to see that Janice wonders why Cora isn't asking. Once Janice started to tell her something, but then turned red to her collar bone and shut up fast.

Janice has continued making good suppers of Cora's favorite foods. Cora is still waiting for the practical joke to come to its finale, but even … or especially if it doesn't end, she knows something's up. She hasn't let down her guard and she's snooped around — even in the basement, but not in the coal room. She didn't notice the padlock on the door. But in the attic she did find a large … very large piece of stiff leather, dried blood along its edges. So brittle she couldn't unfold it to see what it was. It gave her the shivers. Pained her to see it, though she couldn't say why. Perhaps it was the two toenails or claws that were attached to each corner. She'd thought of throwing the dead-looking thing out in the garbage, but after she saw those claws that were part of it, she couldn't bring herself to touch it again.

●　◑　○　◐　●

Everything is ready, but Janice knows Jonesy needs a little more experience and training. She wants to pretend to go down and pick him up at the airport in Detroit. Cora, if she hears about it, will never let Janice go there by herself. But Cora mustn't be there. For lots of reasons, not the least of which that Janice wants the trip to be like a honeymoon. They could sneak out in the middle of the night and they could take two or three or even more days getting down there, and two or three or more days coming back. Maybe a couple of days enjoying Detroit. Jonesy could learn a lot.

Janice has never dared to even think of going on a trip like this before, but with Jones she wouldn't be alone. She sees herself, dressed in her best, sitting across from him (he'll be wearing his pin-striped suit) in restaurants, going to motels, movies, even … . She'd look right doing these things. Like all the other couples. They'd hold hands at the movies. They'd stroll in the evenings after their long drive. Can he stroll? She'll get him a silver-handled walking stick in Detroit. Better than Father's. He may be a cripple, but he'll look like a gentleman. And the better he looks the more jealous Cora will be.

Janice leaves a note for Cora mentioning the airport in Detroit.

● ◗ ○ ◖ ●

And it started out to be a wonderful honeymoon. Janice kept the choke collar under Jonesy's necktie and shirt, running the chain down inside his left sleeve so that when she held his hand she could also hold the chain just to make sure. She also found a way to hold the back of his shirt so she could give a little pull on it, but she seldom had to use any of these techniques. And how could he try to escape, hobbling as he does? Unless he learns to drive the pickup? But Janice wouldn't be a bit surprised if he could learn to drive it. Even before they get to Detroit, Jonesy is dressing himself, uses the right fork in fancy restaurants, can eat a lobster just as neatly as anyone can. (Though he throws it up afterwards.)

Janice keeps a running conversation going, just as if they were communicating. She keeps saying, "Don't you think so, dear?" hoping nobody will notice that he doesn't nod. Except she's sure that lots of husbands are like that. Even Father often didn't answer Mother, lost as he was in his own thoughts all the time. But Mr. Jones doesn't look lost in his thoughts. And he doesn't look as if he feels hopeless anymore. He looks out at everything with such intelligence that Janice is considering calling him *Doctor* Jones.

In Detroit (they are staying at the Renaissance Center) Janice gets the good idea that they should get married right there at City Hall. Before she even tries to do it, she calls Cora up. "I got married," she says, even though it hasn't happened, and whether it does or not, Cora will never know the difference. "And isn't it funny, I'm Mrs. Jones, and I call him Jones, just like Old Jonesy."

Cora can't answer. She just sputters. She's been lonelier without Janice there than she ever thought she would be. She had even wished the little light was still flickering in the orchard. She'd gone out there, hoping to find another nest. Partly she'd been just looking for company. She'd even left the doors unlocked, her window open. But then she'd put two and two together. She's had all these days to wonder and worry and wait, and she's been down in the basement where the coal-room door had been carelessly left open. She's seen the pallet on the floor, the bowl of dusty water, the remains of a last meal (Mother's china, wine glasses), three pairs of Janice's underpants, badly soiled. And she remembers that piece of folded leather with the dried blood all over it that she'd found in the attic and she's gotten the shivers all over again. Cora knows she's been outmaneuvered by Janice, which she never thought could ever come about, but she suddenly realizes that she doesn't care about that anymore.

She sputters into the phone and then, for the first time — at least that Janice ever knew about — Cora bursts into tears. Janice can tell, even though Cora is trying to hide it. All of a sudden Janice wants to say something that will make Cora happy, but she doesn't know what. "You'll like him," she says. "I know you will. You'll *love* him, and he'll love you, too. I know him well enough to know he will. He *will*."

Cora keeps on trying to hide that she's crying, but she doesn't hang up. She's glad, at last, to be connected to Janice however tenuously.

"I'll bring you something nice from Detroit," Janice says.

Cora still doesn't say anything, though Janice can hear her ragged breathing.

"I'll be back real soon." Janice doesn't want to break the connection, either, but she can't think of anything else to say. "I'll see you in two days."

It takes four. Janice comes home alone by taxi, after a series of buses. (The pickup is going to be found two weeks later up in Canada, north of Thunder Bay. Men's clothes will be found in it, including Panama hat, dark glasses, and a silver-handled cane. The radio will have been stolen. There will be maps, and a big dictionary that had never belonged either to Cora or Janice.)

As Janice staggers up the porch steps, Cora rushes down, her arms held out, but Janice flinches away. Janice is wearing a wedding ring and a large, phony diamond engagement ring. She has on a new dress. Even though it's wrinkled and is stained with sweat across the back, Cora can see it was expensive. Janice's hair is coming loose from its Psyche knot and now she's the one who's crying and trying to pretend she's not.

Cora tries to help Janice up the steps. Even though Janice stumbles, she won't let her, but she does let Cora push her on into the living room. Janice collapses onto the couch, tells Cora, "Don't hover." Hovering is something Cora never did before. It's more like something Janice would do.

Even after Cora brings Janice a strong cup of coffee, Janice won't say a single word about anything. Cora says she'll feel better if she talks about it, but she won't. She looks tired and sullen. "You'd like to know everything, wouldn't you just," she says. (What other way to stay one up than not to tell? … than to have secrets?)

Cora almost says, "Not really," but she doesn't want to be, anymore, what she used to be. Janice hasn't had the experience of being in the house all alone for several days. There's a different secret now that Janice doesn't know about yet. Maybe never will unless Cora goes off someplace. But why would she go anyplace? And where? Besides, being one up or being even doesn't matter to Cora anymore. She doesn't care if Janice understands or not. She just wants to take care of her and have her stay. Maybe, after a while, Janice will come to see that things have changed.

Cora goes to the kitchen to make a salad that she thinks Janice will like. She sets the dining room table the way she thinks Janice would approve of, with Mother's best dishes, and with the knives and forks in all the right places, and both water glasses and wine glasses, but Janice says she'll eat later in the kitchen and alone and on paper plates. Meanwhile she'll take a bath.

After Cora eats and is cleaning up the last of her dishes, Janice comes in, wearing her nightgown and Mother's bathrobe. As she leans to get a pan from a lower shelf, the bathrobe falls away. When she straightens up again, she sees Cora staring at her. "What are you ogling?" she says, holding the frying pan like a weapon.

"Nothing," Cora says, knowing better than to make a comment. She's seen more than she wants to see. There are big red choke collar marks all around Janice's neck.

But something must be done or said. Cora wonders what Father would have done? She usually knows exactly what he'd do and does it without even thinking about it. Now she can't imagine Father ever having to deal with something like this. She can't say anything. She can't move. Finally she thinks: No secrets. She says, "Sister." And then … but it's too hard. (Father never would have said it.) She starts. She almost says it. "Sister, I love … ."

At first it looks as if Janice *will* hit her with the frying pan, but then she drops it and just stares.

GRANDMA

GRANDMA USED TO BE A WOMAN OF ACTION. SHE WORE tights. She had big boobs, but a teeny-weeny bra. Her waist used to be twenty-four inches. Before she got so hunched over she could do way more than a hundred of everything, pushups, sit-ups, chinning .... She had naturally curly hair. Now it's dry and fine and she's a little bit bald. She wears a babushka all the time and never takes her teeth out when I'm around or lets me see where she keeps them, though of course I know. She won't say how old she is. She says the books about her are all wrong, but, she says, that's her own fault. For a long while she lied about her age and other things, too.

She used to be on every search and rescue team all across these mountains. I think she might still be able to rescue people. Small ones. Her set of weights is in the basement. She has a punching bag. She used to kick it, too, but I don't know if she still can do that. I hear her thumping and grunting around down there — even now when she needs a cane for walking. And talk about getting up off the couch!

I go down to that gym myself sometimes and try to lift those weights. I punch at her punching bag. (I can't reach it except by standing on a box. When I try to kick it, I always fall over.)

Back in the olden days Grandma wasn't as shy as she is now. How could she be and do all she did? But now she doesn't want to be a bother. She says she never wanted to be a bother, just help out is all.

She doesn't expect any of us to follow in her footsteps. She used to, but not anymore. We're a big disappointment. She doesn't say so, but we have to be. By now she's given up on all of us. Everybody has.

It started … we started with the idea of selective breeding. Everybody wanted more like Grandma: Strong, fast-thinking, fast-acting, and with the desire … that's the most important thing … a desire for her kind of life, a life of several hours in the gym every single day. Grandma loved it. She says (and says and says), "I'd turn on some banjo music and make it all into a dance."

Back when Grandma was young, offspring weren't even thought of, since who was there around good enough for her to marry? Besides, everybody thought she'd last forever. How could somebody like her get old? is what they thought.

She had three … "husbands" they called them (donors, more like it), first a triathlon champion, then a prize fighter, then a ballet dancer.

There's this old wives' tale of skipping generations, so, after nothing good happened with her children, Grandma (and everybody else) thought, surely it would be us grandchildren. But we're a motley crew. Nobody pays any attention to us anymore.

● ☊ ○ ☾ ●

I'm the runt. I'm small for my age, my foot turns in, my

teeth stick out, I have a lazy eye …. There's lots of work to be done on me. Grandma's paying for all of it though she knows I'll never amount to much of anything. I wear a dozen different kinds of braces, teeth, feet, a patch over my good eye. My grandfather, the ballet dancer!

Sometimes I wonder why Grandma does all this for me, a puny, limping, limp-haired girl. What I think is, I'm her real baby at last. They didn't let her have any time off to look after her own children — not ever until now, when she's too old for rescuing people. She not only was on all the search and rescue teams, she was a dozen search and rescue teams all by herself, and often she had to rescue the search and rescue teams.

Not only that, she also rescued animals. She always said the planet would die without its creatures. You'd see her leaping over mountains with a deer under each arm. She moved bears from campgrounds to where they wouldn't cause trouble. You'd see her with handfuls of rattlesnakes gathered from golf courses and carports, flying them off to places where people would be safe from them and they'd be safe from people.

She even tried to rescue the climate, pulling and pushing at the clouds. Holding back floods. Re-raveling the ozone. She carried huge sacks of water to the trees of one great dying forest. In the long run there was only failure. Even after all those rescues, always only failure. The bears came back. The rattlesnakes came back.

Grandma gets to thinking all her good deeds went wrong: Lots of times she had to let go and save … maybe five babies and drop three. I mean even Grandma only had two arms. She expected more of herself. I always say, "You did save lots of people. You kept that forest alive ten years longer than expected. And me. I'm saved." That always makes her laugh, and I am saved. She says, "I guess my one good eye can see well enough to look after you, you rapscallion."

She took me in after my parents died. (She couldn't save them. There are some things you just can't do anything about no matter who you are, like drunken drivers. Besides, you can't be everywhere.)

When she took me to care for, she was already feeble. We needed each other. She'd never be able to get along without me. I'm the saver of the saver.

How did we end up this way, way out here in the country with me her only helper? Did she scare everybody else off with her neediness? Or maybe people couldn't stand to see how far down she's come from what she used to be. And suppose she has gotten difficult, but I'm used to her. I hardly notice. But she's so busy trying not to be a bother, she's a bother. I have to read her mind. When she holds her arms around herself, I get her old red sweatshirt with her emblem on the front. When she says, "Oh dear," I get her a cup of green tea. When she's on the couch and struggles and leans forward on her cane, trembling, I pull her up. She likes quiet. She likes for me to sit by her, lean against her, and listen to the birds along with her. Or listen to her stories. We don't have a radio or TV set. They conked out a long time ago, and no one thought to get us new ones, but we don't need them. We never wanted them in the first place.

Grandma sits me down beside her, the lettuce planted, the mulberries picked, sometimes a mulberry pie already made (I helped), and we just sit. "I had a grandma," she'll say, "though I know, to look at me, it doesn't seem like I could have. I'm older than most grandmas ever get to be, but we all had grandmas, even me. Picture that: Every single person in the world with a grandma." Then she giggles. She still has her girlish giggle. She says, "Mother didn't know what to make of me. I was opening her jars for her before I was three years old. Mother …. Even that was a long time ago."

When she's in a sad mood, she says everything went wrong. People she had just rescued died a week later of something that Grandma couldn't have helped. Hanta virus or some such that they got from vacuuming a closed room, though sometimes Grandma had just warned them not to do that. (Grandma believes in prevention as much as in rescuing.)

● ◑ ○ ◐ ●

I've rescued things. Lots of them. Nothing went wrong, either. I rescued a junco with a broken wing. After rains I've rescued stranded worms from the wet driveway and put them back in our vegetable garden. I didn't let Grandma cut the suckers off our fruit trees. I rescued mice from sticky traps. I fed a litter of feral kittens and got fleas and worms from them. Maybe this rescuing is the one part of Grandma I inherited.

Who's to say which is more worthwhile, pushing atom bombs far out into space or one of these little things I do? Well, I do know which is more important, but if I were the junco I'd like being rescued.

● ◑ ○ ◐ ●

Sometimes Grandma goes out, though rarely. She gets to feeling it's a necessity. She wears sunglasses and a big floppy hat and scarves that hide her wrinkled-up face and neck. She still rides a bicycle. She's so wobbly it's scary to see her trying to balance herself down the road. I can't look. She likes to bring back ice-cream for me, maybe get me a comic book and a licorice stick to chew on as I read it. I suppose in town they just take her for a crazy lady, which I guess she is.

When visitors come to take a look at her, I always say she isn't home, but where else would a very, very, very old lady be but mostly home? If she knew people had come she'd have hobbled out to see them and probably scared them half to death. And they probably wouldn't have believed it was her, anyway. Only the president of the Town and Country Bank — she rescued him a long time ago — I let him in. He'll sit with her for a while. He's old, but of course not as old as she is. And he likes her for herself. They talked all through his rescue and really got to know each other back then. They talked about tomato plants and wildflowers and birds. When she rescued him they were flying up with the wild geese. (They still talk about all those geese they flew with and how exciting that was with all the honking and the sound of wings flapping right beside them. I get goosebumps — geesebumps? — just hearing them talk about it.) She should have married somebody like him, pot-belly, pock-marked face, and all. Maybe we'd have turned out better.

● ◑ ○ ◐ ●

I guess you could say I'm the one that killed her — caused her death, anyway. I don't know what got into me. Lots of times I don't know what gets into me and lots of times I kind of run away for a couple of hours. Grandma knows about it. She doesn't mind. Sometimes she even tells me, "Go on. Get out of here for a while." But this time I put on her old tights and one of the teeny-tiny bras. I don't have breasts yet so I stuffed the cups with Kleenex. I knew I couldn't do any of the things Grandma did, I just thought it would be fun to pretend for a little while.

I started out toward the hill. It's a long walk but you get to go through a batch of piñons. But first you have to go up an arroyo. Grandma's cape dragged over the rocks and sand behind me. It was heavy, too. To look at the satiny red outside you'd think it would be light, but it has a felt lining. "Warm and waterproof," Grandma said. I could hardly walk. How did she ever manage to fly around in it?

I didn't get very far before I found a jackrabbit lying in the middle of the arroyo half-dead (but half-alive, too), all bit and torn. I'll bet I'm the one that scared off whatever it was that did that. That rabbit was a goner if I didn't rescue it. I was a little afraid because wounded rabbits bite. Grandma's cape was just the right thing to wrap it in so it wouldn't.

Those jackrabbits weigh a lot. And with the added weight of the cape ....

Well, all I did was sprain my ankle. I mean I wasn't really hurt. I always have the knife Grandma gave me. I cut some strips off the cape and bound myself up good and tight. It isn't as if Grandma has a lot of capes. This is her only one. I felt bad about cutting it. I put the rabbit across my shoulders. It was slow going, but I wasn't leaving the rabbit for whatever it was to finish eating it. It began to be twilight. Grandma knows I can't see well in twilight. The trouble is, though she used to see like an eagle, Grandma can't see very well anymore either.

● ◐ ○ ◑ ●

She tried to fly as she used to do. She did fly. For my sake. She skimmed along just barely above the sage and bitterbrush, her feet snagging at the taller ones. That was all the lift she could get. I could see, by the way she leaned and flopped like a dolphin, that she was trying to get higher. She was calling, "Sweetheart. Sweetheart. Where are yoouuu?" Her voice was almost as loud as it used to be. It echoed all across the mountains.

"Grandma, go back. I'll be all right." My voice can be loud, too.

She heard me. Her ears are still as sharp as a mule's.

The way she flew was kind of like she rides a bicycle. All wobbly. Veering off from side to side, up and down, too. I knew she would crack up. And she looked funny flying around in her print dress. She only has one costume and I was wearing it.

"Grandma, go back. Please go back."

She wasn't at all like she used to be. A little fall like that from just a few feet up would never have hurt her a couple of years ago. Or even last year. Even if, as she did, she landed on her head.

I covered her with sand and brush as best I could. No doubt whatever was about to eat the rabbit would come gnaw on her. She wouldn't mind. She always said she wanted to give herself back to the land. She used to quote, I don't know from where, "All to the soil, nothing to the grave." Getting eaten is sort of like going to the soil.

● ◐ ○ ◑ ●

I don't dare tell people what happened — that it was all my fault — that I got myself in trouble sort of on purpose, trying to be like her, trying to rescue something.

But I'm not as sad as you might think. I knew she would die pretty soon anyway, and this is a better way than in bed looking at the ceiling, maybe in pain. If that had happened, she wouldn't have complained. She'd not have said a word, trying not to be a bother. Nobody would have known about the pain except me. I would have had to grit my teeth against her pain the whole time.

I haven't told anybody partly because I'm waiting to figure things out. I'm here all by myself, but I'm good at looking after things. There are those who check on us every weekend — people who are paid to do it. I wave at them. "All okay." I mouth it. The president of the Town and Country Bank came out once. I told him Grandma wasn't feeling well. It wasn't exactly a lie. How long can this go on? He'll be the one who finds out first — if anybody does. Maybe they won't.

I'm nursing my jackrabbit. We're friends now. He's getting better fast. Pretty soon I'll let him go off to be a rabbit. But he might rather stay here with me.

I'm wearing Grandma's costume most of the time now. I sleep in it. It makes me feel safe. I'm doing my own little rescues as usual. (The vegetable garden is full of happy weeds. I keep the bird feeder going. I leave scraps out for the skunk.) Those count — almost as much as Grandma's rescues did. Anyway, I know the weeds think so.

I love writing first person unreliable most of all and I do it all the time. I know that's dangerous because people then think what my characters think is what I think. Yet it's the most fun to write. …

I seldom write about people I don't like in some ways even if they are mistaken. I think villains are too easy to write about. I always set myself a more complicated story than straight out evil.

—CAROL EMSHWILLER, 2003

BOYS

WE NEED A NEW BATCH OF BOYS. BOYS ARE SO FOOLHARDY, impetuous, reckless, rash. They'll lead the way into smoke and fire and battle. I've seen one of my own sons, aged twelve, standing at the top of the cliff shouting, daring the enemy. You'll never win a medal for being too reasonable.

We steal boys from anywhere. We don't care if they come from our side or theirs. They'll forget soon enough, which side they used to be on, if they ever knew. After all, what does a seven-year-old know? Tell them this flag of ours is the best and most beautiful, and that we're the best and smartest, and they believe it. They like uniforms. They like fancy hats with feathers. They like to get medals. They like flags and drums and war cries.

Their first big test is getting to their beds. You have to climb straight up to the barracks. At the top you have to cross a hanging bridge. They've heard rumors about it. They know they'll have to go home to mother if they don't do it. They all do it.

You should see the look on their faces when we steal them. It's what they've always wanted. They've seen our fires along the hills. They've seen us marching back and forth across our flat places. When the wind is right, they've heard the horns that signal our getting up and going to bed and they've gotten up and gone to bed with our sounds or those of our enemies across the valley.

In the beginning they're a little bit homesick (you can hear them smothering their crying the first few nights) but most have anticipated their capture and look forward to it. They love to belong to us instead of to the mothers.

If we'd let them go home they'd strut about in their uniforms and the stripes of their rank. I know because I remember when I first had my uniform. I was wishing my mother and my big sister could see me. When I was taken, I fought, but just to show my courage. I was happy to be stolen — happy to belong, at long last, to the men.

● ◑ ○ ◐ ●

Once a year in summer we go down to the mothers and copulate in order to make more warriors. We can't ever be completely sure which of the boys is ours and we always say that's a good thing, for then they're all ours and we care about them equally, as we should. We're not supposed to have family groups. It gets in the way of combat. But every now and then, it's clear who the father is. I know two of my sons. I'm sure they know that I, the colonel, am their father. I think that's why they try so hard. I know them as mine because I'm a small, ugly man. I know many must wonder how someone like me got to be a colonel.

(We not only steal boys from either side but we copulate with either side. When I go down to the villages, I always look for Una.)

TO DIE FOR YOUR TRIBE IS TO LIVE FOREVER. That's written over our headquarters entrance. Under it, NEVER FORGET. We know we mustn't forget but we suspect maybe we have. Some of us feel that the real reasons for the battles have been lost. No doubt but that there's hate, so we and they commit more atrocities in the name of the old ones, but how it all began is lost to us.

We've not only forgotten the reasons for the conflict, but we've also forgotten our own mothers. Inside our barracks, the walls are covered with mother jokes and mother pictures. Mother bodies are soft and tempting. "Pillows," we call them. "Nipples" and "pillows." And we insult each other by calling ourselves the same.

● ◐ ○ ◑ ●

The valley floor is full of women's villages. One every fifteen miles or so. On each side are mountains. The enemy's, at the far side, are called The Purples. Our mountains are called The Snows. The weather is worse in our mountains than in theirs. We're proud of that. We sometimes call ourselves The Hailstones or The Lightnings. We think the hailstones harden us up. The enemy doesn't have as many caves over on their side. We always tell the boys they were lucky to be stolen by us and not those others.

● ◐ ○ ◑ ●

When I was first taken, our mothers came up to the caves to get us back. That often happens. Some had weapons.

Laughable weapons. My own mother was there, in the front of course. She probably organized the whole thing, her face red and twisted with resolve. She came straight at me. I was afraid of her. We boys fled to the back of the barracks and our squad leader stood in front of us. Other men covered the doorway. It didn't take long for the mothers to retreat. None were hurt. We try never to do them any harm. We need them for the next crop of boys.

Several days later my mother came again by herself — sneaked up by moonlight. Found me by the light of the night lamp. She leaned over my sleeping mat and breathed on my face. At first I didn't know who it was. Then I felt breasts against my chest and I saw the glint of a hummingbird pin I recognized. She kissed me. I was petrified. (Had I been a little older I'd have known how to choke and kick to the throat. I might have killed her before I realized it was my mother.) What if she took me from my squad? Took away my uniform? (By then I had a red and blue jacket with gold buttons. I had already learned to shoot. Something I'd always wanted to do. I was the first of my group to get a sharpshooters medal. They said I was a natural. I was trying hard to make up for my small size.)

The night my mother came she lifted me in her arms. There, against her breasts, I thought of all the pillow jokes. I yelled. My comrades, though no older than I and only a little larger, came to my aid. They picked up whatever weapon was handy, mostly their boots. (Thank goodness we had not received our daggers yet.) My mother wouldn't hit out at the boys. She let them batter at her. I wanted her to hit back, to run, to save herself. After she finally did run, I found I had bitten my lower lip. In times of stress I'm inclined to do that. I have to watch out. When you're a colonel, it's embarrassing to be found with blood on your chin.

● ◑ ○ ◐ ●

So now, off to steal boys. We're a troop of older boys and younger men. The oldest maybe twenty-two, half my age. I think of them all as boys, though I would never call them boys to their faces. I'm in charge. My son, Hob, he's seventeen now, is with us.

But we no sooner creep down to the valley than we see things have changed since last year. The mothers have put up a wall. They've built themselves a fort.

I immediately change our plans. I decide this will be copulation day, not boys day. Good military strategy: Always be ready for a quick change of plan.

The minute I think this, I think Una. This is her town. My men look happy, too. This is not only easier, but lots more fun than herding a new crop of boys.

Last time I came down at copulation time I found her — or she found me, she usually does. She's a little old for copulation day, but I didn't want anybody but her. After copulation, I did things for her, repaired a roof leak, fixed a broken table leg .... Then I took her over again, though it wasn't needed, and caused my squad to have to wait for me. Got me a lot of lewd remarks, but I felt extraordinarily happy anyway.

Sometimes on boys night I wonder, what if I stole Una along with boys? What if I dressed her as a boy and brought her to some secret hiding place on our side of the mountain? There are lots of unused caves. Once our armies occupied them all, but that was long ago. Both us and our enemies seem to be dwindling. Every year there are fewer and fewer suitable boys.

Una always seems glad to see me even though I'm ugly and small. (My size is a disadvantage for a soldier, though less so now that I have rank, but the ugliness … that's how I can tell which are my sons … small, ugly boys, both of them. Too bad for them. But I've managed well even so, all the way up to colonel.)

Una was my first. I was her first, too. I felt sorry for her, having to have me for her beginning to be a woman. We were little more than children. We hardly knew what we were doing or how to do it. Afterwards she cried. I felt like crying myself but I had learned not to. Not just learned it with the squad, but I had learned it even before they took me from my mother. I wanted to be taken. I roamed far out into the scrub, waiting for them to come and get me.

The pain in my hip started when I was one of those boys. It wasn't from a wound in a skirmish with the enemy, but from a fight among ourselves. Our leaders were happy when we fought each other. We'd have gotten soft and lazy if we didn't. I keep my mouth shut about my injury. I kept my mouth shut even when I got it. I thought if they knew I could be so easily hurt they'd send me back. Later, I thought if they knew about it, I might not be allowed to come on our raids. Later still I thought I might not be able to be a colonel. I don't let myself limp though sometimes that makes me more breathless than I should be. So far it doesn't seem as if anybody's noticed.

We regroup. I say, "Fellow nipples and fellow pillows … ." Everybody laughs. "When have they ever stopped men? Look how womanish the walls are. They'll crumble as we climb." I scrape at a part with the tip of my cane. (As a colonel, I'm allowed to have a cane if I wish instead of a swagger stick.)

We're not sure if the women want to stop copulation day or boy gathering day. We hope it's the latter.

Boost up the smallest boy with a rope on hooks. The rest of us follow.

I used to be that smallest boy. I always went first and highest. Times like this I was glad for my size. I got medals for that. I don't wear any of them. I like playing at being one of the boys. Being small and being a colonel is a good example for some. If they knew about my bum leg I'd be an even better example of how far you can get with disabilities.

       ● ◑ ○ ◐ ●

We scale the walls and drop into the edges of a vegetable garden. We walk carefully around tomatoes and strawberry plants, squash and beans. After that, raspberry bushes tear at our pants and untie our high tops as we go by. There's a row of barbed wire just beyond the raspberries. Easy to push down.

I feel sad that the women want to keep us out so badly. I wonder, does Una want me not to come? Except they know we're as determined as mothers. At least I am when it comes to Una.

       ● ◑ ○ ◐ ●

Una has always been nice to me. I often wonder why she likes me. I can understand somebody liking me now that I'm a colonel with silver on my epaulets and a silver-handled cane, but she liked me when I was nothing but a runty boy. She's small, too. I always think Una and I fit together except for one thing, she's beautiful.

● ◑ ○ ◐ ●

We swarm in, turn, each to our favorite place, the younger ones to what's left over, usually other young ones. But then here we are, swarming back again, into their central square, the place with the well, and stone benches, and their one and only tree. Around the tree are the graves of babies. The benches are the mourning benches. We sit on them or on the ground. There's nobody here, not a single woman nor girl nor baby.

Then there's the sound of shooting. We move from the central square — we can't see anything from there. We hide behind the houses at the edges of the gardens. Our enemy stands along the top of the wall. We're ambushed. We flop down. We have no rifles with us and only two pistols, mine and my lieutenant's. This wasn't supposed to be a skirmish. We have our daggers, of course.

Those along the wall don't seem to be very good shots. I raised my pistol. I'm thinking to show them what a good shot really is. But my lieutenant yells, "Stop! Don't shoot. It's mothers!"

Women all along the wall! And with guns. Hiding under wall-colored shields. Whoever heard of such a thing.

They shoot, but a lot are missing, I think on purpose. After all, we may be the enemy, but we're the fathers of many of their girls and many of them. I wonder which one is Una.

The women are angrier than we thought. Perhaps they're tired of losing their boys to us and to the other side. I wouldn't put it past them not to be on any side whatsoever.

Our boys begin to yell their war cry but in a half-hearted way. But then … one shot … a real shot this time. Good shot, too. One wonders how a woman could have done it. One wonders if it was a man who taught her. The boys are stunned. To think that one of their mothers or one of their sisters would shoot to kill. This is real. We hadn't thought they'd harm us any more than we ever really harm them.

It was my lieutenant they killed. One bloodless shot to the head. For that boy's sake I'm glad at least no pain. He was wearing his ceremonial hat. I wasn't wearing mine. I never liked that fancy heavy hat. I suppose they really wanted to kill me, but had to take second best since they couldn't tell which one I was. Una would know which one was me.

The boys scatter — back to the center square with its mourning tree. The women can't see them back there. I stay to check on the dead lieutenant and to get his dagger and pistol. Then I limp back to where the boys are waiting for me to tell them what to do. Limp. I relax into it. I don't care who sees. I haven't exactly given up, though perhaps I have when it comes to my future. I'll most likely be demoted. To be captured by women …. All twenty of us. If I can't get out of this in an efficient and capable way, there goes my career.

I hope they have the sense to come rescue us with a large group. They'll have to make a serious effort. I hope they no longer fight and at the same time try to save the women for future use.

But then we hear shooting again and we look out from behind the huts near the wall and see the women have turned their guns outwards. At first we think it's us, come to rescue us, but it's not. That's not our battle cry, not our drum beats …. We can't see from behind the walls so some of us go up on the roofs. There's no danger, all the rifles are facing outwards, but our boys would have braved the roof without a word, as they always do.

It's not our red and blue banners. It's their ugly green and white. It's the enemy come to take advantage of our capture. We wish the women would get out of the way and let us go so we could fight for ourselves. Those women are breaking every rule of battle. They're lying flat along their wall. Nobody can get a fair shot at them.

It goes on and on. We get tired of watching and retreat to the square. We reconnoiter food from the kitchens. We eat better than we usually do. The food is so good we wish the women would let up a bit so we can enjoy it without that racket. Where did they get all these weapons? They must have found our ammunition caves and those of our enemy, too.

● ○ ○ ◐ ●

The women do a pretty good job. By nightfall our enemy has fled back into their mountains and the women are still on top of their wall. It looks as if they're going to spend the night up there. It's a wide wall. Not as badly built as I told the boys it was.

We find beds for ourselves, all of them better than our usual sleeping pads. I go to Una's hut and lie where I had hoped to have a copulation.

Cats prowl and yowl. All sorts of things live with the

women. Goats wander the streets and come in any house they want to. All the animals expect food everywhere. Like the women, our boys are soft hearted. They feed every creature that comes by. I don't let on that I do too.

This whole thing makes me sad. Worried. If I could just have Una in my arms, I might be able to sleep. I have a day dream of her creeping in to me in the middle of the night. I wouldn't even care if we had a copulation or not.

● ◑ ○ ◐ ●

In the morning boys climb to the roofs again to see what's up. They describe women lying under shields all along the walls and they can see some of the enemy lying dead away from the walls. I need to climb up and see for myself. Besides it's good for the boys to see me taking the same chances they do.

I send the boys off and I take their place. I look down on the women along the wall. I see several rifles pointed at me. I stand like a hero. I dare them to shoot. I take all the time I want. I see wall sections less crowded with women. I take out my notebook (no leader is ever without one) and draw a diagram. I take my time until I have the whole wall mapped out.

I could take out my pistol and threaten them. I could shoot one but it wouldn't be very manly to take advantage of my high point. Were they men I'd do it. But then they do the unmanly thing. They shoot me. My leg. My good leg. I go down, flat on the roof. At first I feel nothing but the shock ... as if I'd been hit with a hammer. All I know is I can't stand up. Then I see blood.

Though they're on the wall, they're lower. They can't see me as long as I keep down. I crawl to the edge where boys help me.

They carry me back to Una's bed. I feel I'm about to pass out or throw up and I become aware that I've soiled myself. I don't want the boys to see. I've always been a source of strength and inspiration in spite of or because of my size.

One of those boys is Hob, come to help me, my arm across his shoulders. I lean in pain but keep my groans to myself.

"Sir? Colonel?"

"I'm fine. Will be. Go."

I wish I could ask him if he really is my son. They say sometimes the women know and tell the boys.

"Don't you want us to … ."

"No. Go. Now. And shut the door."

They leave just in time. I throw up over the side of the bed. I lie back — Una's pillow all sweated up, not to mention what I've done to her quilt.

Una can make potions for pain. I wish I knew which of the herbs hanging from her ceiling might help me. But I'd not be able to reach them anyway.

I lie, half conscious, for I don't know how long. Every time I sit up to examine my leg, I feel nausea again and have to lie back. I wonder if I'll ever be able to lead a charge or a raid for boys or a copulation day. And I always thought, when I became a general (and lately I felt sure I'd be one) maybe I'd find out what we're fighting for — beyond, that is, the usual rhetoric we use to make ourselves feel superior. Now I suppose I'll never know the real reasons.

● ◑ ○ ◐ ●

The boys knock. I rouse myself and say, "Come." Try, that

is. At first my voice won't sound out at all and then it sounds more like a groan than a word. The boys tell me the women have called down from the wall. They want to send in a spokesman. The boys want to let him in and then hold him hostage so that we'll all be let out safely.

I tell them the women will probably send in a woman.

That bothers the boys. They must have had torture or killing in mind but now they look worried.

"Tell them yes," I say.

It must smell terrible in here. I even smell terrible to myself, and it's uncomfortable sitting in my own mess. I prop myself up as best I can. I hope I can keep to my senses. I hope I don't throw up in the middle of it. I put my dagger, unsheathed, under the pillow.

At first I think the boys were right, it's a man, of course a man. Where would they have found him, and is he from our side or theirs? That's important. I can't tell by the colors. He's all in tan and gray. He's not wearing any stripes at all so I can't tell his rank. He stands, at ease. More than at ease, utterly relaxed, and in front of a colonel.

But then … I can't believe it, it's Una. I should have known. Dressed as a man down to the boots. I have such a sense of relief and after that joy. Everything will be all right now.

I tell the boys to get out and shut the door.

I reach for her, but the look on her face stops me.

"You shot me in the leg on purpose, didn't you! My good leg!"

"I meant to shoot the bad one."

She opens all the windows, and the door again, too, and shoos the boys away.

"Let me see."

She's gentle. As I knew she'd be.

"I'll get the bullet out, but first I'll clean you up." She hands me leaves to chew for pain.

As she leans, so close above me, her hair falls out of her cap and brushes my face, gets in my mouth as it does when we have copulation day. I reach to touch her breast but she pushes me away.

I should kill her for the glory of it … the leader of the women. I'd not be thought a failure then. I'd be made a general in no time.

But, as she pulls away the soiled quilts, she finds my dagger first thing. She puts it in the drawer with her kitchen knives.

I think again how … (and we all know, only too well) how love is a dangerous thing and can spoil the best of plans. Even as I think it, I want to spoil the very plans I think of. I mean if she's the leader then I could deal with her right now, as she leans over me — even without my dagger. They may be good shots, but can they wrestle a man? Even a wounded one?

"I chose you because I thought, of all of them, you might listen."

"You know I won't ever be let come down to copulation day again."

"Don't go back then. Stay here and copulate."

"I have often thought to bring you up to the mountain dressed as a man. I have a place all picked out."

"Stay here. Let *everybody* stay here and be as women."

I can't answer such a thing. I can't even think about it.

"But what else do you know except how to be a colonel?"

She washes me, changes the bed, and throws the bed

clothes and my clothes out the door. Then she gets the bullet out. I'm half out of my head from the leaves she had me chew so the pain is dulled. She bandages me, covers me with a clean blanket, puts her lips against my cheek for a moment.

Then stands up, legs apart. She looks like one of our boys getting ready to prove himself. "We'll not stand for this anymore," she says. "It has to end and we'll end it, if not one way, then another."

"But this is how it's always been."

"You could be our spokesman."

How can she even suggest such a thing. "Pillows," I say. "Spokesman for the nipples."

Goodness knows what the mothers are capable of. They never stick to any rules.

"If the answer is no, we'll not have any more boy babies. You can come down and copulate all you want but there'll be no boys. We'll kill them."

"You wouldn't. You couldn't. Not you, Una."

"Have you noticed how there are fewer and fewer boys? Many have already done it."

But I'm in too much pain and dizzy from the leaves she gave me to think clearly. She sees that. She sits beside me, takes my hand. "Just rest," she says. How can I rest with such ideas in my head? "But the rules."

"Hush. Women don't care about rules. You know that."

"Come back with me." I pull her down against me. This time she lets me. How good it feels to have us chest to chest, my arms around her. "I have a secret place. It's not a hard climb to get there."

She pulls back. "Colonel, sir!"

"Please don't call me that."

Then I say … what we're not allowed to say or even think. It's a mother/child thing, not to be said between a man and a woman. I say, "I love you."

She leans back and looks at me. Then wipes at my chin. "Try not to bite your lip like that."

"It doesn't matter anymore."

"It does to me."

"I liked … . I like … ." I already used the other word, why not yet again. "I love copulation day only when with you."

I wonder if she feels the same about me. I wish I dared ask her. I wonder if my son … . Is Hob hers and mine together? I've always hoped he was. She's made no gesture towards him. She hasn't even looked at him any more than any other boy. This would have been his first copulation day had the women not built their wall.

"Rest," she says. "We'll discuss later."

"Is it just us? Or are you saying the same thing to the enemy? They could win the war like that. It would be your fault."

"Stop thinking."

"What if no more boys on either side, ever?"

"What if?"

She gives me more of those leaves to chew. They're bitter. I was in too much pain to notice that the first time. I feel even sleepier right away.

● ◑ ○ ◐ ●

I dream I'm the last of all the boys. Ever. I have to get somewhere in a hurry, but there's a wall so high I'll never get over it. Beside, my legs are not there at all. I'm nothing but a torso. Women watch me. Women, off across the valley floor as far as I can see and none will help. There's nothing to do but lie there and give the war cry.

I wake shouting and with Una holding me down. Hob is there, helping her. Other boys are in the doorway looking worried.

I've thrown the blanket and the pillow to the floor and now I seem to be trying to throw myself out of bed. Una has a long scratch across her cheek. I must have done that.

"Sorry. Sorry."

I'm still as if in a dream. I pull Una down against me. Hold her hard and then I reach out for Hob, too. My poor ugly boy. I ask the unaskable. "Tell me, is Hob mine and yours together?"

Hob looks shocked that I would ask such a thing, as well he should. Una pulls away and gets up. She answers as if she was one of the boys. "Colonel, sir, how can you, of all people, ask a thing like that." Then she throws my own words back at me. "This is how it's always been."

"Sorry. Sorry."

"Oh, for Heaven's sake stop being so *sorry!*"

She shoos the boys from the doorway but she lets Hob stay. Together they rearrange the bed. Together she and Hob make broth for me and food for themselves. Hob seems at home here. It's true, I'm sure. This is our son.

But I suppose all this yearning, all this wondering, is due to the leaves Una had me chew. It's not the real me. I'll not pay any attention to myself.

But there's something else. I didn't get a good look at my leg yet, but it feels like a serious wound. If I can't climb up to our stronghold, I'll not ever be able to go home. I shouldn't, even so, and though my career is in a shambles … I shouldn't let myself be lured into staying here as a copulator for the rest of my life. I can't think of anything more dishonorable. I should send Hob back to the citadel to report on what's happened and to get help. If he was found trying to escape, would Una let the women kill him?

I try to get Hob alone so I can whisper his orders to him. Only when Una goes out to the privy do I get the chance. "Get back to the citadel. Cross the wall tonight. There's no moon." I show him my map and where I think there are fewer women. I want to tell him to take care, but we don't ever say such things.

● ◑ ○ ◐ ●

In the morning I tell Una to tell my leaders to come in to me. I'm in pain, in a sweat, my beard is itchy. I ask Una to clean me up. She treats me as a mother would. Back when my mother did it, I pulled away. I wouldn't let her get close to me. I especially wouldn't let her hug or kiss me. I wanted to be a soldier. I wanted nothing to do with mother things.

All the boys are looking scruffy. We take pride in our cleanliness, in shaving every day, in our brush cuts, and our enemy is as spic and span as we are. I hope they don't launch an offensive today and see us so untidy.

I'm glad to see Hob isn't with them.

I find it hard to rouse myself to my usual humor. I say, "Pillows, nipples," but I'm too uncomfortable to play at being one of the boys.

I'd prefer to recuperate some, but the boys are restless

already. I can't be thinking of myself. We'll storm the wall. I show them the map. I point out the less guarded spots. I grab Una. Both her wrists. "Men, we'll need a battering ram."

Wood isn't easy to get out here on the valley floor. This is a desert except along the streams, but every village has one tree in the center square that they've nurtured along. As here, baby's graves are always around it. In other villages, most are cottonwood, but this one is oak. It's so old I wouldn't be surprised if it hadn't been here since before the village. I think the village was built up around it later.

"Chop the tree. Ram the wall," I tell them. "Go back to the citadel. Don't wait around for me. Tell the generals never to come here again, neither for boys nor for copulation. Tell them I'm of no use to us anymore."

The women won't be able to shoot at the boys chopping it down. It's hidden from all parts of the wall.

When they hear the chopping, the women begin to ululate. Our boys stop chopping, but only for a moment. I hear them begin again with even more vigor.

Here beside me Una ululates, too. She struggles against me but I hang on.

"How could you? That's the tree of dead boys."

I let go.

"All the babies buried there are boys. Some are yours."

I can't let this new knowledge color my thinking. I have to think of the safety of my boys. "Let us go, then."

"Tell them to stop."

"Would you let us go for the sake of a tree?"

"We would."

I give the order.

The women move away from a whole section of the wall, they even provide their ladders. I tell the boys to go. There's no way they could carry me back and no way I could ever climb to the citadel again.

No sooner are the boys gone, even to the last tootle of the fifes, the last triumphant drum beat … . (We always march home as though victorious whether victorious or not.) Hearing them go, I can't help but groan, though not from pain this time. No sooner have the mothers come down from the wall but that I hear ululating again. Una stamps in to me.

"What now?"

"It's Hob. Your enemy … . *Your* enemy has dropped him off at the edge of your foothills."

I can see it on her face.

"He's dead."

"Of course he's dead. You are all as good as dead."

She blames me for Hob. "I blame myself."

"I hate you. I hate you all."

I don't believe we'll be seeing many boys anymore. I would warn us if I was able, I would be the spokesman, though I don't suppose I'll ever have the chance.

"What will the women do with me?"

"You were always kind. I'll not be any less to you."

What am I good for? What use am I but to stay here as the father of females? All those small, ugly, black-haired girls … . I suppose all of them biting their lower lips until they bleed.

AL

SORT OF A PLANE CRASH IN AN UNCHARTED REGION OF the park.

● ◑ ○ ◐ ●

We were flying fairly low over the mountains. We had come to the last ridge when there, before us, appeared this incredible valley . . . .
Suddenly the plane sputtered. (We knew we were low gas but we had thought to make it over the mountains. "I think I can bring her in." (John's last words.)
I was the only survivor.

● ◑ ○ ◐ ●

A plane crash in a field of alfalfa, across the road from it the Annual Fall Festival of the Arts. An oasis on the edge of the parking area. One survivor. He alone, Al, who has spent considerable time in France, Algeria, and Mexico, his paintings without social relevance (or so the critics say) and best in the darker colors, not a musician at all yet seems to be one of us. He, a stranger, wandering in a land he doesn't remember and not one penny of our kind of money, creeping from behind our poster, across from it the once-a-year art experience for music lovers. Knowing him as I do now, he must have been wary then; view from our poster, ENTRANCE sign, vast parking lot, our red and white tent, our EXIT on the far side, maybe the sound of a song — a frightening situation under the circumstance, all the others dead and Al having been unconscious for who knows how long? (the scar from that time is still on his cheek), stumbling across the road then and into our ticket booth.

"Hi."

I won't say he wasn't welcome. Even then we were wondering, were we facing stultification? Already some of our rules had become rituals. Were we, we wondered, doomed to a partial relevance in our efforts to make music meaningful in our time? And now Al, dropped to us from the skies (no taller than we are, no wider and not even quite so graceful). Later he was to say: "Maybe the artful gesture is lost forever."

We had a girl with us then as secretary, a long-haired changeling child, actually the daughter of a prince (there still are princes), left out in the picnic area of a western state forest to be found and brought up by an old couple in the upper middle class (she still hasn't found this out for sure, but has always suspected something of the sort), so when *I* asked Al to *my* (extra) bedroom it was too late. (By that time he had already pounded his head against the wall some so he seemed calm and happy and rather well adjusted to life in our valley.) The man from the *Daily* asked him how did he happen to become interested in art? He said he came from a land of cultural giants east of our outermost islands where the policemen were all poets. That's significant in two ways.

About the artful gesture being lost, so many lost arts and also soft, gray birds, etc., etc., etc. (The makers of toe shoes will have to go when the last toe dancer dies.)

However, right then, there was Al, mumbling to us in French, German and Spanish. We gave him two tickets to our early-evening concert even though he couldn't pay except in what looked like pesos. Second row, left side. (Right from the beginning there was something in him I couldn't resist.) We saw him craning his neck there, somehow already with our long-haired girl beside him. She's five hundred years old though she doesn't look a day over sixteen and plays the virginal like an angel. Did her undergraduate work at the University of Utah (around 1776, I would say). If she crossed the Alleghenies *now* she'd crumble into her real age and die, so later on I tried to get them to take a trip to the Ann Arbor Film Festival together, but naturally she had something else to do. Miss Haertzler.

● ◗ ○ ◑ ●

As our plane came sputtering down I saw the tents below, a village of nomads, God knows how far from the nearest outpost of civilization. They had, no doubt, lived like this for thousands of years.

These thoughts went rapidly through my mind in the moments before we crashed and then I lost consciousness.

● ◗ ○ ◑ ●

"COME, COME YE SONS OF ART." That's what our poster across the street says, quotes, that is. Really very nice in Day-Glo colors. "COME, COME AWAY …" etc., on to "TO CELEBRATE, TO CELEBRATE THIS TRIUMPHANT DAY," which meant to me, in some symbolic way even at that time, the day Al came out from behind it and stumbled across the road to our booth, as they say, "a leading force, from then on, among the new objectivists and continues to play a major role among them up to the present time" (which was a few years ago). Obtained his bachelor's degree in design at the University of Michigan with further study at the Atelier Chaumière in Paris. He always says, "Form speaks." I can say I knew him pretty well at that time. I know he welcomes criticism but not too early in the morning. Ralph had said (he was on the staff of the Annual Fall Festival), "Maybe artistic standards are no longer relevant." (We were wondering at the time how to get the immediacy of the war into our concerts more meaningfully than the "1812 Overture." Also something of the changing race relations.) Al answered, but just then a jet came by or some big oil truck and I missed the key word. That leaves me still not understanding what he meant. The next morning the same thing happened and it may have been more or less the answer to everything.

By then we had absorbed the major San Francisco influences. These have remained with us in some form or other up to the present time. Al changed the art exhibit we had in the vestibule to his kind of art as soon as Miss Haertzler went to bed with him. We had a complete new selection of paintings by Friday afternoon, all hung in time for the early performance (Ralph hung them) and by then, or at least by Saturday night, I knew I was, at last, really in love for the first time in my life.

● ◑ ○ ◐ ●

When I came to, I found we had crashed in a cultivated field planted with some sort of weedlike bush entirely unfamiliar to me. I quickly ascertained that my three companions were beyond my help, then extricated myself from the wreckage and walked to the edge of the field. I found myself standing beneath a giant stele where strange symbols swirled in brilliant, jewellike colors. Weak and dazed though I was, I felt a surge of delight. Surely, I thought, the people who made this cannot be entirely uncivilized.

● ◑ ○ ◐ ●

Miss Haertzler took her turn on stage like the rest of us. She was the sort who would have cut off her right breast the better to bow the violin, but, happily, she played the harpsichord. Perhaps Al wouldn't have minded, anyway. Strange man. From some entirely different land and I could never quite figure out where. Certainly he wouldn't have minded. She played only the very old and the very new, whereas *I* had suddenly discovered Beethoven (over again) and I talked about Romanticism during our staff meetings. Al said, "In some ways a return to Romanticism is like a return to the human figure." I believe he approved of the idea.

He spent the first night, Tuesday night, that was, the twenty-second, in our red and white tent under the bleachers at the back. A touch of hay fever woke him early.

By Wednesday Ralph and I had already spent two afternoons calculating our losses due to the rain, and I longed for a new experience of some sort that would lift me out of the endless problems of the Annual Fall Festival of the Arts. I returned dutifully, however, to the area early the next day to continue my calculations in the quiet of the morning and found him there.

"Me. Al. You?" Pointing finger.

"Ha, ha." (I *must* get rid of my nervous laugh!)

● ◑ ○ ◐ ●

I wanted to redefine my purposes not only for his sake, but for my own.

I wanted to find out just what role the audience should play.

I wanted to figure out, as I mentioned before, how we could best incorporate aspects of the war and the changing race relations into our concerts.

I wondered how to present musical experiences in order to enrich the lives of others in a meaningful way, how to engage, in other words, their total beings. I wanted to expand their musical horizons.

"I've thought about these things all year," I said, "ever since I knew I would be a director of the Annual Fall Festival. I also want to mention the fact," I said, "that there's a group from the college who would like to disrupt the unity of our performances (having other aims and interests) but," I told him, "the audience has risen to the occasion, at least by last night, when we had not only good weather, but money and an enthusiastic reception."

"I have recognized," he replied, "here in this valley, a fully realized civilization with a past history, a rich present, and a future all its own, and I have understood, even in my short time here, the vast immigration to urban areas that must have taken place and that must be continuing into the present time."

How could I help but fall in love with him? He may have spent the second night in Miss Haertzler's bed (if my conjectures are correct) but, I must say, it was with me he had all his discussions.

● ◑ ○ ◐ ●

I awoke the next morning extremely hungry, with a bad headache and with sniffles and no handkerchief, yet somehow, in spite of this, in fairly good spirits though I did long for a good hot cup of almost anything. Little did I realize then, or I might not have felt so energetic, the hardships I was to encounter here in this strange, elusive, never-never land. Even just getting something to eat was to prove difficult.

● ◑ ○ ◐ ●

Somewhat later that day I asked him out to lunch and I wish I could describe his expression eating his first grilled cheese and bacon, sipping his first clam chowder ....

Ralph, I tell you, this really happened and just as if we haven't *all* crash-landed here in some sort of (figurative) unknown alfalfa field. As if we weren't *all* penniless or about to be, waiting for you to ask us out to lunch. Three of our friends are dead and already there are several misunderstandings. You may be in love with me for all I know, though that may have been before I had gotten to be your boss in the Annual Fall Festival.

That afternoon I gave Al a job, Ralph, cleaning up candy wrappers and crumpled programs with a nail on a stick, and I invited him to our after-performance party for the audience. Paid him five dollars in advance. That's how much in love I was, so there's no sense in you coming over anymore. Besides, I'm tired of people who play instruments by blowing.

● ◑ ○ ◐ ●

I found the natives to be a grave race, sometimes inattentive, but friendly and smiling, even though more or less continuously concerned about the war. The younger ones frequently live communally with a charming innocence, by threes or fours even up to sixes or eights in quite comfortable apartments, sometimes forming their own family groups from a few chosen friends, and, in their art, having a strange return to the very old or the primitive along with their logical and very right interest in the new, though some liked Beethoven.

● ◑ ○ ◐ ●

We had invited the audience to our party after the performance. The audience was surprised and pleased. It felt privileged. It watched us now with an entirely different point of view and it wondered at its own transformation while I wondered why I hadn't thought of doing this before and said so to Al as the audience gasped, grinned, clapped, fidgeted and tried to see into the wings.

We had, during that same performance, asked the audience to come forward, even to dance if it was so inclined. We had discussed this thoroughly beforehand in our staff meetings.

It wasn't as though it was not a completely planned thing, and we had thought some Vivaldi would be a good way to start them off. Al had said, "Certainly something new must happen every day." Afterward I said to the audience, "Let me introduce Al, who has just arrived by an unfortunate plane crash from a far-off land, a leading force among the new objectivists, but penniless at the moment, sleeping out under our bleachers … ." However, that very night I heard that Miss Haertzler and Al either went for a walk after our party up to the gazebo on the hill or they went rowing on the lake, and I heard someone say, though not necessarily referring to them, "Those are two thin young people in the woods and they're quite conscious that they don't have clothes on and that they're very free spirits." And someone said, "She has a rather interesting brassiere," though that was at a different time, and also, "I wonder if he's a faggot because of the two fingers coming down so elegantly."

● ☽ ○ ☾ ●

I found it hard to adjust to some of the customs of this hardy and lively people. This beautiful, slim young girl invited me to her guest room on my second night there and then entered as I lay in bed, dropping her simple, brightly colored shift at her feet. Underneath she wore only the tiniest bit of pink lace, and while I was wondering, was she, perhaps, the king's daughter or the chief's mistress? what dangers would I be opening myself up to and thinking besides that this was my first night in a really comfortable bed after a very enervating two days, also my first night with a full stomach and would I be able to? she moved, not toward me, but to the harpsichord.

I had much to learn.

●　◑　○　◐　●

Mornings, sometimes as early as nine-thirty, Al could be found painting in purples, browns, grays, and blacks in the vestibule area at the front of our tent. The afternoons many of us, Al included, frequently spent lounging on the grass outside the tent (on those days when it didn't rain), candidly confessing the ages of and the natures of our very first sexual experiences and discussing other indiscretions, with the sounds of the various rehearsals as our background music. (Miss Haertzler's first sexual experience, from what I've been told, may have actually taken place fairly recently and in our own little red ticket booth.) Thinking back to those evening concerts I can still see Al, as though it were yesterday, in his little corner backstage scribbling on his manifesto of the new art:

"Why should painting remain shackled by outmoded laws? Let us proclaim, here and at once, a new world for art where each work is judged by its own internal structures, by the manifestations of its own being, by its self-established decrees, by its self-generated commands.

"Let us proclaim the universal properties of the thing itself without the intermediary of fashion.

"Let us proclaim the fragment, the syllable, the single note (or sound) as the supreme elements out of which everything else flows …."

And so forth.

(Let us also proclaim what a friend [Tom Disch] has said: "I don't understand people who have a feeling of comfortableness about art. There's a kind of art that they feel comfortable seeing and will go and see that kind of thing again and again. I get very bored with known sensations ....")

But, even as Al worked, seemingly so contented, and even as he welcomed color TV, the discovery of DNA and the synthesizing of an enzyme, he had his doubts and fears just like anyone else.

●   ○   ○   ◐   ●

Those mountains that caught the rays of the setting sun and burned so red in the evenings! That breathtaking view! How many hours did I spend gazing at them when I should have been writing on my manifesto, aching with their beauty and yet wondering whether I would ever succeed in crossing them? How many times did my conversation at that time contain hidden references to bearers and guides? Once I learned of a trail that I might follow by myself tf I could get someone to furnish me with a map. It was said to be negotiable only through the summer to the middle of October and to be too steep for mule or motorcycle. Later on I became acquainted with a middle-aged homosexual flute player named Ralph, who was willing to answer all my questions quite candidly. We became good friends and, as I got to know him better, I was astounded at the sophistication of his views on the nature of the universe. He was a gentle, harmless person, tall and tanned from a sun lamp. Perhaps I should mention that he never made any sexual advances to me, that I was aware of at any rate.

●   ○   ○   ◐   ●

"After the meeting between Ralph A. and Al W.," the critics write, "Ralph A.'s work underwent an astonishing change. Obviously he was impressed by the similarities between art and music and he attempted to interpret in musical terms those portions of Al W.'s manifesto that would lend themselves to this transposition. His 'Three Short Pieces for Flute, Oboe and Prepared Piano' is, perhaps, the finest example of his work of this period."

By then Al had lent his name to our town's most prestigious art gallery. We had quoted him often in our programs. I had discussed with him the use of public or private funds for art. I had also discussed, needless to say, the problem of legalized abortion and whether the state should give aid to parochial schools. Also the new high-yield rice. I mentioned our peace groups including our Women's March for Peace. I also tried to tell him Miss Haertzler's real age and I said that, in spite of her looks, it would be very unlikely that she could ever have any children, whereas I, though not particularly young anymore, could at least do that, I'm (fairly) sure.

And then, all too soon, came the day of the dismantling of the Annual Fall Festival tent and the painting over of our billboard, which Al did (in grays, browns, purples, and blacks), making it into an ad for the most prestigious art gallery, and I, I was no longer a director of anything at all. The audience, which had grown fat and satiated on our sounds, now walked in town as separate entities … factions … fragments … will-o'-the-wisp … meaningless individuals with their separate reactions. Al walked with them, wearing his same old oddy cut clothes as unselfconsciously as ever, and, as ever, with them but not of them. He had worked for us until the very last moment, but now I had no more jobs to give. He couldn't find any other work and, while the critics and many others, too, liked his paintings, no one wanted to buy them. They were fairly expensive and the colors were too somber. I helped him look into getting a grant, but in the end it went to a younger man (which I should have anticipated). I gave him, at about that time, all my cans of corned beef hash even though I knew he still spent some time in Miss Haertzler's guest room, though, by then, a commune (consisting of six young people of both sexes in a three-room apartment) had accepted him as one of them. (I wonder sometimes that he never asked Miss Haertzler to marry him, but he may have been unfamiliar with marriage as we know it. We never discussed it that I remember and not too many people in his circle of friends were actually married to each other.)

Ralph had established himself as the local college musical figure, musician in residence really, and began to walk with a stoop and a slight limp and to have a funny way of clearing his throat every third or fourth word. I asked him to look into a similar job for Al, but they already had an artist in residence, a man in his sixties said to have a fairly original eye and to be profoundly concerned with the disaffection of the young, so they couldn't do a thing for Al for at least a year, they said, aside from having him give a lecture or two, but even that wouldn't be possible until the second semester.

Those days I frequently saw Al riding around on a borrowed motor scooter (sometimes not even waving), Miss Haertzler on the back with her skirts pulled up. He still painted. The critics have referred to this time in his life as one of hardship and self-denial while trying to get established.

Meanwhile it grew colder.

Miss Haertzler bought him a shearling lamb jacket. Also one for herself. I should have suspected something then, but I knew it was the wrong time of year for a climb. There was already a little bit of snow on the top of the highest of our mountains and the weatherman had forecast a storm front on the way that was to be there by that night or the next afternoon. We all thought it was too early for a blizzard.

I was to find Miss (Vivienne) Haertzler an excellent traveling companion. Actually a better climber than I was myself in many ways and yet, for all that vigor, preserving an essential femininity. Like many others of her race, she had small hands and feet and a fair-skinned look of transparency, and yet an endurance that matched my own. But I did notice about her that day an extraordinary anxiety that wasn't in keeping with her nature at all (nor of the natives in general). I didn't give a second thought, however, to any of the unlikely rumors I had heard, but I assumed it was due to the impending storm that we hoped would hide all traces of our ascent.

A half day later a good-sized group of our more creative people were going after one of the most exciting minds in the arts with bloodhounds. A good thing for Miss Haertzler, too, since the two of them never even got halfway. I saw them back in town a few days afterward, still looking frostbitten, and it wasn't long after that that I had a very pleasant discussion with Al. I had asked him out to our town's finest continental restaurant. We talked, among other things, about alienation in our society, population control, impending world famine, and other things of international concern, including the anxiety prevalent among our people of impending atomic doom. In passing I mentioned a psychologist I had once gone to for certain anxieties of my own of a more private nature. Soon after that I heard that Al was in therapy himself and had learned to accept his perennial urge to cross the mountains and, as the psychologist put it, "leave our happy valley in his efforts to escape from something in himself." It would be a significant moment in both modern painting and modern music (and perhaps in literature, too) when Al would finally be content to remain in his new-found artistic milieu. I can't help but feel that the real beginning of Al's participation (sponsored) within our culture as a whole was right here on my couch in front of the fireplace with a cup of hot coffee and a promise of financial assistance from two of our better-known art patrons. It was right here that he began living out some sort of universal human drama of life and death in keeping with his special talents.

THE BIRD PAINTER IN TIME OF WAR

I PAINT BIRDS IN ENEMY TERRITORY. I RISK MY LIFE TO paint them. My people are desert people. They think I've made the birds up — that I'm painting fairy tales just so I can sell them to the gullible. I don't think I could invent such fancy birds by myself. So far I've only been able to smuggle some feathers to prove to my own people that there do, indeed, exist birds of a beauty they've never even thought of.

The enemy farmers know I'm a foreigner but they don't guess where I'm from. I ask, with some of their words and with drawings, if such and such a bird is around. I pay them in pictures. I don't have any of their kind of money. I don't even have my own kind. That would be a sure giveaway.

If their soldiers catch me, they'll take me for a spy. They'll think my paintings full of secret messages. *Who cares about birds?* they'd say. And they'd be right. Who does? Not very many in any country.

I doubt if I'd have the energy or the will to defend myself. I stutter. Even more so when I'm nervous. The birds don't care. I can imitate their calls. I can whistle, squawk, quack and squeak. I'm good at those, no problem.

I eat what comes to hand but I won't eat birds. I can usually find tree ears or chanterelles and there are roots. But I won't eat quail or duck or sage hen as most do. I do eat fish and crayfish.

I used to photograph wars, but that was before I looked up, not for the hiss of a mortar but for a different, exciting sound, and there, in long lines, were the snow geese flying north.

That was a long time ago, and an entirely different war.

I prefer the people here where I don't talk their language that well. Then not talking is normal. A silent cup of tea with gestures. A place by the fire on a rainy night. These people are not great talkers, anyway. I and the farmer can sit and smoke and nod, his wife and children nearby, happy, or so it seems, for each other's silent company.

If I see a good barn I may not even ask. I may just bed down there secretly. Of course there'll be a dog, but I'm good with dogs. I always sit a bit before imposing myself on their space. Sometimes I manage to get out a series of Gs. Guh, guh, ghu, ghu, good dog.

Children ask what's wrong with me. I always say, "L, l, l, *lots* of things."

●　◒　○　◐　●

To avoid detection, when I leave my desert for their mountains, I always cross the border where the cliffs are steep and the forest thick. It's not easy with my folio and sketch books on my back.

After climbing the ridge, I'll hit the road to the village. I never get far. I'm always looking down at the plants along the roadside, as much as I look up to see what's flying by. I don't bother with the names of either birds or plants. Words are my adversaries. Besides, the names will be different in their language.

It's the perfect time of year. All sorts of birds are passing through. Half way up the hills on their side of the border, I stop, turn around, and rest. I can see the tops of the flags that fly from their fort just below me. I'm well past their lines. From now on I'll just look like one more farmer with a big bundle.

But there's not a single bird call nor rustle of ground squirrels. I hold still — just as everything else does. I hear the snap of twigs. Something's happening just above the fort.

Then I see soldiers in the colors of my own side, circling past not far below me. They're going to hit from behind, where the cliffs look down on the fort. They'll drop mortars right into the central courtyard.

These days forts aren't worth much. I don't think the enemy uses this one for anything but barracks. Those cannons along the ramparts are a hundred years old. I heard reveille as I passed by. The enemy will be there. My side could do a lot of damage.

I wonder if I should try to warn the enemy. What would save the most bloodshed?

I climb higher, wondering what to do.

But then I hear a sound from above. I stop again. Hold still …

… and a soldier backs up right into me. This time a soldier of the enemy, looking down on those skulking soldiers of my own side. He's alone, but loaded down with rifle and grenades.

At first I think a boy and I think, does the enemy use children as its soldiers? But I start to suspect. I look down at her body.

She sees my look. "Yes," she says, in the enemy language, "I am," and points her gun at my chest. "What are you doing out here? Trying to sneak across the border?"

Exactly what I *am* doing. Of course what I answer is my usual. "I, I, I, I, I."

"What's in your bundle?"

I hand it to her. She moves away, tries to keep her gun on me, and open the bundle at the same time. Not easy.

Then she forgets all about the gun. She even forgets about me.

I have two smaller paintings I brought with me to trade for a meal, or a bed in case the weather turns bad. One is of the bird I call a golden wing. The other is of a pair of black and white longtails with red heads. I tried to capture the luminosity of their throats. There are flowers in each painting. People like that. In one there's dew on the petals and a sunrise in the background. They're not completely realistic. After all, I was a photographer, I got tired of reality.

She can't stop looking. Ten … maybe fifteen minutes. I sit down. Later she turns to me, a look of wonder on her face. All she says is, "You!"

I nod.

She sits beside me, the paintings at our feet. She gives three big sighs in a row, says, "I'd like to forget all about the war. I'd like to run away and never come back."

I keep nodding. I don't want to have to try to say anything.

She looks at me again — all admiration. "Easy to see you're not a soldier."

Then she looks at the signature.

My name will tell her I'm a foreigner.

"Nor. Nor? Where's that from?"

I took that name from the word for bird in my language.

I don't lie. "I, I'm yu, yu, your … enemy."

"Not *my* enemy."

Her eyes are greenish blue.

Then, below us, the bombardment begins. My people against her people.

She picks up her rifle. She's about to take off, but I grab her arm.

"N, n, n, nothing you can d … ."

A trumpet sounds down in the fort.

"You're trying to save them."

"No. S, s, save … . *You!*"

But she twists away and off she goes.

I pack up my paintings and head up. I want to be back where the birds are singing. I need to paint. It calms me.

I don't stop until the sound is muffled and distant and until I start to hear birds again and the rustle of ground creatures.

I get out my sketch pad and a crow quill pen and sit, hardly moving. And soon, here comes a redheaded yellowbeak with topknot and right behind him his drab but, in her own way, equally beautiful mate. I start to sketch, then give each drawing a wash of water color, wait a few minutes until they dry and pack up.

I was concentrating so hard I didn't notice that the distant explosions had stopped, though there's a volley of rifle shots now and then.

I climb out on a jutting rock. I'm almost at the top of the cliff. Behind me is the high flat land of the enemy. I watch the sun setting across the valley where my people live. I watch a flock of snow geese fly by. I hear them. They're low, getting ready to land for the night. I watch until even the stragglers pass. Then I climb below the jutting rock and lie down.

I wonder how things went at the fort and with the girl. I wonder if she's still alive or if she rushed in, threw her grenades and was shot right away. I hope she had more sense.

Can a mere bird painter rescue somebody? Especially a bird painter who can hardly talk?

I feel bad that I let myself spend the afternoon sketching — making myself forget while others were in danger and maybe pain … of course it's pain they've gotten themselves into. Even she. But the joy on her face when she looked at my paintings! And then at me! It's enough to make me fall in love. But I don't ever let myself. How could I say what needs to be said? With secret signs and hand signals? A wink? A leer? Maybe with a parrot on my shoulder to talk for me in squawks? I refuse.

Besides, I have my birds.

But could I rescue?

I give up on sleeping.

I can at least see if she made it down to her own people. After I find out, I'll escape back to my solitude.

●   ◐   ○   ◑   ●

I leave my bundle under the jutting rock. No moon. There's an owl. That reassures me. I disturb things that skitter away. Then I trip and fall flat. Branches scratch my face. I hit my chin on a rock and almost knock myself out. There's a mini landslide. I make a terrible racket. I lie still and listen.

Nothing.

But right after that, my own side captures me. They don't treat me very well. Before they ask me anything or try to find out who I am, they throw me down and kick me a few times. Then bring me to a bonfire and to a colonel. I stutter more than usual. I don't make any sense at all. They take me for a moron — it's not the first time — and chain me to a tree.

I'm worried about my paintings and sketch books under that overhang (they're not well hidden), but I'm mostly worried about the girl. I don't even know her name. I can't ask about her. But then I can't ask about her anyway. They don't have time to listen to me trying to get the words out.

● ◑ ○ ◐ ●

In the morning I open my eyes to white feathers. A fog of white. Tiny bits of down. I'm hurting and stiff but I'm charmed. Enchanted. It's as if I've found my way into a bird world. I sit up and then I realize there's nothing to be enchanted about.

Every little group of soldiers has a camp fire with a spit and something cooking. The battle was long over, but that evening they had nothing else to shoot so they shot the snow geese as they came down low, looking for a resting place.

They eat and then bring me their leftovers, but, hungry as I am, I won't eat snow goose.

Finally they unchain me, bring me down to the ruined fort where they've set up headquarters. The outer walls still stand, but inside it's a mess. The inner walls are stone, too, but the roofs were mostly wood and they're splintered and broken. Everything in the rooms is scattered and covered with debris.

They have ways of hurting that don't leave a mark. If I could think of a secret I'd try to tell it to them, but I never pay attention to anything except birds and flowers. And the more I need to talk, the worse my sputtering gets. I find myself making the bird sounds that come to me so easily, quacks and screeches and squawks.

Afterwards they don't bother tying me up. They let me lie in the courtyard. Discarded. Soldiers walk back and forth around me and don't pay any attention.

●　◗　○　◖　●

Later I hear somebody calling, "Nor, Nor. Get up, Nor. Please. Can you get up?"

It's dusk. The fort is quiet. Quieter than it should be, not a soldier in sight. It seems the army has left for some other battle.

"Nor."

I know who it is.

I stand up and hobble over to a tiny window in a stone wall. She reaches out. I grab her hand. Without thinking I kiss it and then hold it to my cheek. Then I worry about what I've done, but she reaches with her other hand and places it over my hand. Perhaps words aren't so necessary after all.

"Are y, y, you aw … ."

"What have they done to you? You look … ."

I'm thinking: Nothing you can see, but then I remember my bruised chin and scratched face from my fall.

"They've gone," she says. "Can you let me out."

The door is chained shut, but I use a piece of debris as a crow bar and pry the hinges out.

We run out the broken gates, around the fort, and start up behind it. I'm, yet again, climbing the cliffs at the hardest place. I know the way well but now I'm hurting. I wonder if I have a cracked rib.

● ◑ ○ ◐ ●

It's exactly under that jutting rock where I hid my things that we finally stop, and there's my bundle, slashed. Everything scattered. My paintings are not only cut, but shot at. I suppose the next best thing to shooting real birds is shooting paintings of them. They burned the sketch books. Just the metal rings are left. They cooked another snow goose there.

I sit down, discouraged. It's the girl that yells, "Oh no! Oh no!" over and over. She runs around gathering up pieces and trying to fit them back together.

I say, "D, d, don't."

She says, "But I want these. Can I have them?"

I shrug.

I sit beside the dead campfire, while the girl, on her knees, keeps trying to piece together parts of the paintings and I finally remember to ask her name. It's Milla. I think it means cloud. It fits her.

She keeps looking up at me with the same admiration as before and I realize I've done it — I've actually rescued her. If not for me coming down for her, who would have been there to let her out?

She pieces together about half of one of my paintings. The middle is full of bullet holes and cuts.

"Look. The sunset and the flock of ducks in the distance is

still there. I want it. Please."

"C, c, 'course."

"Except you could sell this as it is."

"No. You c, c."

"But what can I do for you that would be worth as much?"

"N, n, no."

Then we hear honking way above us. Another batch of geese but high. You can just barely hear them.

Then there's gunfire below us. None of the geese fall, they're way too high. Somebody is shooting just for the fun of it. It stops after the ducks pass, but the shooters are so near, we think we'd better get out of there.

But they've heard us. They start shooting in our direction before they know which side we are, or we them. We flop down flat.

But it might be my own side.

I stand up. I shout, "S, s, stop," in my own language.

Behind me Milla shouts, "Stop," in her language.

Good. We have both languages going. Then one of them says, "Stop," in the enemy's language. It's Milla's people.

Right in front of me, and in flower, is the bush the hummingbirds love best, and there, the hummingbird. How can it be? Right between shots? I still have a red feather in my button hole. I don't know how it lasted here through all this. The bird hovers over it. I stand still. It hovers over my face. Checking, am I food or not? Perhaps my scratches are red enough to tempt it.

●　◑　○　◐　●

I come to, to someone crying. I'm comfortable. There's a pillow. There's a feather bed. I think: *Some day there will be nothing to cry about. Or at least there'll be no shooting and plenty of feather beds.* Then I think: *Hummingbird!*

I open my eyes and sit up.

The crying stops.

There's a little girl standing in the doorway. She says, "Oh!" And then, in the enemy language, "I thought you were dead."

I'm not a good judge of children's ages, but she can't be more than six or seven.

I say, "N, n, not yet."

She says, "You had blood."

"D, did I?"

"You stayed in bed all day. I wouldn't like that."

"I, I, I … ."

"You talk funny."

"I, I … . Yup."

"They didn't want me to see you but I did anyway. Lots of times. Like now. You're a secret. But how come you get all these nice things?"

"Wh, what? N, nice?"

Then I see, beside the bed, there are sketch books, pens, and paints, and a large tablet of watercolor paper.

"I wish *I* could have them. Or even just one little bitty thing."

"Which?"

"Paints."

"I … I'll … share."

Then Milla comes in, carrying a tray.

"Sassuna! What are you doing here?"

She's wearing slacks and a flowery blouse. Everything much more revealing than her uniform.

"He said he'd share."

"Go!"

The girl is so happy she actually skips out.

"I hope she didn't wake you."

"I … l … like … ."

She puts the tray on a little table by the bed.

I try to get up and fall flat. Bang my chin yet again, knock over the tray — the tea, the bread — in a great clatter.

But she's kneeling beside me. I'm in her arms.

Again I'm thinking: *Maybe words aren't that important.*

Sassuna must have heard everything crashing down. She's back. As before she says, "Oh!" Stands in the doorway watching us.

Milla kisses my forehead and then my cheeks. I reach up to hold her head so I can kiss her lips.

Sassuna keeps on looking. We keep right on kissing.

●　◑　○　◐　●

Milla tells me the soldiers of my side are entering houses hunting for soldiers of their side. They're killing animals to eat and killing animals for fun. The place is overrun by *us*. So far they haven't come here. This farm is set well back from the main road and hidden in trees.

I was shot in the thigh. Another shot creased my ribs under my arm. When I fell, I fell hard and hit my head.

After they shot me, Milla's side apologized to her. They even helped carry me out to the road, but refused to do more.

They thought my side was right behind them. Milla found an old man with a cart and had him haul me here.

There's an old lady here (Sassuna's grandmother) and a boy who sleeps in the barn and helps out. They know I rescued Milla and she showed them the pieces of my paintings. Boasted about me. Only Sassuna doesn't look at me as if I was special. She says she can draw and paint just as well as I can. I say we'll go out and paint as soon as I'm well enough. Of course I don't say it as easily as that but Sassuna waits for me to sputter it out.

● ◑ ○ ◐ ●

Later they wheel me into the yard to paint and soon we hike the fields and orchard. Milla comes, too. She likes to sit behind my left shoulder and watch my paintings grow, little by little by little.

Everything we paint is hung up in the main room right away, mine and Sassuna's side by side.

Now, to everybody's exasperation, Sassuna limps and stutters as much as I do. Nobody can stop her.

Sassuna says, if she was a bird, she'd like to be the red and blue one with the topknot. I say I'd like to be a crow or raven because they're clever and tricky.

And Milla and I …

Sassuna's grandmother lets us do as we do without disapproval.

Neither of us talk much. Touch is how we love each other.

● ◑ ○ ◐ ●

But they come. My side. In the middle of the night, of course. They take me and Milla.

I can't explain anything, even in my own language, but I don't want to. I want to go with Milla. Milla tells them I'm on their side, but they don't believe her.

I'm still wearing my shirt and pants with bullet holes. Bullet holes in civilian clothes means to them I'm worse than a soldier, I'm a spy. They think my stuttering is a ruse. Or they think I was picked to be a spy because I couldn't divulge secrets when tortured.

They tie us up and throw us in a truck bed and drive us back to the old fort. I have a kind of fit. I *will* not let this happen. I refuse. I struggle. Milla keeps yelling for me to stop. "It won't do any good." At the end of twenty minutes I'm exhausted.

They lock the others near the gate but they take me to a cell on the far side of the fort. I'm in a room with hardly space enough for a cot. And there's no cot. In fact there's nothing. There's a barred window in the door just big enough for somebody to look in and see if I'm still here.

There are ravens all over the yard. Perhaps the bombing scattered garbage.

One comes to my tiny window, pecks at the bars. "Hello," he says. And then, "Fire in the hole. Boom."

I caw and then coo. I'm thinking: *Go tell my love I love her.* I say, "I, I … t, t, tell her l, l … ." And shoo him away. He says, "Goodbye," and does a barrel role before flying off. It cheers me up.

I kick aside chunks of plaster and pieces of a beam and lie down on the earth floor and look at the half ruined ceiling. Could I pull it apart even more and escape? There's nothing to stand on to reach it. Maybe at the door, perching on the lintel? I leap up the wall but fall flat. I do it again.

When I was young I took needless risks in order to test myself. Perhaps it was because I couldn't talk. I had to prove myself some way. I'd stay out in a cold rain without a raincoat. I'd climb the hardest cliffs, and climb higher and longer than anybody else. I was a pacifist, but I went to photograph wars to prove myself as brave as any soldier. I thought I had gotten over that need.

But I leap up the wall yet again and fall flat, as if hurting myself proved something.

I'm about ready to have another fit.

I calm myself by imagining Milla yelling, Stop. I lie down, and study the ceiling again. Finally I doze.

Evening comes. No one brings food or water.

I watch out my little window. There's a mortar launcher set up in the yard, but nobody near it. Soldiers are walking about now and then, though not as many as you'd think if they're serious about holding the fort. Just enough to look after the prisoners — which they're not doing, at least as far as food and drink is concerned. I wonder if Milla got fed.

I call out a couple of times but nobody pays attention. Crazy man, stuttering out consonants. "P, p, p, p, please," like a motor boat that won't start.

● ◑ ○ ◐ ●

At dark the bombing begins. This time it will be Milla's people trying to get their fort back. What's the sense of all this back and forth? This fort isn't worth much to either side. When they win it what will they have won?

At the next volley my roof collapses. Thank goodness there wasn't much of it left to fall on me. One of the beams lies wedged, half way down, and at an angle. I can reach it and climb out.

Mortars are falling everywhere. As I watch, the mortar launcher in the yard is blasted apart.

And then her side does an old fashioned thing. They shoot arrows wrapped with burning rags into the broken wooden roofs. It only takes a minute for smoke to cover everything. Soldiers run around choking and yelling.

All I think about is Milla. I run through the smoke to where she was locked up but when I get there, the door is lying on its side burning. I try to go in but I can't walk over the fallen and burning ceiling and I can't see in all the smoke. I call out. Nobody answers.

But I'm the only one they thought was a spy. Maybe they let her go. Or could she have knocked the door down, or maybe got out through the roof as I did before it burned?

Would she have left without me? She might. She might have been thinking of Sassuna and Grandma.

I head for the gate.

But their side is picking off the soldiers as they run out. No questions asked — as usual.

I pull my shirt up around my face and turn back into the smoke.

I get lost right away. I fall. Then I hear, "Hello. Hello."

I caw.

"Hello there. Fire in the hole. Boom."

I've always trusted birds.

I get up and run, following that crazy, raucous voice.

"Hello. Hello there."

Just when I think I can't take one more smoky breath, there I am, bumping into the back wall of the fort, suffocating and nowhere to go. But there's an impatient, "craw, craw, craw," from somewhere near me. I turn towards the crawing and feel a gust of fresh air. There's a narrow stone doorway and a stone stairway just inside. It's not smoky in there. The air is cool and smells of mold. I climb the steps for what seems like three stories and end up, high, on the ancient battlements. The wind is blowing in the other direction. The rest of the fort is completely hidden in smoke but I'm in the clear.

Back here, the battlements are right against the cliff. The ancient cannons can't have been of any use at all, and yet there's one every ten or twelve steps. For Heaven's sake, facing the cliff! As if to follow some military rule that said, in all forts, it must be so.

The raven is perched on one of the cannons.

Then the fire hits the arsenal. The whole front of the fort blows up.

We — raven and I — are far enough back and high enough not to be hurt by debris, but we're both knocked down. I'm on my back and the raven ... at first I think he's dead, splayed out flat, feathers every which way, but he gets up and flutters to shake his feathers back in place.

"Fire in the hole. Boom."

"Ex, ex ... actly."

He starts to preen, trying to put himself back together.

This section of the fort is all that's left. Not much use now, even as a prison.

I hear a squawking and look in the mouth of the cannon and there's a nest and three baby ravens in there. They're not even dusty. When they see me peering in, they squawk louder. All you can see are three wide open red mouths.

I make a fluttering sound in the back of my throat. "Rroo, rroo, rroo," trying to imitate the sounds parents make to their chicks. I sit down beside the cannon.

Some things, even fragile things, still live and thrive. But Milla? Is she part of this dust billowing around us? Am I breathing her?

What if I hadn't made it this far before that blast? What if I … ? Blown to bits, too, flying, as maybe Milla is flying around me right now.

I have wished I could fly.

I don't want to be birds made of a hundred little bits. Unless Milla … .

The raven hops up on the side of the cliff.

"Hello. Boom! Hello. Boom!" As if telling me to follow.

But only finger holds and toe holds here. If that. Does he think I'm a mountain goat? Or does he think I, too, can fly?

But I've lost all fear for my own safety. I have nothing else to lose and nothing to do but trust my raven.

Now he's even higher.

"Crox. Creeks. Crow. Boom!"

I find a tiny finger hold. I begin.

● ◗ ○ ◖ ●

Without my raven's repertoire of caws and cricks and buzzes and booms, I'd not have had the guts to do it. He gives me confidence and, even in the midst of all this, amuses me. If such a creature still talks and crows his way through life, his chicks on the very edge of disaster — if he tries to help me for no reason whatsoever, it must be worth hanging on … and literally hanging on.

I thought maybe with my wounded leg I wouldn't be able to do it … that I'd end up flat out beside the chicks. Good food for carrion crows. At least I'd end up of some use.

It gets easier. In a few minutes I'm back on the wooded pathways I usually travel. Cinders fly up around me, some as white and magical as the feathers of the snow geese. I grab at them but they're as illusive as down.

I turn around. I want to circle to the gates of the fort and try to find out what happened to Milla.

My raven calls, "Hello. Hello. Hello."

I keep going.

He flies into my face.

In spite of a face full of feathers, I keep going back.

He dive bombs my head.

"Aw, r, r, right," and turn around. "D, d, d, *damn!*"

I don't believe this. Birds are smart in their own way, but not in our ways.

He leads me up my usual pathway. We don't go far when I see a small bundle wrapped in red cloth and partly covered in leaves and brush.

The raven coos — as if to his chicks.

It isn't! But it is!

I squat beside her. "S, s, s, Sa, suna!"

She sits up and grabs me so hard she knocks me over.

I never saw such a sad, pale, dirty, tear-streaked face. Ever.

"I couldn't find you. I couldn't find Milla."

Has she been out here all night?

"H … how? How long?"

She starts to cry. By the looks of her I wouldn't have thought she had the energy.

"And then I couldn't get back home."

"Fire in the hole. Boom! Hello."

"It, it,'s all right n, now."

"Don't go."

"C,'course not."

When I look up to see where the raven's got to, he's gone.

We'll have to hurry back. The night will be cold. Sassuna only has her jacket and I have nothing but my shirt. I take it off and wrap it around her, tie it on by the sleeves. I put her piggy back, and start on up. My body will help to warm her.

I've climbed up and down here so often, and with a big bundle of paper and paints. Sassuna isn't much heavier.

What a dangly age she is, nothing but arms and legs.

"Nor."

"Mmm hmm."

"I love you."

As I was following the raven up the cliff, I had thought to find a way to get myself blown to bits or burned to ashes — anything that would take wing, but I guess not. At least not yet.

She falls asleep there on my back and drools on my shoulder. As evening comes it does get cold and me with no shirt. It'll take another couple of hours before I can find my way back to Grandma's.

But my leg wound and lack of food catches up with me. I stop under the overhanging rock. Just one more short climb and we'll be up where it's flat and easy but I have to rest. I put Sassuna down next to the dead fire where Milla and I sat side by side and she tried to put my paintings back together.

I'm freezing. I gather up wood and brush, make a small fire and lie down beside it.

I think of those raven chicks, right on the edge of war, and the hummingbird there, practically between shots. Why can't some of us resign from all sides? Fly over it. Not even be bothered? Build our nests above it all?

I wake to shooting. Sassuna and I are caught between it. She cries out in panic.

"Shhh. Shhh. B, b, b, be a bird."

"How?"

And now my words come out perfectly. No hesitation.

"Remember the shiny red and blue one you wanted to be? Be it."

Shots are all around from both above us and below. A grenade lands next to us, right where the cinders still … .

● ◑ ○ ◐ ●

I rise, a shiny red and blue bird beside me. There's a great rush of wings as a flock of ravens rises up with us.

"Hello. Hello. Hello."

ALL OF US CAN ALMOST

… FLY, THAT IS. OF COURSE LOTS OF CREATURES CAN almost fly. But all of us are able to match any others of us, wing span to wing span. Also to any other fliers. But though we match each other wing to wing we can't get more than inches off the ground. If that. But we're impressive. Our beaks look vicious. We could pose for statues for the birds representing an empire. We could represent an army or a president. And, actually, we are the empire. We may not be able to fly, but we rule the skies. And most everything else, too.

Creatures come to us for advice on flying. They see us kick up dust and flap and stretch and are awed.

We croak out what we have to say in quacks. We tell them, "The sky is a highway. The sky is of our time and recent. The sky is flat. It's blue because it's happy." They thank us with donations. That's how we live.

The sound of our clacking beaks carries across the valley. It adds to our reputation as powerful — though what good is it really? It's just noise.

Nothing said of us is true, but must we live by truths? Why not keep on living by our lies?

Soaring! Think of it! The stillness of it. Not even the sound of flapping. They say we once did that. Perhaps we still can and just forgot how to begin. How make that first jump? How get the lift? But we grew too large. We began to eat the things that fell and lots of things fall.

I could leap off a cliff. Test myself. But I might become one of those things tumbling down. Even my own kind would tear me apart.

Loosely … very loosely speaking, I do fly. My sleep is full of nothing but that. The joy of it.

But where's the joy in *almost* doing it. Flapping in circles. Making a great wind for nothing but a jump or two. We don't even look good to ourselves.

I don't know what we're made for. It's neither sky nor water nor … especially not … the waddle of the land. We can't sing. Actually we can't do anything. Except look fierce.

Pigeons circle overhead. Meadowlarks sing. Geese and ducks, in Vs, do their seasonal things. We stay. We *have* to. Winter storms come and we're still here. We puff up as much as we can and wrap our wings around ourselves. Perhaps that's what our wings were for in the first place. We're designed merely to shelter ourselves. Even our dreams of flying are yet more lies.

But none others are as strong as we are … at least none *seem* to be. We win with looks alone and a big voice. We stand, assured and sure.

When creatures ask me for a ride I say, "I'd take you up any time you want — hop and skip and up we go — except you're too heavy. Next time measure wings, mine against some other of us. You'll need a few inches more on each side. Tell a bigger one I said to take you up."

"Take to the air along with us," I say. "Follow me up and up." I'm shameless. But I suspect it's only the young that really believe. The older ones pretend to because of our beaks, because of the wind we can stir up — our clouds of dust.

Still, I go on, "Check out my wing span. Check out my evil eye. Listen. *My* voice."

They jump at my squawk.

They bring me food just to watch me tear at it. At least I'm good at that. I put on a good show. Every creature backs away.

One of the young ones keeps wanting me to take him up. He won't stop asking. I say, "A sparrow could do better." That's true, but he takes it as a joke. I say, "Why not at least ask a male."

"Males scare me."

Finally, just to shut him up, I say, "Yes, but not until the next section of time."

He runs off yelling, "Whee! Whee! Whee! She's taking me up!"

Now how will I get out of it? I only have from one moon to the other. But who knows, one of the big males may have eaten him by that time. They don't care where their food comes from. He was right to be scared.

● ◑ ○ ◐ ●

Who knows how we lost our ability to fly? Maybe we're just lazy. Maybe we just don't exercise our flying muscles. How could we fly, sitting around eating dead things all the time? If anyone can fly, it seems to me more likely one of us smaller females could than a big male.

● ◑ ○ ◐ ●

That little one keeps coming back and saying, "*Really?* Are you *really* going to take me up?"

And I keep saying, "I said I would didn't I? When have any of us ever lied?" (Actually, when have we ever told the truth?)

He keeps yelling back and forth to all who'll listen. The way he keeps on with it, I could eat him myself.

But we have to be careful. Sometimes those ground dwellers get together and decide not to feed us. Whoever they don't feed always dies. He'll waddle around trying to get someone of us to share, but we don't. We're not a sharing kind.

I *should* like these ground dwellers because of the food they bring, but I don't. I pretend to, just like they pretend to believe us. They call us Emperor, Leader, Master, but why are they doing this? It could be a conspiracy to keep us fat and lazy so we won't be lords of the sky anymore. So we're tamed and docile. Maybe they started this whole thing, stuffing us with their leftovers. Maybe they're the real emperors of the sky. Master of the sky though never in it anymore than we are. At least they can climb trees.

I wonder what they want us for? Or maybe it's the best way to know where we are and what we're doing.

Feed your enemies. Tame them.

● ◑ ○ ◐ ●

I ask some of us, "Where is that cliff they say we used to soar out from?"

"Was there a cliff? Did there used to be a cliff?"

I'm sure there must have been one. How could birds the size of us get started without one — a high one? Maybe that's our problem, we've lost our cliff. We forgot where it is.

● ◑ ○ ◐ ●

Evenings when all are in their burrows, and my own kind, wrapped in their wings, are clustered under the lean-tos set out for us by lesser beings, I stretch and flap. Reach. Jump. Only the nightingale sees me flop. It's a joy to be up to hear her and to be flipping and flopping.

I'll take that pesky little one all the way to wherever that cliff of ours is. Wouldn't that be something? See the sights? Be up in what we always call "Our element."

● ◑ ○ ◐ ●

But there's a male, has his eye on me. Has had for quite some time. That's another good reason to take off. I'd like to get out of here before the time is ripe.

Or perhaps he's heard the little one yelling, "Whee, Whee," and likes the idea of me with one of those little ones on my back. Easy pickin's, *both* of us. Little one for one purpose and me for another. I can just see it, me distracted, defending the little, and the big taking care of both things while I struggle, front *and* back.

He may be the biggest, but I don't want him. Maybe that's how we got too big to fly, we kept mating with the biggest. It's our own fault we got so big. I'm not going to do that. Well, also the big ones are the strongest. This biggest could slap down all the other males.

If not for the fact that we hardly speak to each other, we females could get together and stop it. Go for the small and the nice. If there are any nice. Not a single one of us is noted for being nice.

I hate to think what mating will be like with one so huge. I'd ask other females if we were the kind who asked things of each other.

He keeps following me around. I don't know how I'm going to avoid him if he's determined. I won't get any help from any of the others. They'll just come and watch. Probably even squawk him onward. I've done it myself.

● ◑ ○ ◐ ●

I'm thinking of ways to avoid that male, so when that little one comes to ask, yet again, "Why wait for next moon?" I say, "You're right. We'll do it now but I have to find our platform."

"Why?"

"Have you ever seen any of us take off from down here? Of course you haven't. I need a place to soar from."

"Can't we start flying from right here so everybody can see me?"

"No. I have to have a place to take off from. Get on my back. I'll take you there."

"I can walk faster than this all by myself."

"I know, but bear with me."

"My name is Hobie. What's yours?"

"We don't have names. We don't need them."

The big one comes waddling after us. A few of us follow him, wanting to see what's going to happen. I don't think the big realizes how far I'm going. Nobody does.

When we get to the end of the nesting places, Hobie says, "I've never been this far. Is this all right to do?"

"It's all right."

"Your waddling is making me sick."

"We'll rest in a few minutes."

I don't dare stop now, so near the nests. Everybody will waddle out to us. We have to get out of sight. Out there I could eat Hobbie myself if need be. I don't suppose anybody will be feeding us way out here.

I don't stop soon enough. Hobie throws up on my back. It smells of dirt dweller's food. And we're still not out of sight.

"Hang on. I'll stop at that green patch just ahead."

I waddle a little faster but that just makes him fall off. I'm thinking, *Oh well, go on back and let the big male do what he has to do. It can't last more than a couple of minutes. If he breaks my legs it might be better than what I'm going through now.*

But I wait for Hobie to get back on. I say, "Not much farther." He climbs on slowly. I wonder if he suspects I might eat him.

That big is coming along behind us but he's slower even than I am. Who'd have thought I was worth so much trouble.

In the green patch there's a stream. We both drink and I start washing my back. Hobie keeps saying, "I couldn't help it."

"I know that. Now stop talking so I can think."

I leave foot prints. Maybe best if I go along the stream for a while. Then we can drink any time we want. I turn towards the high side, where the stream comes from. If there really is a take off platform it's got to be high.

"Where are we going?"

"There's a place in the sky that'll give me a good lift.

"What kind of a place?"

"A cliff."

"How far is it?"

"Oh for the sky's sake keep quiet."

"Why does your kind always say, for the sky's sake?"

"Because we're sky creatures. Not like you. Now let me think about walking."

Even in this little stream there's fish. Wouldn't it be nice if I could catch one by myself?

"Hang on!"

I dive. But I forgot about the water changing the angle of view. I miss. I say, "Next time."

Hobie says, "I can."

I let him off to stand on the bank and dive and he does it. Gives the fish to me even though I'll bet he's getting hungry, too.

"Thank you, Hobie. Now get one for yourself."

● ◑ ○ ◐ ●

At dusk we find a nice place to nest in among the trees along the stream — soft with leaves. Hobie curls up right beside my beak. Practically under it. I'm more afraid of my bite than he is. I hope I don't snap him up in my sleep.

Towards morning we hear something coming … lumbering along. Sounding tired for sure. We both know who. Hobie doesn't like big males any more than I do. He scrambles up on my back and says, "Shouldn't we go?"

Because I'm so much smaller than any male, I waddle a lot

faster. It gets steeper but I'm still doing pretty well. It's so steep I have hopes of finding our cliff. I turn around and look back down and here comes the big, but a long ways off. Staggering, stumbling. Am I really worth all this effort?

"Are we far enough ahead? Are we getting some place? How long now?"

"Do you ever say anything that isn't a question?"

"You do it. That's a question."

● ☽ ○ ☾ ●

I'm not used to waddling all day long, especially not uphill. It's the hardest thing I've ever done. But the big …. He's still coming. It's getting steeper. I hope one as large as he is can't get up here. This is just what I wanted. The launching platform has got to be here. How did it ever come to be that we got stuck down in the flat places?

And finally here it is, *the* launch place at the top of the cliff. I look over the edge. I'm so scared just looking I start to feel sick. I'm not sure I can even pretend to jump.

"Why are you shaking so much? It's going to make me sick again."

Should I eat Hobie now before he tells everybody I not only can't fly, I can't even get close to the edge without trembling and feeling sick?

But it's been nice having company. I've gotten used to his paws tangled in my feathers, making a mess of them. And I'd miss his questions.

I move back and look over the other side. It's steep on that side, too, though not so much. This platform is a promontory going off into nothing on all sides but one. It must have been perfect for fliers.

I look around to see if I can see any signs that it was used as a launching place, but there's nothing. I suppose, up here so high, the weather would have worn away any signs of that. I wonder if that big male knows anything more about it than I do.

*   ◐   ○   ◑   ●

It's breezy up here. I flap my wings to test myself, but I do it well away from the edges.

Hobie says, "Go, go, go."

Maybe I should just get closer and closer to edge … get used to it little by little … until I don't feel quite so scared.

I look over the side again, though from a few feet away. I see the big male is still coming. I see him turn around and look down at exactly the same spot where we did. Then he looks up. Right at us. He spreads his wings at us so I'll see his wing-span. Then he turns side view. That's so I'll get a good look at his profile … the big hooked beak, the white ruff …. Then he starts up again.

I look over the more sloping side again. I think I might be able to slide down there though it's a steep slide. At the bottom there's a lot of trees and brush. That would break our fall.

That big one is getting so close I can hear him shuffling and sliding just like I did. I sit over by the less steep side and wait.

Pretty soon I see the fierce head looking up at us, the beady eye, and then the whole body. He has an even harder time than I had lifting himself on to the launching platform.

Hobie says, "I'm scared of males," and I say, "I am, too."

As soon as the big catches his breath he says, "You're beautiful."

I say, "That's neither here nor there."

He says, "I love you." As if any of us knew what that word meant.

I say, "Love is what you feel for a nice piece of carrion."

He looks a mess. I must, too. Dusty, feathers every which way. Hobie and I filled up on fish back at the stream, but I don't think he did. He looks at Hobie like the next meal. I back up a little closer to the sliding side. I say, "This one's mine." *That*, he'll understand.

He's inching closer. He thinks I don't notice. If he grabs me there's no way I can escape. I back up even more.

And then …. I didn't mean to. Off we go. Skidding, sliding, but like flying. Almost! Almost!

Hobie is yelling, "Whee. Whee. Whee." At least he's happy.

When we get down as far as the trees and bushes, I grab at them with my beak to slow us. And then I hear the big coming behind us. I never thought he … such a big one … would dare follow.

There's a great swish of gravel sliding with us. Even more as the big comes down behind us. Here he is, landed beside us, but, thank goodness, not exactly on.

Hobie and I are more or less fine. Scratched and bruised and dusty, but the big is moaning.

We're in a sort of ditch full of lots of brush and trees. It looks to be up hill on all sides. I wonder if either of us … the big and I could waddle out of it. Hobie could.

Hobie and I dust off.

Hobie says. "That was great. I wish the others could have seen me."

He can't, can he? Can he *possibly* think that was flying?

Then I see that the big one's legs slant out at odd angles. His weight was his undoing. My lightness saved me.

The big says, "Help me." But why should I? I say, "It's all your fault in the first place."

He's in pain. I brush him off. I even dare to preen him a bit. I don't think he'll hurt me or try to mate. He couldn't with those broken legs, anyway. He needs me. He has to be nice. That'll be a change.

These big males are definitely bigger than they need to be. He's twice my size. Where will all this bigness lead? Just to less and less, ever again, the possibility of flight, that's where.

Hobie doesn't even need to be asked. "I'm hungry. Can I go get us some food?"

"Of course you can."

"After you flew me I owe you lots."

Off he goes into the brush. I take a look at the big one's legs and wonder what to do. Can I make splints? And what to use to bind them with? Though there's always lots of stringy things in our meals if Hobie finds us food.

"You're not only never going to fly, you may never waddle either."

He just groans again.

"I'll try to straighten these out." I give him a stick to bite on. And then I do it. After I look for sticks as splints.

In no time Hobie brings three creatures. I think one for each of us but he says he ate already. He's says this place is all meals. Nothing has been hunting here in a long time, maybe never. He says, "You could even hunt for yourself."

Now there's a thought. I think I will.

I leave the three creatures for the big male and start out but the big says, "Don't leave me." Just like a chick.

I say, "If you eat Hobie that's the last you'll ever see of me." And I go.

• ◑ ○ ◐ ●

Hobie is right, all the little meals are easy to catch. I eat four and keep all the stringy things. I also look around at where we are and if we could ever get out. There's that little stream below, cool and clear, bubbling along not far from where we fell. Beside it there's a nice place for a nest. I think about chicks. How I'd try to get them flapping right from the start. Even the baby males. And maybe, if we all were thinner and had to scramble for our food like I just had to do, and if all the food would get to know the danger and make us scramble harder and we'd get even thinner and stronger, and first thing you know we wouldn't have to climb out, we'd fly. All of us. Could that really come to be?

I throw away the stringy things I was going to make splints with. I have everything under control. I'll tell Hobie he can go on home if he wants to, though I'll tell him I do wish he'd stay, just for the company. And just in case we never do learn to fly again, we'd need his help when the food gets smarter and scarcer.

PELT

She was a white dog with a wide face and eager eyes, and this was the planet, Jaxa, in winter.

She trotted well ahead of the master, sometimes nose to ground, sometimes sniffing the air, and she didn't care if they were being watched or not. She knew that strange things skulked behind iced trees, but strangeness was her job. She had been trained for it, and crisp, glittering Jaxa was, she felt, exactly what she *had* been trained for, *born* for.

I love it, I love it … that was in her pointing ears, her waving tail … I *love* this place.

It was a world of ice, a world with the sound of breaking goblets. Each time the wind blew they came shattering down by the trayful, and each time one branch brushed against another it was, Skoal, Down the hatch, To the Queen … tink, tink, tink. And the sun was reflected as if from a million cut-glass punch bowls under a million crystal chandeliers.

She wore four little black boots, and each step she took sounded like two or three more goblets gone, but the sound was lost in the other tinkling, snapping, cracklings of the silver, frozen forest about her.

She had figured out at last what that hovering scent was. It had been there from the beginning, the landing two days ago, mingling with Jaxa's bitter air and seeming to be just a part of the smell of the place, she found it in criss-crossing trails about the squatting ship, and hanging, heavy and recent, in hollows behind flat-branched, piney-smelling bushes. She thought of honey and fat men and dry fur when she smelled it.

There was something big out there, and more than one of them, more than two. She wasn't sure how many. She had a feeling this was something to tell the master, but what was the signal, the agreed upon noise for: We are being watched? There was a whisper of sound, short and quick, for: Sighted close, come and shoot. And there was a noise for danger (all these through her throat mic to the receiver at the master's ear), a special, howly bark: Awful, awful — there is something awful going to happen. There was even a noise, a low rumble of sound for: Wonderful, wonderful fur — drop everything and come after *this* one. (And she knew a good fur when she saw one. She had been trained to know.) But there was no sign for: We are being watched.

She'd whined and barked when she was sure about it, but that had got her a pat on the head and a rumpling of the neck fur. "You're doing fine, Baby. This world is our oyster, all ours. All we got to do is pick up the pearls. Jaxa's what we've been waiting for." And Jaxa was, so she did her work and didn't try to tell him anymore, for what was one more strange thing in one more strange world?

She was on the trail of something now, and the master was behind her, out of sight. He'd better hurry. He'd better hurry or there'll be waiting to do, watching the thing, whatever it is, steady on until he comes, holding tight back, and that will be hard. Hurry, hurry.

She could hear the whispered whistle of a tune through the receiver at her ear and she knew he was not hurrying but just being happy. She ran on, eager, curious. She did not give the signal for hurry, but she made a hurry sound of her own, and she heard him stop whistling and whisper back into the mike, "So, so, Queen of Venus. The furs are waiting to be picked. No hurry, Baby." But morning was to her for hurry. There was time later to be tired and slow.

That fat-man honeyish smell was about, closer and strong. Her curiosity became two pronged — this smell or that? What *is* the big thing that watches? She kept to the trail she was on, though. Better to be sure, and this thing was not so elusive, not twisting and doubling back, but up ahead and going where it was going.

She topped a rise and half slid, on thick furred rump, down the other side, splattering ice. She snuffled at the bottom to be sure of the smell again, and then, nose to ground, trotted past a thick and tangled hedgerow.

She was thinking through her nose, now. The world was all smell, crisp air and sour ice and turpentine pine … and this animal, a urine and brown grass thing … and then, strong in front of her, honey-furry-fat man.

She felt it looming before she raised her head to look, and there it was, the smell in person, some taller than the master and twice as wide. Counting his doubled suit and all, twice as wide.

This was a fur! Wonderful, wonderful. But she just stood, looking up, mouth open and lips pulled back, the fur on the back of her neck rising more from the suddenness than from fear.

It was silver and black, a tiger-striped thing, and the whitish parts glistened and caught the light as the ice of Jaxa did, and sparkled and dazzled in the same way. And there, in the center of the face, was a large and terrible orange eye, rimmed in black with black radiating lines crossing the forehead and rounding the head. That spot of orange dominated the whole figure, but it was a flat, blind eye, unreal, grown out of fur. At first she saw only that spot of color, but then she noticed under it two small, red glinting eyes and they were kind, not terrible.

This was the time for the call: Come, come and get the great fur, the huge-price-tag fur for the richest lady on earth to wear and be dazzling in and most of all to pay for. But there was something about the flat, black nose and the tender, bow-shaped mouth and those kind eyes that stopped her from calling. Something master-like. She was full of wondering and indecision and she made no sound at all.

The thing spoke to her then, and its voice was a deep lullaby sound of buzzing cellos. It gestured with a thick, fur-backed hand. It promised, offered, and asked; and she listened, knowing and not knowing.

The words came slowly.

This ... is ... world.

Here is the sky, the earth, the ice. The heavy arms moved. The hands pointed.

We have watched you, little slave. What have you done that is free today? Take the liberty. Here is the earth for your four shoed feet, the sky of stars, the ice to drink. Do something free today. Do, do.

Nice voice, she thought, nice thing. It gives and gives ... something.

Her ears pointed forward, then to the side, one and then the other, and then forward again. She cocked her head, but the real meaning would not come clear. She poked at the air with her nose.

Say that again, her whole body said. I almost have it. I *feel* it. Say it once more and maybe then the sense of it will come.

But the creature turned and started away quickly, very quickly for such a big thing, and disappeared behind the trees and bushes. It seemed to shimmer itself away until the glitter was only the glitter of the ice and the black was only the thick, flat branches.

The master was close. She could hear his crackling steps coming up behind her.

She whined softly, more to herself than to him.

"Ho, the Queen, Aloora. Have you lost it?" She sniffed the ground again. The honey-furry smell was strong. She sniffed beyond, zig-zagging. The trail was there. "Go to it, Baby." She loped off to a sound like Chinese wind chimes, business-like again. Her tail hung guilty, though, and she kept her head low. She had missed an important signal. She'd waited until it was too late. But was the thing a man, a master? Or a fur? She wanted to do the right thing. She always tried and tried for that, but now she was confused.

She was getting close to whatever it was she trailed, but the hovering smell was still there too, though not close. She thought of gifts. She knew that much from the slow, lullaby words, and gifts made her think of bones and meat, not the dry fishy biscuit she always got on trips like this. A trickle of drool flowed from the side of her mouth and froze in a silver thread across her shoulder.

She slowed. The thing she trailed must be there, just behind the next row of trees. She made a sound in her throat ... ready, steady … and she advanced until she was sure. She sensed the shape. She didn't really see it … mostly it was the smell and something more in the tinkling glassware noises. She gave the signal and stood still, a furry, square imitation of a pointer. Come, hurry. This waiting is the hardest part.

He followed, beamed to her radio. "Steady, Baby. Hold that pose. Good girl, good girl." There was only the slightest twitch of her tail as she wagged it, answering him in her mind.

He came up behind her and then passed, crouched, holding the rifle before him, elbows bent. He knelt then, and waited as if at a point of his own, rifle to shoulder. Slowly he turned with the moving shadow of the beast, and shot, twice in quick succession.

They ran forward then, together, and it was what she had expected—a deer-like thing, dainty hoofs, proud head, and spotted in three colors, large grey-green rounds on tawny yellow, with tufts of that same glittering silver scattered over.

The master took out a sharp, flat bladed knife. He began to whistle out loud as he cut off the handsome head. His face was flushed.

She sat down nearby, mouth open in a kind of smile, and she watched his face as he worked. The warm smell made the drool come at the sides of her mouth and drip out to freeze on the ice and on her paws, but she sat quietly, only watching.

Between the whistlings he grunted and swore and talked to himself, and finally he had the skin and the head in a tight, inside-out bundle.

Then he came to her and patted her sides over the ribs with a flat, slap sound, and he scratched behind her ears and held a biscuit to her on his thick-gloved palm. She swallowed it whole and then watched him as he squatted on his heels and himself ate one almost like it.

Then he got up and slung the bundle of skin and head across his back. "I'll take this one, Baby. Come on, let's get one more something before lunch." He waved her to the right. "We'll make a big circle," he said.

She trotted out, glad she was not carrying anything. She found a strong smell at a patch of discolored ice and urinated on it. She sniffed and growled at a furry, mammal-smelling bird that landed in the trees above her and sent down a shower of ice slivers on her head. She zig-zagged and then turned and bit, lips drawn back in mock rage, at a branch that scraped her side. She followed for a while the chattery sound of water streaming along under the ice, and left it where an oily, lambish smell crossed. Almost immediately she came upon them—six small, greenish balls of wool with floppy, woolly feet. The honey-fat man smell was strong here too, but she signaled for the lambs, the Come and shoot sound, and she stood again waiting for the master.

"*Good* girl!" His voice had special praise. "By God, this place is a gold mine. Hold it, Queen of Venus. Whatever it is, don't let go."

There was a fifty-yard clear view here and she stood in plain sight of the little creatures, but they didn't notice. The master came slowly and cautiously, and knelt beside her. Just as he did, there appeared at the far end of the clearing a glittering, silver and black tiger-striped man.

She heard the sharp inward breath of the master and she felt the tenseness come to him. There was a new, faint whiff of sour sweat, a stiff silence and a special way of breathing.

What she felt from him made the fur rise along her back with a mixture of excitement and fear.

The tiger thing held a small packet in one hand and was peering into it and pulling at the opening in it with a blunt finger. Suddenly there was a sweep of motion beside her and five fast, frantic shots sounded sharp in her ear. Two came after the honey-fat man had already fallen and lay like a huge, decorated sack.

The master ran forward and she came at his heels. They stopped, not too close and she watched the master looking at the big, dead tiger head with the terrible eye. The master was breathing hard and seemed hot. His face was red and puffy looking, but his lips made a hard whitish line. He didn't whistle or talk. After a time he took out his knife. He tested the blade, making a small, bloody thread of a mark on his left thumb. Then he walked closer and she stood and watched him and whispered a questioning whine.

He stooped by the honey-fat man and it was that small, partly opened packet that he cut viciously through the center. Small round chunks fell out, bite sized chunks of dried meat and a cheesy substance and some broken bits of clear, bluish ice. The master kicked at them. His face was not red anymore, but olive-pale. His thin mouth was open in a grin that was not a grin.

He went about the skinning then.

He did not keep the flat-faced, heavy head nor the blunt-fingered hands.

●　◗　○　◖　●

The man had to make a sliding thing of two of the widest kind of flat branches to carry the new heavy fur, as well as the head and the skin of the deer. Then he started directly for the ship.

It was past eating time but she looked at his restless eyes and did not ask about it. She walked before him, staying close. She looked back often, watching him pull the sled thing by the string across his shoulder and she knew, by the way he held the rifle before him in both hands, that she should be wary.

Sometimes the damp-looking, inside-out bundle hooked on things, and the master would curse in a whisper and pull at it. She could see the bundle made him tired, and she wished he would stop for a rest and food as they usually did long before this time.

They went slowly, and the smell of honey-fat man hovered as it had from the beginning. They crossed the trails of many animals. Even, they saw another deer run off, but she knew that it was not a time for chasing.

Then another big silver and black tiger stood exactly before them. It appeared suddenly, as if actually it had been standing there all the time, and they had not been near enough to see it, to pick it out from its glistening background.

It just stood and looked and dared, and the master held his gun with both hands and looked too, and she stood between them glancing from one face to the other. She knew, after a moment, that the master would not shoot, and it seemed the tiger thing knew too, for it turned to look at her and it raised its arms and spread its fingers as if grasping at the forest on each side. It swayed a bit, like bigness off balance, and then it spoke in its tight-strung, cello tones. The words and the tone seemed the same as before.

Little slave, what have you done that is free today? Remember this is world. Do something free today. Do, do.

She knew that what it said was important to it, something she should understand, a giving and a taking away. It watched her, and she looked back with wide, innocent eyes, wanting to do the right thing, but not knowing what.

The tiger-fat man turned then, this time slowly, and left a wide back for the master and her to see, and then it half turned, throwing a quick glance over the heavy humped shoulder at the two of them. Then it moved slowly away into the trees and ice, and the master still held the gun with two hands and did not move.

The evening wind began to blow, and there sounded about them that sound of a million chandeliers tinkling and clinking like gigantic wind chimes. A furry bird, the size of a shrew and as fast, flew by between them with a miniature shriek.

She watched the master's face, and when he was ready she went along beside him. The soft sounds the honey-fat man had made echoed in her mind but had no meaning.

●　◗　○　◖　◉

That night the master stretched the big skin on a frame and afterwards he watched the dazzle of it. He didn't talk to her. She watched him a while and then she turned around three times on her rug and lay down to sleep.

The next morning the master was slow, reluctant to go out. He studied charts of other places, round or hourglass-shaped maps with yellow dots and labels, and he drank his coffee standing up looking at them. But finally they did go out, squinting into the ringing air.

It was her world. More each day, she felt it was so, right feel, right temperature, lovely smells. She darted on ahead as usual, yet not too far today, and sometimes she stopped and waited and looked at the master's face as he came up. And sometimes she would whine a question before she went on … Why don't you walk brisk, brisk, and call me Queen of Venus, Aloora, Galaxa, or Bitch of Betelgeuse? Why don't you sniff like I do? Sniff, and you will be happy with this place … And she would run on again.

Trails were easy to find, and once more she found the oily lamb smell, and once more came upon them quickly. The master strode up beside her and raised his gun … but a moment later he turned, carelessly, letting himself make a loud noise, and the lambs ran. He made a face, and spit upon the ice. "Come on Queen. Let's get out of here. I'm sick of this place."

He turned and made the signal to go back, pointing with his thumb above his head in two jerks of motion.

But why, why? This is morning now and our world. She wagged her tail and gave a short bark, and looked at him, dancing a little on her back paws, begging with her whole body.

"Come on," he said.

She turned then, and took her place at his heel, head low, but eyes looking up at him, wondering if she had done something wrong, and wanting to be right and noticed and loved because he was troubled and preoccupied.

They'd gone only a few minutes on the way back when he stopped suddenly in the middle of a step, slowly put both feet flat upon the ground and stood like a soldier at a stiff, off-balance attention. There, lying in the way before them, was the huge, orange-eyed head and in front of it, as if at the end of outstretched arms, lay two leathery hands, the hairless palms up.

She made a growl deep in her throat and the master made a noise almost exactly like hers, but more a groan. She waited for him, standing as he stood, not moving, feeling his tenseness coming in to her. Yet it was just a head and two hands of no value, old ones they had had before and thrown away.

He turned and she saw a wild look in his eyes. He walked with deliberate steps, and she followed, in a wide circle about the spot. When they had skirted the place, he began to walk very fast.

They were not far from the ship. She could see its flat blackness as they drew nearer to the clearing where it was, the burned, iceless pit of spewed and blackened earth. And then she saw that the silver tiger men were there, nine of them in a wide circle, each with the honey-damp fur smell, but each with a separate particular sweetness.

The master was still walking very fast, eyes down to watch his footing, and he did not see them until he was there in the circle before them all, standing there like nine upright bears in tiger suits.

He stopped and made a whisper of a groan, and he let the gun fall low in one hand so that it hung loose with the muzzle almost touching the ground. He looked from one to the other and she looked at him, watching his pale eyes move along the circle.

"Stay," he said, and then he began to go toward the ship at an awkward limp, running and walking at the same time, banging the gun handle against the air lock as he entered.

He had said, Stay. She sat watching the ship door and moving her front paws up and down because she wanted to be walking after him. He was gone only a few minutes, though, and when he came back it was without the gun and he was holding the great fur with cut pieces of thongs dangling like ribbons along its edges where it had been tied to the stretching frame. He went at that same run-walk, unbalanced by the heavy bundle, to one of them along the circle. Three gathered together before him and refused to take it back. They pushed it, bunched loosely, back across his arms again and to it they added another large and heavy package in a parchment bag, and the master stood, with his legs wide to hold it all.

Then one honey-fat man motioned with a fur-backed hand to the ship and the bundles, and then to the ship and the master, and then to the sky. He made two sharp sounds once, and then again. And another made two different sounds, and she felt the feeling of them … Take your things and go home. Take them, these and these, and go.

They turned to her then and one spoke and made a wide gesture. *This is world. The sky, the earth, the ice.*

They wanted her to stay. They gave her … was it their world? But what good was a world?

She wagged her tail hesitantly, lowered her head and looked up at them … I do want to do right, to please everybody, everybody, but … Then she followed the master into the ship.

The locks rumbled shut. "Let's get out of here," he said. She took her place, flat on her side, take-off position. The master snapped the flat plastic sheet over her, covering head and all and, in a few minutes, they roared off.

Afterwards he opened the parchment bag. She knew what was in it. She knew he knew too, but she knew by the smell. He opened it and dumped out the head and the hands. His face was tight and his mouth stiff.

She saw him almost put the big head out the waste chute, but he didn't. He took it in to the place where he kept good heads and some odd paws or hoofs, and he put it by the others there.

Even she knew this head was different. The others were all slant-browed like she was and most had jutting snouts. This one seemed bigger than the big ones, with its heavy, ruffed fur and huge eye staring, and more grand than any of them, more terrible … and yet a flat face, with a delicate, black nose and tender lips.

The tenderest lips of all.

CREATURE

THIS CREATURE LOOKS MORE SCARED THAN I AM. COME knocking … pawing … scratching at my door. Come, maybe in search of me (I'm easy prey for the weak and scared and hungry), or maybe in search of help and shelter … . (I'm peering out my window, hoping it won't see me.) It's been snowing — seems like three or four days now. The first really bad weather of the year so far.

It looks so draggled and cold … . I open the door. I welcome it. I say, "Hello new and dangerous friend." My door's a normal size, but too small for it. It pushes and groans and squeezes itself in. Then collapses on the floor in my one and only room, its big green head facing the stove. It takes up all the space and makes puddles.

There's a tag stapled in its ear — rather tattered (both ear and tag), green (both ear and tag), with a number so faded I can hardly make it out. It might be zero seven. Strange that it has ears at all considering what it (mostly) looks like. But they're small — tiny vestigial … no, the opposite, evolving ears. They look as if made purely as place to put a tag.

It's wearing a large handmade camouflage vest with lots of pockets. Now, while it's still out of breath and collapsed, I check for weapons, though with those claws, why would it need any? What it has is old dried crumbs of pennyroyal, left over from some warmer season and some higher mountain, a few interesting stones, one streaked green with copper and one that glitters with fool's gold, two books, one of poetry (*100 Best-Loved Poems*) and one on plants of the area. Both well worn. A creature of my own heart. Perhaps.

It looks half starved — more than half. I have broth. I help it raise its heavy head. It sips, nods as if in thanks, but then shows its teeth, blinks its glittery eyes. I jump back. Try to, that is, but I bump into my table. There's no room with it in here. It shakes its head, no, no, no. Seems to say it. "Mmmnno."

But how can such a creature talk at all with such a mouth? But then come words, or parts of words. "Thang … kh … mmmyou … kind. Kindly. Thang you." Then it seems to faint, or collapses, or sleeps — instantly snow melting from its eyelashes (it has eyelashes) and rolling off its back, icy mud drying between its claws. The tiny arms look as if made for nothing but hugging.

While it seems in such an exhausted sleep, or maybe passed out, I take pliers and carefully remove the staple that holds the zero seven ear tag. I notice several claw marks along its back and it's lost a large chunk off the end of its tail.

Now where in the world did this thing come from?

I've heard tales. I thought they were the usual nonsense … like sasquatch, yeti, and so forth, abominable this or that. (And here, for sure, the most abominable of all.) But I've heard tales of secret weapons, too. I've heard there are creatures made specifically to patrol this empty border land. Supposed to be indestructible in so far as a living breathing creature can ever be. Supposed to attack everything that moves in this no man's land where nothing is supposed to be, but another of its own kind.

I'd probably help even a suffering weapon, I probably wouldn't be able to keep myself from it, but this one seems odd for a weapon, too polite, and with vest pockets full of dried bits of flowers, that book of poetry … .

I drink the rest of the broth myself and stare at the creature for a while. No sense in trying to mop up with this thing in the way and still dripping. I can't even get across the room without leaning against a wall or climbing over my chair or cot. I step over its legs. I squinch over to my front door. I take my jacket. I'm not worried about leaving the thing alone. It doesn't seem the sort to do any harm — unless by mistake.

I whisper, "Sleep, my poor wet friend. I'll be back soon," in case it hears me leave. It doesn't move. I might as well be talking to myself. I do that all the time anyway. I used to talk to my dog, Rosie, but since she died I haven't stopped. I jabber on. No need for a dog for talking. They used to say we men were the silent sex, at least compared to women, but not me. Rosie just made it worse. She would look up at me, trying hard to get every word. Seemed to smile. I'd talk all the more. And now, as if she was still here, I talk. I talk to anything that moves.

●　◑　○　◐　●

As I go out, right outside the door there's some juniper branches threaded together as though it had made itself a wind shield of some sort and dropped it before it came in. Farther along I see broken branches around my biggest limber pine. It must have sheltered there — leaned against the leeward side. Hard to think of such a creature giving out.

I lean against the leeward side, too. You'd think it would have smelled my fire and me. Perhaps it was already weak and sick. I don't dare leave it by itself for long but I need space. That was like being in a squeeze gate. Still, I like company. Watch the fire together. Come better weather, we could make the shack bigger. It was polite, even.

I say, "Rosie, Rosie." The wind blows my words off into the hills before I hardly get them said. That name has already bounced off these cliffs sunrise to sunset. Not a creature here that hasn't heard it. I've called her, sometimes by mistake, sometimes on purpose. Sometimes knowing she was dead, sometimes forgetting.

After she died I ran out in a snowstorm naked — and not just once or twice — hoping for … what? Death by freezing? I yelled, answering the coyotes, until I was so hoarse I couldn't have spoken if there'd been somebody to speak to. After that I whispered. Then I sat, brooding over the knots in the logs as I had when I first came out here. Rosie needed me. She kept me human. Or should I say, and better yet, she kept me animal. I don't know what I've become. I need this creature as much as it needs me. I'd make it a good meal. Maybe that's what I want to be.

I squat down, my back against the tree. I shouldn't go far. I should listen. Even just waking up and stretching, it could mess things up.

● ◐ ○ ◑ ●

I chose this no man's land. I came here ten years ago. There's a war been going on for a long time, but never any action here

— not since I've been around. Missiles fly overhead, satellites float in the night sky, but nothing ever happens here. The war goes on, back and forth above me. Sometimes I can see great bursts of light. I wonder if there's anything left on either side. No man's land is the safest place to be. Had I had the sense to bring my wife and child here, they'd still be alive. Of course I didn't think to come here myself until they were gone and my life was over.

● ◑ ○ ◐ ●

I don't know how long I sit, the sun is hidden, but I've had no need for time since I came. I don't even keep track of my age, let alone the time of day.

I've never seen a single one of these thick-skinned things until now. I wasn't sure they existed. I didn't want them to. I felt sorry for them even when I didn't believe in them. How can they have any sort of life at all? Seeing this one, I think perhaps they can. (Or this one can.) But here they are in the world in spite of themselves. No fault of theirs. And in all kinds of weather. If they get sick, I suppose they pine and die on their own.

The creature seemed … rather sweet, I thought. Fine fingered hands. Womanly arms. Perhaps it really is female.

● ◑ ○ ◐ ●

Then I hear the scraping and thumping of something who hasn't hardly room enough to turn around. My poor friend, Zero Seven. I hurry back as best I can, clumping through snow a foot deep in spots. I open my door and go from a wall of softly falling flakes (softly now) to a wall of shiny green.

I push my fist into its side as one does to move a horse. I hope it feels my push. I hope it's as sensitive as a horse. "Let me in, friend." It moves. I hear something falling over on its far side.

"Do gum in. I'mmmm afraig I … . Mmmmm … as you ksee."

I slide myself in — scrape myself in, that is: It's the wrong direction for the scales.

It turns toward me as best it can and seems to almost bow, or perhaps it's a nod, one elegant little hand at its mouth as if embarrassed. I do believe I'm right about the sex. It must be female.

"Kh kvery, kvery, sssssorry. I'll leave mmmm-nnnow."

With me in the way it can't turn around to go. Perhaps not even with me not in the way. It'll have to back out.

"Don't go. Sit down." It's in a half-crouch already. It goes down into a squat, its stomach on the floor, feet splayed on each side — long-toed, gruesome feet with claws I wouldn't want to argue with.

I slide myself around the creature to the stove on the far side. I should have had the dishes washed and put away. Well, no matter, they're tin. A few more bumps and scratches won't make any difference.

No doubt about it, it's sick. I could even feel that as I move around it. Though how do you know if a reptile is sick? But there's an odd stickiness to it and I imagine it normally doesn't have any smell at all.

"Stay. You're sick. I'll make stew. Rest again."

It shakes its head. "Mmmmmukst go."

"I don't want to find you out there dead."

"Dhuh dhead in here iks worssse for mmgh … mmyou."

It shows its teeth. There are lots of them. Is that a grin? Can that be? That the creature has a sense of humor? Rosie seemed to grin, too. I take a chance. I laugh. It opens its mouth wider but there's no sound. We look each other in the eye. Some kind of understanding, lizard to mammal, passes between us. Then the creature shivers. I pull a blanket off the bunk, big Hudson Bay, but it only covers the creature's top half like a shawl. It helps to hold it on with those tiny arms, and nods again.

"I'll build up the fire and get us something to eat. You just rest."

"I hhhelp-puh."

"Please don't."

It grins again, mouth wide, that row of teeth gleaming, then huddles close against the wall opposite my kitchen area, trying to make itself small. Still, I step on its toes as I work. When I do, we both say, "Sorry." "Khsssorry." We both laugh … . Well, I laugh and it shows its teeth.

How nice to have somebody … some*thing* around that has a sense of humor. They must have left in some odd rogue genes by mistake.

I start to make stew. I have lots of dried chanterelles and I hope it likes wild garlic. It watches me as Rosie did, mouth open. I hum a song my grandma taught me. I thought hardly anybody knew that song but me, but then I hear the creature buzzing along with me, no doubt about it, the same song. I look at it. It blinks a slow blink, as if for a wink.

We eat my hare stew, it out of my wash basin. Licks it clean like Rosie always did. At least it hasn't lost its appetite.

"Have you a name other than that Zero Seven on your tag? By the way, I took that off. I had a dog, Rosie. She died. I keep almost calling you Rosie by mistake. It's the only name I've said for years."

There's that smile again. "Rrrrosie is kfine. Kfine." Then Kfine turns into a cough. I heat up some wild rose hips tea. I always have lots of that.

Then it stretches out again. I pile on more blankets.

"Mmmmmnnno mmno. Mmdon't."

"I insist. You must stay warm. If the lamp doesn't bother you I'll read for a while, but you should sleep. I'll make the fire high. Wake me if it gets cold. You should be warm."

(My lamp is just a bowl of volcanic tuff with exactly the right hole in the center. I have a big one and a little one. The oil I've rendered even from creatures with not much fat. Even deer.)

I settle myself with a book. I like having company even if the company takes up most of the room. I think it's already asleep, but then, "Khind, kh hind ssssir. I like being Rrrrosie." (It gargles it out as if it was French.) "Bhut who are mmmm kh you? *If* khyou don't mmmmind."

"Ben. I'm Ben."

"Ah, easy khto kkh ssssay."

I think: She. She is a she.

When I douse the lamp (by putting on the lid) and it's pitch black in here, I do have a moment when I worry. She *is* starving. I might be her next meal and a better one than I've prepared for her so far, or at least bigger. What's a little broth and then a little rabbit stew? But I won't be facing anything my wife and child didn't face already though my fate might not be as instantaneous as theirs. But I hear her breathing, snuffling, snorting in her sleep just like Rosie. I'm comforted and reassured by her snores.

● ◑ ○ ◐ ●

Sometime during the night the snow stops. Dawn, in my one and only window, shows a cloudless sky. I watch the oblong of sunlight move down and across the far wall until it lights on her. She's a bundle of blankets, but what little I can see of her shines out. Certainly she's not made for a winter climate. Probably most comfortable in a hot place with lots of shiny green leaves to hide in.

She feels the sun the moment it touches her. (Thick-skinned but infinitely sensitive.) Turns and looks at me. Grins her Rosie-grin. Like Rosie she doesn't have to say it, it's all over her face: Hey, a new day. What's up now? And: Let's get going. "You look better."

She nods. Says, "Mmmmm, nnnn. Mmmmm, nnnn."

"We'll go out, if you like. You must feel cramped in here."

"Mmmmmmm, nnnn."

I've jerky and hard tack. We breakfast on that, and more rose hip tea — a pitcher of it for her.

"Keep a blanket around your shoulders. And I think you'll have to back out."

Like my Rosie was before she got old, this Rosie peers, sniffs, hops up on boulders, jumps for no reason whatsoever, she skips in the bare spots where the snow has blown off. Sings a ho dee ho dee ho kind of song. A young thing that, sick or not, starving or not, can't sit still. I saw that in my boy.

I take her to my viewing spot. You can see the whole valley. I often see deer from here.

As we watch, another of these creatures comes down the valley heading south. I haven't seen any until this one sitting beside me, and here comes yet another, and then two more not far behind. Driven down from the mountain passes on purpose? Or is it the cold?

We watch. Not moving. Rosie looks at me, at them, at me. I love that look all young things have, animal or human, of wondering: What's up? What's going on? Is everything all right?

Then those first two turn and trumpet at the others. Rosie's arms are just long enough for her to cover her ears. (She must hear extraordinarily well to need to do that from way up here.) Hard to tell from this distance, but those others all seem much larger than she is.

When, a moment later, she takes her fingers from her ears, I ask her, "Have you had experiences with others of your own kind before?" She nods.

"The scars."

"Mmmnnn."

"You weren't supposed to fight each other."

"Mmmnnn."

I want to comfort her. Put my arms around this green scaly thing. (My son had an iguana. We never hugged it.) She reaches toward me as if to hug, too. But even those little arms … those claws … . And my head could fit all the way in her mouth, no problem. I flinch away. I see her eyes turn reptilian — lose their wide childlike look. She says, "Kh … khss sssorry."

"No, it's I who should be … *am* sorry."

I reach and I do hug and let myself be hugged. I get my parka ripped on her claws. Well, it's not the first rip.

Far below us, the things fight and trumpet, smash trees, trample brush. I can see, even from up here, spit fly out. There's no blood. Their hide is too tough.

They fight with their feet, leaping as cocks do. One is losing. It's on its back, talons up. Even from way up here, I can see a little herd of panicked deer galloping off toward the hills. Rosie covers her eyes this time and leans over as if she has a stomachache. Says, "Mmmmmmmmmnnn. Not Kkkh kkh krright.'

"What *were* you supposed to do?"

"Kkh … khill … . Mmmm those like kh you. Khill you."

Below us, the creature that was on its back tries to escape but the others leap high and claw at it, pull it down, then one bites the under part of the neck. Now there *is* blood.

I turn to see Rosie's reaction, but she's not here. Then I see her, way, way back, curled up behind a tree.

I go back to her. I put my arm around her again. "Old buddy." Then, "How did you ever turn out as you are?"

"Mmmm mmistake. Gh gho," Rosie says, carefully not looking down at them. "Ghho. Mmmmnn … *mnnnow!*" And she's already on her way, back to the shack. I follow. Watching her. Her arms, so like ours, look like an afterthought. Obviously there's a bit of the human in her. I see it in the legs, too. Also in those half-formed ears.

Those others below could push down my shack in half a minute. I need Rosie on my side. "Stay. I need you. I'll push out a wall. I'll make the door bigger."

She stops, stares. I wish I knew what's going on inside that big fierce head of hers.

"I'll start getting the logs for it today."

"I kh … kh … khelph."

But my food won't last long with her eating washbasins full. Besides, she's starving. We'll have to get food first.

"How have you lived all this time? What have you eaten?"

"Ghhophers mmm mostly. *When* mmmwere gh hophers. Khrabbits. When them. When kh llleaves, leaves. Mmmmushrooms. Rrrroots. Mmmmbark nnnot good but kh ate it. Khfish. Hhhard to kh kfish when kh h ice."

We climb higher than my shack so Rosie can fish. The streams up there are too fast to freeze over. She uses her foot. Hooks them on a claw. Her arms seem even too small to help with balancing. It's her big green head and the half of her leftover tail, waving from side to side, that balances her as she reaches. She gets seven.

"Kkhfried?" she says. "In khfat? With khh kh corn mmmeal? Like Mmmmmama? Mushka?"

"You betcha. You had a mama?"

"Mmmmmmnnnn. Mmmmmm. Mmone kh like mmyou."

She bounces off down the path ahead of me, singing an oolie, oolie, doodlie do kind of song. I guess she's no longer sick. Or she's too happy to care. And certainly not thinking about those others fighting in the valley.

(I'm carrying the fish. I strung them through their gills on to a willow stick. I hadn't brought my stringer. I guess I don't have to worry about getting enough food for her. Yet she was starving. Perhaps she doesn't like things raw?)

Back home we eat fried fish. I eat two and Rosie eats five. She watches as I cook just as the dog did, exact same expression, mouth half open. A dog sort of smile. We settle down afterward and I read to her from one of my books: *Moby Dick*. (I only brought three.) I read that to my son and wife, one on each side of me, and all of us on the couch. Rosie lies, head toward me, eyes almost shut, commenting now and then, her voice breathy, like one would imagine a snake would talk. I'm sitting on my cot. We sip our rosehips tea. We're both covered with blankets.

Then, "Time's up," I say. "You need sleep." But she doesn't want us to stop reading. "I insist," I say. She groans. "*I* kh kread. *You* ssssleep." She reaches for the book with those womanly shiny green fingers. I put it down and take her hand. "Ooobie baloobie, *do* it," I say. (Ooobie baloobie is another of her songs.) She laughs. (It's more like panting than laughing, but so hard I think she must be little more than seven years old — her equivalent of seven — to think that's so funny.) But she settles down right after. Says, "Kh … koh khay." Wraps her little arms around herself. I tuck the blankets closer and douse the lamp with its lid.

This time I don't worry if I might be her next meal, but I have a hard time sleeping anyway. I keep wondering what might happen it those others find my shack. They could break it down just leaning on it by mistake.

Since *they* all seem to be coming down, we'll go up. We'll take some supplies to the pass and hide. I've spent the night there many a time. We'll be all right as long as there isn't another storm that goes on for days and days. At least we'll have fish.

I always did like camping out. The view is always worth more than the discomfort. Besides I do without right here every day. It never bothers me, washing up in a washbowl or an icy stream. Only here is it worth the bother of looking out the window.

Or now, at Rosie, too. She really is quite beautiful, her yellow underbelly and the darker green along the ridge of her back. She's even reddish in spots.

● ◑ ○ ◐ ●

Rosie hears them first, wakes me with her, "Kh … kh … kh." There's sounds of crashing through the brush. A tree splintering. From the look of the big dipper, straight out my little north window, it's probably three or four A.M.

They're coming closer. For sure they saw our smoke and smelled us. They push on our walls. I hear them breathe and hiss. No, it's only one, I *think* only one, pushing the wall on one side. The caulking falls out. Rosie braces herself against that wall to hold it. She picks up the rhythm of the other's pushing, leans when it pushes. It works, the wall holds. At one point there's a large hole where the caulking's gone and I see the creature looking in — one light greenish eye like Rosie's. The thing gives a throaty hiss. Rosie answers with the same hiss. It gives up. We hear it smashing away. We look at each other.

"You did it!"

Rosie's mouth is open in that smile that looks so much like my old Rosie's and she nods yes so hard I'm thinking she'll put her neck out of joint. "Kh khdid! Khdid!"

"Pack up. We'll go camp out up beyond where we fished."

She goes right for the frying pan and the bag of corn meal and puts them in her vest pockets. She's still nodding yes but she stops when I tell her we have to bring blankets and a tarp.

"Kh … kh … kh … . *Kno! Nnnnnooo!*"

"Yes! It's colder up there. You need shelter as much as I do. Maybe more so."

Like Rosie, she gives up easily. "Kh … kh-kho kay." I don't know what I'd do if she didn't. She helps me roll the blankets in the tarp. Says, "I kh kcarry mmmmthat."

I have to stop her from taking her books and her fancy green rock. She insists she can carry all the things we need and those too.

"I kh likhe ghrrrrreeeen."

"That's good. Then you like yourself."

●　◐　○　◑　◕

She starts up, hop, skip, and jump … even with all that to carry. I can't believe it, she's leaping from rock to rock — even across talus. I keep telling her that stuff is unstable. "Dangerous even for you," I say, but she does it anyway. The rocks do teeter, but she's sure-footed. That leaping doesn't last long, thank goodness. She doesn't realize how much all that weight she's carrying will tire her. I warned her, but since when do the young listen to warnings of that sort. She's jumped and skipped and leaped until now she lags behind and blows like a horse at every other step. I take the tarp and blankets from her. I'd take that frying pan, too, but she won't let me. "Kh … kan do it. I *kan!*"

I don't let Rosie stop until the halfway spot. "We'll get up where we can see," I say, "then we'll rest."

"Oh pf … pfhooo," she says, but she goes on, sighing now.

"You can do it. Fifty more steps."

● ◑ ○ ◐ ●

A few minutes later we put down our bundles, Rosie takes off her vest, and we climb out to the edge of the scarp we just zigzagged up to see what we can see. And it's as I feared, they've found my cabin. Looks like there's not much left of it already, walls pushed in, roof collapsed. I had doused the fire but there must have been some cinders left. A fire has started, at the cabin and on the ground around it.

She sits as I sit, legs hanging over. How much like a human she is. Sometimes you don't see it at all, but in certain positions you do. Now she looks as if she's going to cry. (Can they cry? Only humans, seals, and sea birds have tears. Anyway, you don't need tears for sadness.) I feel like crying, too. Rosie can tell just like my old Rosie could. We lean against each other.

"At least your stones are all right."

She doesn't even answer with an Mmmnnnn.

I look to see if any trees are waving around down there from being bumped into, but there's nothing. Odd.

● ◑ ○ ◐ ●

After we start on up, Rosie is droopy, not only tired but sad. She thunks along. I feel sorry that she jumped and hopped so much in the beginning. My other Rosie was like that. She never realized she had to save her strength.

Most of my talking has been to keep her going. "Count steps. Maybe a hundred more." "Come on, poor tired friend." "See that rock? We'll stop just beyond that." Now I mumble to myself— about when I'll be back to sift through my things. I didn't bring

any souvenirs of my wife and child. When I fled out here …
escaped … I didn't even want pictures. I was running away from
memories. Of course memories come and go as they please.

Just around the corner and we'll be able to see the little
lake I'm heading for, the stepping stones crossing the creek that
pours down from it, beyond, the trees and boulders where I had
hoped to hide us this first night, but I decide we have to stop
now. We stand … that is, I stand, Rosie collapses. We're both
too tired to get out food other than jerky. I tuck Rosie in under
an overhang. Just her big back end with the half-bitten-off
tail hanging out. I cover her with blankets and the tarp. She's
asleep before she can finish her jerky. I pick the chunk out of
her mouth to save it for breakfast.

● ◑ ○ ◐ ●

In the morning I wake to the sound of a helicopter. I know
right away. Why … *why* didn't I suspect before? Rosie not only
had an ear tag, but she has a chip imbedded in her neck.

There's no place for a helicopter to land, the mountains
are too closed in and too many boulders, but we're not safe
anyway. There could be more things in Rosie's neck than just
an ID chip. That could be why we didn't hear those creatures
down there anymore.

Rosie's in an exhausted sleep. "You have to wake up. *Now.*
I have to get your chip out." I don't mention what else might
be there. Those others may have been disposed of … without a
trace, I'll bet. Or little traces scattered all over the place so no
one will know there ever were creatures like this.

"Did you know you have a chip?"

I feel around Rosie's neck.

"Hang on, friend, this will hurt."

I don't care about those others, but I'd never like the forest without Rosie in it, skipping and hopping along, picking flowers, collecting green rocks or glittery fool's gold, singing doodlie do songs.

She looks at the helicopter, then at me, then the copter again, then back at me. Again it's that: Should I be frightened or not? Except now *I'm* frightened. I try not to show it but she senses it. I see her getting scared, too.

The copter circles. I have to hurry — but I don't want to hurt her but her skin is so tough! And who knows, if I do find one or two things, will that be all that's hidden there?

"Hang on."

She hugs herself with those inadequate arms. Even before I start she makes little doglike … or, rather, birdlike sounds.

"Sing," I say. "Sing your oobie do."

I feel two lumps. I dig in. I say, "Almost done," when I've hardly begun.

●   ◐   ○   ◑   ●

Then we run. Without our blankets, without our food, except what Rosie has in her vest.

"They can't follow now." I *hope* that's true.

We stick to the old path that circles over the pass. We try to stay close to rocks and under what trees there are. Even running as we do, I can't not think about how beautiful it is up here. When I first saw it, years ago, I shouted when I came around the corner.

She's way ahead of me in no time — those long strong legs. And we're not carrying much of anything. I catch up when she finally turns to look for me. We both look back. The helicopter still hovers. I left the chip and button bullet back there at our camping spot. They think she's still there. Maybe they don't know about me.

She's different from those others. What was she for? That is, besides killing those like me?

It starts to snow. Thank God or worse luck, I don't know which. It'll hide our tracks and the helicopter won't fly, but we don't have food or blankets.

We cross the pass and dip into the next valley. We find a sheltered spot among a mass of fallen boulders where the whole side of a cliff came down. Some boulders are on top of each other making a roof. Boulders over, boulders under — not a particularly comfortable spot but we huddle there and rest. We take stock. All we have is what's in Rosie's vest, a little leftover jerky (we eat it), the frying pan, and cornmeal. We can make corn cakes if we don't catch fish.

This is just a mountain storm. If we can get far enough down we'll walk out of it. If we're lucky it'll last just long enough to cover our tracks. I tell Rosie. She lies at my feet still panting, I stoke her knobby head.

"How's your neck?"

"Hh … hoo khay."

She sleeps. Murmuring a whole series of Mmmms, and then Mmmush, and Mmmushka.

As the storm eases and we're some rested, I wake her and we start down. After an hour we're out of the snow and wind and into a hanging meadow. I've been over this pass but not this far.

I'm worried. Rosie is sluggish and dreamy, flopping along, tripping a lot. Poor thing, all she has on is her vest. She's cold and with reptiles … or part-reptiles … . I don't want to build a fire but I must. The copter's gone, maybe it's all right to now.

"My poor fierce friend," I say. She grins. I take her hand and sit her down. "We're going to have a nice big fire. You rest. I'll find the wood."

"I'll hhh … hhh … hhh."

"No you won't. I'm going by myself. I'll be back before you know it."

She mews, turns away, and curls up.

● ◑ ○ ◐ ●

On this side there's a lot less snow, so not hard going. I gather brush, dead limbs, and drag the whole batch back to her, flop down, my arm around her. I see her eyes flicker, though the nictitating membrane closes as she does it. She doesn't wake. I'll have to make the fire right now.

How does a sick reptile show how sick it is? All I know is, she doesn't look right and doesn't feel right.

I build the fire as close to her as I dare. Finally she seems in a more normal sleep. I sleep, too.

● ◑ ○ ◐ ●

I wake with a start. *Hibernate!* Do they? All those others, too. But she's been mixed with other genes. For sure, some human.

I wake her by mistake as I get out the frying pan and the

cornmeal. I'm melting snow, first to drink and then to make corncakes. She drinks as if she's been out in the desert for days. Then, "I'mm mmhungry." Then she sees what little cornmeal we have and says, "Mmmm *nnnot* ssso . . . . *Nnnot* hungry," she says again. "Ooobie, baloobie, *nnnnot*."

"Ooobie, baloobie, *do* eat me. Roll me in corn meal. I'm old and I'm tired."

All of a sudden it's not a joke.

"Kkkh kkkh! Kh khcan't dooo that! Oooooh!"

"I thought that's what you were made for … born for."

"Kkh can't."

"You'll die. Look how thin you are."

"I'mmm tem *po* rary. Temmm *po po* rary." She sings it like a song like she doesn't care. Does she understand what it means? I wonder if it's true. Perhaps they all are — were.

"Mmmmmm *all* temmm *po po!* rary."

"What makes you think you're temporary?"

"Mmmmush kh knew."

"She *told* you? How could she!"

"Kkh kh *ntmno!* I sssaw kher eyes. Sssscared. I kh khfound out. I kh … kh … kread."

"You're only half grown."

"Have a kh kh tth timer."

I don't know what I see in those lizardy eyes of hers. "Don't you like it here? Don't you care anything about being alive?"

"Oh! Kh! *Oooh!* Kh!" She does a hopping, twisting dance, those tiny arms raised. It tells how she feels, better than her words ever could.

"Mmmmy kh heart," she says, "hasss kth th timer."

"How long is temporary."

"I sh should dannnce. Ssssing. *Mnnnow!* And lllook. Lllook a *lllot! Yesssss!* Lottts. Mmm then kh kgo for goood mmmmbig bh bones."

We'll build another cabin. Here in this hanging valley, sheltered under boulders and trees and next to a good fishing stream. With her help we'll have one up in no time. We'll dance and sing and look around a lot. At the smallest and the largest … the near and the far … stars, mountain peaks, beetles … .

As to any "meaning" I'm trying to get across, there isn't any. It's just that I've somehow ended up with a "meaning" in most of what I write, though I never think about meanings. I never knew what "theme" meant either until I had students that didn't seem to have a point to their stories. I would wonder why in the world they'd bothered to write that story? Did they care? I don't know where my "meanings" come from. I just try to write a good, well-formed story.

—CAROL EMSHWILLER, 2001

SEX AND/OR MR. MORRISON

I CAN SET MY CLOCK BY MR. MORRISON'S STEP UPON THE stairs, not that he is that accurate, but accurate enough for me. Eight-thirty, thereabouts. (My clock runs fast, anyway.) Each day he comes clumping down and I set it back ten minutes, or eight minutes or seven. I suppose I could just as well do it without him but it seems a shame to waste all that heavy treading and those puffs and sighs of expanding energy on only getting downstairs, so I have timed my life to this morning beat. Funereal tempo, one might well call it, but it is funereal only because Mr. Morrison is fat and therefore slow. Actually he's a very nice man as men go. He always smiles.

I wait downstairs, sometimes looking up and sometimes holding my alarm clock. I smile a smile I hope is not as wistful as his. Mr. Morrison's moon face has something of the Mona Lisa to it. Certainly he must have secrets.

"I'm setting my clock by you, Mr. M."

"Heh, heh ... my, my," grunt, breath. "Well," heave the stomach to the right, "I hope ..."

"Oh, you're on time enough for *me*."

"Heh, hch. Oh. Oh, yes." The weight of the world is surely upon him or perhaps he's crushed and flattened by a hundred miles of air. How many pounds per square inch weighing him down? He hasn't the inner energy to push back. All his muscles spread like jelly under his skin.

"No time to talk," he says. (He never has time.) Off he goes. I like him and his clipped little Boston accent, but I know he's too proud ever to be friendly. Proud is the wrong word (so is shy) but I'l leave it at that.

He turns back, pouting, and then winks at me as a kind of softening of it. Perhaps it's just a twitch. He thinks, if he thinks of me at all: What can she say and what can I say talking to her? What can she possibly know that I don't know already? And so he duck-walks, knock-kneed, out the door.

And now the day begins.

There are really quite a number of things that I can do. I often spend time in the park. Sometimes I rent a boat there and row myself about and feed the ducks. I love museums and there are all those free art galleries and there's window-shopping and if I'm very careful with my budget, now and then I can squeeze in a matinee. But I don't like to be out after Mr. Morrison comes back. I wonder if he keeps his room locked while he's off at work.

His room is directly over mine and he's too big to be a quiet man. The house groans with him and settles when he steps out of bed. The floor creaks under his feet. Even the side walls rustle and the wallpaper clicks its dried paste. But don't think I'm complaining of the noise. I keep track of him this way. Sometimes, here underneath, I ape his movements, bed to dresser, step, clump, dresser to closet and back again. I imagine him there, flatfooted. Imagine him. Just imagine those great legs sliding into pants, their godlike width (for no mere man could have legs like that), those Thor legs into pants holes wide as caves. Imagine those two landscapes, sparsely fuzzed in a faint, wheat-colored brush, finding their way blindly into the waist-wide skirt-things of brown wool that are still damp from yesterday. Ooo. Ugh. Up go the suspenders. I think I can hear him breathe from here.

I can comb my hair three times to his once and I can be out and waiting at the bottom step by the time he opens his door.

"I'm setting my clock by you, Mr. M."

"No time. No time. I'm off. Well …" and he shuts the front door so gently one would think he is afraid of his own fat hands.

And so, as I said, the day begins.

The question is (and perhaps it is the question for today): Who is he really, one of the Normals or one of the Others? It's not going to be so easy to find out with someone so fat. I wonder if I'm up to it. Still, I'm willing to go to certain lengths and I'm nimble yet. All that rowing and all that walking up and down and then, recently, I've spent all night huddled under a bush in Central Park and twice I've crawled out on the fire escape and climbed to the roof and back again (but I haven't seen much and I can't be sure of the Others yet).

I don't think the closet will do because there's no keyhole though I could open the door a crack and maybe wedge my shoe there. (It's double A.) He might not notice it. Or there's the bed to get under. While it's true that I am thin and small, almost child-sized, one might say, still it will not be so easy, but then neither has it been easy to look for lovers on the roof.

Sometimes I wish I were a little, fast-moving lizard, dull green or a yellowish brown. I could scamper in under his stomach when he opened the door and he'd never see me though his eyes are as quick as his feet are clumsy. Still I would be quicker. I would skitter off behind the bookcase or back of his desk or maybe even just lie very still in a corner, for surely he does not see the floor so much. His room is no larger than mine and his presence must fill it, or rather his stomach fills it and his giant legs. He sees the ceiling and the pictures on the wall, the surfaces of night table, desk and bureau, but the floor and the lower halves of everything would be safe for me. No, I won't even have to regret not being a lizard, except for getting in. But if he doesn't lock his room it will be no problem and I can spend all day scouting out my hiding places. I'd best take a snack with me, too, if I decide this is the night for it. No crackers and no nuts, but noiseless things like cheese and fig newtons.

It seems to me, now that I think about it, that I was rather saving Mr. Morrison for last, as a child saves the frosting of the cake to eat after the cake part is finished. But I see that I have been foolish. As he is really one of the most likely prospects, he should have been first.

And so today the day begins with a gathering of supplies and an exploratory trip upstairs.

The room is cluttered. There is no bookcase but there are books and magazines by the hundreds. I check behind the piles. I check the closet, full of drooping, giant suit coats I can easily hide in. Just see how the shoulders extend over the ordinary hangers. I check under the bed and the kneehole of the desk. I squat under the night table. I nestle among the dirty shirts and socks tossed in the corner. Oh, it's better than Central Park for hiding places. I decide to use them all.

There's something very nice about being here for I do like Mr. Morrison. Even just his size is comforting for he's big enough to be everybody's father. His room reassures with all his father-sized things in it. I feel lazy and young here.

I eat a few fig newtons while I sit on his shoes in the closet, soft, wide shoes with their edges all collapsed and all of them shaped more like cushions than shoes. Then I take a nap in the dirty shirts. It looks like fifteen or so but there are only seven and some socks. After that I hunch down in the knee-hole of the desk, hugging my knees, and I wait and I begin to have doubts. That pendulous stomach, I can already tell, will be larger than all my expectations. There will certainly be nothing it cannot overshadow or conceal, so why do I crouch here clicking my fingernails against the desk leg when I might be out feeding pigeons? "Leave now," I tell myself. "Are you actually going to spend the whole day, and maybe night, too, cramped and confined in here?" Yet haven't I done it plenty of times lately and always for nothing, too? Why not one more try? For Mr. Morrison is surely the most promising of all. His eyes, the way the fat pushes up his cheeks under them, look almost Chinese. His nose is Roman and in an ordinary face it would be overpowering, but here it is lost. Dwarfed. "Save me," cries the nose. "I'm sinking." I would try, but I will have other, more important duties, after Mr. Morrison comes back, than to save his nose. Duty it is, too, for the good of all and I do mean all. Do not think that I am the least bit prejudiced in this.

You see, I *did* go to a matinee a few weeks ago. I saw the Royal Ballet dance *The Rite of Spring* and it occurred to me then … Well, what would you think if you saw them wearing their suits that were supposed to be bare skin? Naked suits, I called them. And all those well-dressed, cultured people clapping at them, accepting even though they knew perfectly well … like a sort of Emperor's New Clothes in reverse. Now just think, there are only two sexes and every one of us is one of those and certainly, presumably that is, knows something of the other. But then that may be where I have been making my mistake. You'd think … why just what I did start thinking, that there must be Others among us.

But it is not out of fear or disgust that I am looking for them. I am open and unprejudiced. You can see that I am when I say that I've never seen (and doesn't this seem strange?) the very organs of my own conception, neither my father's nor my mother's. Goodness knows what they were and what this might make me.

So I wait here, tapping my toes inside my slippers and chewing hangnails off my fingers. I contemplate the unvarnished underside of the desk top. I ridge it with my thumbnail. I eat more cookies and think whether I should make his bed for him or not but decide not to. I suck my arm until it is red in the soft crook opposite the elbow. Time jerks ahead as slowly as a school clock, and I crawl across the floor and stretch out behind the books and magazines. I read first paragraphs of dozens of them. What with the dust back here and lying in the shirts and socks before, I'm getting a certain smell and a sort of gray, animal fuzz that makes me feel safer, as though I really did belong in this room and could actually creep around and not be noticed by Mr. Morrison at all except perhaps for a pat on the head as I pass him.

Thump … pause. Clump … pause. One can't miss his step. The house shouts his presence. The floors wake up squeaking and lean toward the stairway. The banister slides away from his slippery ham-hands. The wallpaper seems suddenly full of bugs. He thinks (if he thinks of me at all): Well, this time she isn't peeking out of her doorway at me. A relief. I can concentrate completely on climbing up. Lift the legs against the pressure. Ooo. Ump. Pause and seem to be looking at the picture on the wall.

I skitter back under the desk.

It's strange that the first thing he does is to put his newspaper on the desk and sit down with his knees next to my nose, regular walls, furnaces of knees, exuding heat and dampness, throwing off a miasma, delicately scented, of wet wool and sweat. What a wide roundness they have to them, those knees. Mother's breasts pressing toward me. Probably as soft. Why can't I put my cheek against them? Observe how he can sit so still with no toe-taping, no rhythmic tensing of the thigh. He's not like the rest of us, but could a man like this do *little* things?

How the circumstantial evidence piles up, but that is all I've had so far and it is time for something concrete. One thing, just one fact is all I need.

He reads and adjusts the clothing at his crotch and reads again.

He breathes out winds of sausages and garlic and I remember that it's after supper and I take out my cheese and eat it as slowly as possible in little rabbit bites. I make a little piece last half an hour.

At last he goes down the hall to the bathroom and I shift back under the shirts and socks and stretch my legs. What if he undresses like my mother did, under a nightgown? Under, for him, some giant, double-bed-sized thing?

But he doesn't. He hangs his coat on the little hanger and his tie on the closet doorknob. I receive his shirt and have to make myself another spy hole. Then off with the tortured shoes, then socks. Off come the huge pants with slow, unseeing effort (he stares out the window). He begins on his yellowed undershorts, scratching himself first behind and starting earthquakes across his buttocks.

Where could he have bought those elephantine undershorts? In what store were they once folded on the shelf? In what factory did women sit at sewing machines and put out one after another after another of those otherworldly items? Mars? Venus? Saturn more likely. Or perhaps, instead, a tiny place, some moon of Jupiter with less air per square inch upon the skin and less gravity, where Mr. Morrison can take the stairs three at a time and jump the fences (for surely he's not particularly old) and dance all night with girls his own size.

He squints his Oriental eyes toward the ceiling light and takes off the shorts, lets them fall loosely to the floor. I see Alleghenies of thigh and buttock. How does a man like that stand naked before even a small-sized mirror? I lose myself, hypnotized. Impossible to tell the color of his skin, just as it is with blue-gray eyes or the ocean. How tan, pink, olive and red and sometimes a bruised elephant-gray. His eyes must be used to multiplicities like this, and to plethoras, conglomerations, to an opulence of self, to an intemperate exuberance, to the universal, the astronomical.

I find myself completely tamed. I lie in my cocoon of shirts not even shivering. My eyes do not take in what they see. He is utterly beyond my comprehension. Can you imagine how thin my wrists must seem to him? He is thinking (if he thinks of me at all), he thinks: She might be from another world. How alien her ankles and leg bones. How her eyes do stand out. How green her complexion in the shadows at the edges of her face (for I must admit that perhaps I may be as far along the scale at my end of "humanity" as he is at his).

Suddenly I feel like singing. My breath purrs in my throat in hymns as slow as Mr. Morrison himself would sing. Can this be love? I wonder. My first *real* love? But haven't I always been passionately interested in people? Or rather in those who caught my fancy? But isn't this feeling entirely different? Can love really have come to me this late in life? (La, la, lee la, from whom all blessings flow …) I shut my eyes and duck my head into the shirts. I grin into the dirty socks. Can you imagine *him* making love to *me!*

Well below his abstracted, ceilingward gaze, I crawl on elbows and knees back behind the old books. A safer place to shake out the silliness. Why, I'm old enough for him to be (had I ever married) my youngest son of all. Yet if he were a son of mine, how he would have grown beyond me. I see that I cannot ever follow him (as with all sons). I must love him as a mouse might love the hand that cleans the cage, and as uncomprehendingly, too, for surely I see only a part of him here. I sense more. I sense deeper largenesses. I sense excesses of bulk I cannot yet imagine. Rounded afterimages linger on my eyeballs. There seems to be a mysterious darkness in the corners of the room and his shadow covers, at the same time, the window on one wall and the mirror on the other. Certainly he is like an iceberg, seven-eighths submerged.

But now he has turned toward me. I peep from the books, holding a magazine over my head as one does when it rains. I do so more to shield myself from too much of him all at once than to hide.

And there we are, confronting each other eye to eye. We stare and he cannot seem to comprehend me any more than I can comprehend him, and yet usually, his mind is ahead of mine, jumping away on unfinished phrases. His eyes are not even wistful and not yet surprised. But his belly button … here is the eye of God at last. It nestles in a vast, bland sky like a sun on the curve of the universe flashing me a wink of heat, a benign, fat wink. The stomach eye accepts and understands. The stomach eye recognizes me and looks at me as I've always wished to be looked at. (Yea, though I walk through the valley of the shadow of death.) I see you now.

But I see him now. The skin hangs in loose, plastic folds just there, and there is a little copper-colored circle like a quarter made out of pennies. There's a hole in the center and it is corroded green at the edges. This must be a kind of "naked suit" and whatever the sex organs may be, they are hidden behind this hot, pocked, and pitted imitation skin.

I look into those girlish eyes of his and there is a big nothing, as blank as though the eyeballs are all whites … as blank as having no sex at all … like being built like a boy doll with a round hole for the water to empty out (something to frighten little-boy three-year-olds).

God, I think. I am not religious but I think: My God, and then I stand up and somehow, in a limping run, I get out of there and down the stairs as though I fly. I slam the door of my room and slide in under my bed. The most obvious of hiding places, but after I am there I can't bear to move out. I lie and listen for his thunder on the stairs, the roar of his feet splintering the steps, his hand tossing away the banister as he comes like an engulfing wave.

I know what I'll say. "We accept. We accept," I'll say. "We will love" (I love already) "whatever you are."

I lie listening, watching the hanging edges of my bedspread in the absolute silence of the house. Can there be anyone here at all in such a strange quietness? Must I doubt even my own existence?

"Goodness knows," I'll say, "if I'm a Normal myself." (How is one to know such things when everything is hidden?) "Tell all of them that we accept. Tell them it's the naked suits that are ugly. Tell them the truth is beautiful. Your dingles, your dangles, wrinkles, ruts, bumps, and humps, we accept. (We will love.) Your loops, strings, worms, buttons, figs, cherries, flower petals, your soft little toad shapes, warty and greenish, your cats' tongues and rats' tails, your oysters one-eyed between your legs, garter snakes, snails, we accept. (Isn't the truth always more lovable?)

But what a long silence this is. Where is he? For he must (mustn't he?) come after me for what I saw. If there has been all this hiding and if he must wear that cache-sex thing across his front, then he must silence me somehow, destroy me even. But where is he? Perhaps he thinks I've locked my door. But I haven't. I haven't.

Why doesn't he come?

I LIVE WITH YOU AND YOU DON'T KNOW IT

I LIVE IN YOUR HOUSE AND YOU DON'T KNOW IT. I NIBBLE at your food. You wonder where it went … where your pencils and pens go …. What happened to your best blouse. (You're just my size. That's why I'm here.) How did your keys get way over on the bedside table instead of by the front door where you always put them? You do always put them there. You're careful.

I leave dirty dishes in the sink. I nap in your bed when you're at work and leave it rumpled. You thought you had made it first thing in the morning and you had.

●　◑　○　◐　●

I saw you first when I was hiding out at the bookstore. By then I was tired of living where there wasn't any food except the muffins in the coffee bar. In some ways it was a good place to be … the reading, the music. I never stole. Where would I have taken what I liked? I didn't even steal back when I lived in a department store. I left there forever in my same old clothes though I'd often worn their things at night. When I left, I could see on their faces that they were glad to see such a raggedy person leave. I could see they wondered how I'd gotten in in the first place. To tell the truth, only one person noticed me. I'm hardly ever noticed.

But then, at the bookstore, I saw you: Just my size. Just my look. And you're as invisible as I am. I saw that nobody noticed you just as hardly anybody notices me.

I followed you home — a nice house on the outskirts of town. If I wore your clothes, I could go in and out and everybody would think I was you. But I wondered how to get in in the first place? I thought it would have to be in the middle of the night and I'd have to climb in a window.

●　◐　○　◑　●

But I don't need a window. I hunch down and walk in right hehind you. You'd think somebody that nobody ever notices would notice other people, but you don't.

Once I'm in, right away I duck into the hall closet.

You have a cat. Isn't that just like you? And just like me also. I would have had one were I you.

●　◐　○　◑　●

The first few days are wonderful. Your clothes are to my taste. Your cat likes me (right away better than he likes you). Right away I find a nice place in your attic. More a crawl space but I'm used to hunching over. In fact that's how I walk around most of the time. The space is narrow and long, but it has little windows at each end. Out one, I can look right into a treetop. I think an apple tree. If it was the right season I could reach out and pick an apple. I brought up your quilt. I saw you looking puzzled after I took the hall rug. I laughed to myself when you changed the locks on your doors. Right after that I took a photo from the mantel. Your mother, I presume. I wanted you to notice it was gone, but you didn't.

I bring up a footstool. I bring up cushions, one by one until I have four. I bring up magazines, straight from the mailbox, before you have a chance to read them.

What I do all day? Anything I want to. I dance and sing and play the radio and TV.

When you're home, I come down in the evening, stand in the hall and watch you watch TV.

I wash my hair with your shampoo. Once, when you came home early, I almost got caught in the shower. I hid in the hall closet, huddled in with the sheets, and watched you find the wet towel — the spilled shampoo.

You get upset. You think: I've heard odd thumps for weeks. You think you're in danger, though you try hard to talk yourself out of it. You tell yourself it's the cat, but you know it's not.

You get a lock for your bedroom door — a deadbolt. You have to be inside to push it closed.

● ◑ ○ ◐ ●

I have left a book open on the couch, the print of my head on the couch cushion. I've pulled out a few gray hairs to leave there. I have left a half-full wine glass on the counter. I have left your underwear (which I wore) on the bathroom floor, dirty socks under the bed, a bra hanging on the towel rack. I left a half-eaten pizza on the kitchen counter. (I ordered out and paid with your stash of quarters, though I know where you keep your secret twenties.)

I set all your clocks back fifteen minutes but I set your

alarm clock to four in the morning. I hid your reading glasses. I pull buttons off your sweaters and put them where your quarters used to be. Your quarters I put in your button box.

●   ◑   ○   ◐   ●

Normally I try not to bump and thump in the night, but I'm tired of your little life. At the bookstore and grocery store at least things happened all day long. You keep watching the same TV programs. You go off to work. You make enough money (I see the bank statements), but what do you do with it? I want to change your life into something worth watching.

I begin to thump, bump, and groan and moan. (I've been feeling like groaning and moaning for a long time, anyway.) Maybe I'll bring you a man. I'll buy you new clothes and take away the old ones, so you'll have to wear the new ones. The new clothes will be red and orange and with stripes and polka dots. When I get through with you, you'll be real … or at least realer. People will notice you. Your red cheeks. Your frown.

Now you groan and sigh as much as I do. You think: This can't be happening. You think: What about the funny sounds coming from the crawl space? You think: I don't dare go up there by myself, but who could I get to go with me? (You don't have any friends that I know of. You're like me in that.)

●   ◑   ○   ◐   ●

Monday you go off to work wearing a fuzzy blue top and red leather pants. You had a hard time finding a combination without stripes or big flowers or dots on it.

I watch you from your kitchen window. I'm heating up your leftover coffee. I'm making toast. (I use up all the butter. You thought there was plenty for the next few days.)

●　◗　○　◖　●

You almost caught me the time I came home late with packages. I had to hide behind the curtains. I could tell that my feet showed out the bottom, but you didn't notice.

Another time you saw me duck into the hall closet but you didn't dare open the door. You hurried upstairs to your bedroom and pushed the deadbolt. That evening you didn't come down at all. You skipped supper. I watched TV … any show I wanted.

I can go in your bedroom and lock you out just like you locked me out. I could bring up a good supper and the cat. Then you'd have to go sleep in the crawl space. It's not bad up there. Lots of your things are handy, a bedside lamp, a clock … .

I put another deadbolt on the *outside* of your bedroom door. Just in case. It's way up high. I don't think you'll notice. It might come in handy.

●　◗　○　◖　●

(Lacy underwear with holes in lewd places. Nudist magazines. Snails and sardines — smoked oysters. Neither one of us like them. All the things I get with your money are for you. I don't steal.)

●　◗　○　◖　●

How do you get through Christmas all by yourself? You're lonely enough for both of us. You wrap empty boxes in Christmas paper just to be festive. You buy a tree, a small one. It's artificial and comes with lights that glimmer on and off. The cat and I come down to sleep near its glow.

● ◑ ○ ◐ ●

But the man. The one I want to bring to you. I look over the personals. I write letters to possibilities but, as I'm taking them to the post office, I see somebody. He limps and wobbles. (The way he lurches sideways looks like sciatica to me. Or maybe arthritis.) He needs a haircut and a shave. He's wearing an old plaid jacket and he's all knees and elbows. There's a countrified look about him. Nobody wears plaid around here.

I limp behind him. Watch him go into one of those little apartments behind a main house and over a garage. It's not far from our house.

It can't be more than one room. I could never creep around in that place and not be noticed.

A country cousin. Country uncle more likely, he's older than we are. Is he capable of what I want him for?

● ◑ ○ ◐ ●

Next day I watch him in the grocery store. Like us, he buys living-alone kind of food, two apples, a tomato, crackers, oatmeal. Poor people's kind of food. I get in line with him at the checkout. I bump into him on purpose as he pays and peek into his wallet. That's all he has — just enough for what he buys. He counts out the change a penny at a time and he hardly has a nickel left over. I get ready to give him a bit extra if he needs it.

He's such an ugly, rickety man … . Perfect.

There's no reason to go into his over-the-garage room, hut I want to. This is important. I need to see who he is.

I use our credit card to open his lock.

What a mess. He needs somebody like us to look after him. His bed is piled with blankets. The room isn't very well heated. The bathroom has a curtain instead of a door. There's no tub or even shower. I check the hot water in the sink. It says HOT, but both sides come out cold. All he has is a hot plate. No refrigerator. There's two windows, but no curtains. Isn't that just like a man. I could climb up on the back fence and see right in.

There's nothing of the holidays here. Nothing of any holidays and not a single picture of a relative. And, like our house, nothing of friends. You and he are made for each other.

What to do to show I've been here? But this time I don't feel much like playing tricks. And it's so messy he wouldn't notice, anyway.

It's cold. I haven't taken my coat off all through this. I make myself a cup of tea. (There's no lemons and no milk. Of course.) I sit in his one chair. It's painted ugly green. All his furniture is as if picked up on the curb and his bedside table is one of those fruit boxes. As I sit and sip, I check his magazines. They look as though stolen from somebody's garbage. I'm shivering. (No wonder he's out. I suppose it's not easy to shave. He'd have to heat the water on the hot plate.)

He needs a cat. Something to sleep on his chest to keep him warm like your cat does with me. Should I bring ours over?

It would take you a week to notice he was gone. I could nibble at the cat food. I have already.

I have our groceries in my backpack. I leave two oranges and a doughnut in plain sight beside the hot plate. I leave several of our quarters. I leave a note: I put in our address. I sign your name. I write: Come for Christmas. Two o'clock. I'll be wearing red leather pants! Your neighbor, Nora.

(I wonder which of us should wear those pants.)

I clean up a little bit but not so much that he'd notice if he's not a noticing person. Besides, people only notice when things are dirty. They never notice when things are cleaner.

As I walk home, I see you on your way out. We pass each otber. You look right at me. I'm wearing your green sweater and your black slacks. We look at each other, my brown eyes to your brown eyes. Only difference is, your hair is pushed back and mine hangs down over my forehead and I have to admit my nose is less aristocratic. You go right on by. I turn and look back. You don't. I laugh behind my hand that you had to wear those red leather pants and a black and white striped top.

● ◑ ○ ◐ ●

He's too timid and too self-deprecating to come. He doesn't like to limp in front of people and he's ashamed not to have enough money hardly even for his food, and not to have a chance to shave and take a bath. Though if he's scared by me coming into his room, he might come. He might want to see who Nora is and if the address is real. His pretext will be that he wants to thank you for the food and quarters. He might even want to give them back. He might be one of those rich people who live as if they were poor. I should have looked for money or bank books. I will next time.

● ◑ ○ ◐ ●

When the doorbell rings, who else could it be? You open the door.

"Are you Nora?"

"Yes?"

"I want to thank you."

I knew it. I suppose he wants more money.

"But I want to bring your quarters back. That was kind of you but I don't need them."

You don't know what to say. You suspect it's all because of me. That I've, yet again, made your life difficult. You wonder what to do. He doesn't look dangerous but you never can tell. You want to get even with me some way. You suppose, if he *is* dangerous, it would be bad for both of us so it must be all right. You ask him in.

He hobbles into your livingroom. You say, sit down, that you'll get tea. You're stalling for time.

He still holds the handful of quarters. He puts them on the coffee table. It's hard for him to sit. Good the chair has arms.

You don't know how those quarters got to him or even if they really are your quarters. "No, no," you say, and, "Where did these come from?"

"They were in my room with a note from you and this address. You said, Come for Christmas."

You wonder what I'll like least. Do I want you to invite him to stay for supper? Unlikely, though, since you only have one

TV dinner and you know I know that.

"Somebody is playing a joke on me. But the tea … ."

You need help getting started so I trip you in the hall as you come back into the room. Everything goes down. Too bad, too, because you'd used your good china in spite of how this man looks.

Of course he pushes himself up and hobbles to you and helps pick up the things and you. You say you could make more but he says. It doesn't matter. Then you both go out to the kitchen. I go, too. Sidling. Slithering. The cat slides in with us. Both your and his glasses are thick. I'm counting on your blindness. I squat down. He puts the broken cups on a corner of the counter. You get out two more. He says, these are too nice. You say, they're Mother's. He says, "You shouldn't use the Rosenthal, not for me."

There now, are you both rich yet never use your money?

The cat jumps on the table and you swipe him off. No wonder he likes me better than you. I always let him go where he wants and I like him on the table.

You're looking at our man — studying his crooked nose. You see what neither of us has noticed until now. The hand that reaches to help you wears a ring with a large stone. Some sort of school ring. You're thinking: Well, well, and changing your mind. As am I.

He's too good for you. Maybe might be good enough for me.

We are all, all three, the same kind of person. When you leave in the morning, I've seen you look out the door to make sure there's nobody out there you might have to say hello to.

But now you talk. You think. You ask. You wonder out

loud if this and that. You look down at your striped shirt and wish you were wearing your usual clothes. I'm under the table wearing your brown blouse with the faint pattern of fall leaves. I look like a wrinkled up paper bag kicked under here and forgotten. The cat is down here with me purring.

It never takes long for two lonely people living in their fantasies to connect — to see all sorts of things in each other that don't exist.

You've waited for each other all your lives. You almost say so. Besides, he'd have a nice place to live if … if anything comes of this.

I think about that black lacy underwear. That pink silk nightie. As soon as I have a chance, I'll go get them. I might need them for myself.

But how to get you moving? You're both all talk. Or you are, he's not talking much. Perhaps one look at the nightie might get things rolling. That'll have to be for later. Or on the other hand … .

I reach back to the shelf behind me and, when neither he nor you are looking, I bring out the sherry. You'll both think the other one got the bottle out.

(You do.)

You get wine glasses. You even get out your TV dinner and say you'll split it. It's turkey with stuffing. You got it special for Christmas.

Of course he says for you to eat it all, but you say you never do, anyway, so you split it.

I'm getting hungry myself. If it was just you, I would sneak a few bites, but there's little enough for the two of you. I'll have to find another way.

You both get tipsy. It doesn't take much. You hardly ever drink and it looks like he doesn't either. And I think you want to get drunk. You want something to happen as much as I do.

Every now and then I take a sip of your drinks. And on an empty stomach it takes even less. With the drone of your talk, talk, talking, I almost go to sleep.

●　　◓　　○　　◑　　◕

But you're heading upstairs already.

I crawl out from under the table and climb the stairs behind you. I'm as wobbly as you are. Actually I'm wobblier. We, all three, go into your bedroom. And the cat. You push the dead-bolt. He wonders why. "Aren't you alone here?"

You say, "Not exactly." And then, "I'll tell you later."

(You're right, this certainly isn't the time for a discussion about me.)

First thing I grab our sexy nightie from the drawer. I get under the bed and put it on. That's not easy, cramped up under there. For a few minutes I lose track of what's happening above me. I comb my hair as you always have it, hack away from your face. I have to use my fingers and I don't have a mirror so I'm not sure how it comes out. I pinch my cheeks and bite my lips to make them redder.

The cat purrs.

I lean up to see what's going on.

Nothing much so far. Even though tipsy, he seems shy. Inexperienced. I don't think he's ever been anybody's grandfather.

(We're, all of us, all of a piece. None of us has ever been anybody's relative.)

You look pretty much passed out. Or you're pretending. Either way, it's a good time for me to make an appearance.

I crawl out from under the bed and check myself in the mirror behind them. My hair is a mess but I look good in the silky nightgown. Better than you do in your stripes and red pants. By far.

I do a little sexy dance. I say, "She's not Nora, I'm Nora. I'm the one wrote you that note."

You sit up. You were faking being drunk. You think: Now I see who you are. Now I'll get you. But you won't.

I stroke the cat. Suggestively. He purrs. (The cat, I mean.) I purr. Suggestively.

I see his eyes light up. (The man's, I mean.) Now there'll be some action. I say, "I don't even know your name."

He says, "Willard."

I'm on his good side because I asked, and you're not because you didn't. All this talk, talk, talk, talk and you didn't.

You slither away, down under the bed. You feel ashamed of yourself and yet curious. You wonder: How did you ever get yourself in this position, and what to do now? But I do know what to do. I give you a kick and hand you the cat.

Willard. Willard is a little confused. But eager. More than before. He likes the nightgown and says so.

I take a good long look at him. Those bushy eyebrows. Lots of white hairs in them. I help him take off his shirt. His is not my favorite kind of chest. He does have a nice flat stomach though. (I liked that about him from the start — back when I first saw him wobbling down the street.) I look into his green/gray/tan eyes.

But what about, I love you?

I say it. "What about I love you?"

That stops him. I didn't mean to do that. I wanted to give Nora a good show. Of course it's much too soon for any sort of thing that might resemble love.

"I take that back," I say.

But it's too late. He's putting on his shirt. (It's a dressy white one. He's even wearing cufflinks engraved with WT.)

Is it really over already?

I pick up the cat, hurry out, slam the door, and push the deadbolt on the outside, then turn back and look through the keyhole. I can see almost the whole bed.

Now look, his hands are … all of a sudden … on her and on all the right places. He knows. Maybe he actually *is* somebody's grandfather after all. And you … you are feeling things that make your back arch.

He tells you he loves you. Now he says it. He can't tell us apart. He'll love anything that comes his way.

I have what I thought I wanted … a good view of something interesting for a change, except … .

Actually I can't see much, just his back and then your back and then his back and then yours. (How do they do that, still attached?)

Until we're all, all of us, exhausted.

● ◑ ○ ◐ ●

I go downstairs … . (I like how this nightgown feels. I'm so slinky and slippery. I bump and grind just for myself.)

I make myself a peanut-butter sandwich. I feel better after eating. Things are fine.

I might leave you milk and cookies. Bring it now while you

sleep so I can lock you both in again. But I don't suppose that lock will hold against two people who *really* want to get out.

I think about maybe both of you up in my crawl space. He's taller than we are. He'd not like it. I think about your job at the ice cream factory unfolding boxes to put the ice cream in. I wouldn't mind that kind of job. You sit and daydream. I saw you. You hardly talk to anybody.

I think about how you can't prove you're you. You'll go to the police. You'll say you're you, but they'll laugh. Your clothes are all wrong for the you you used to be. They'll say, the person who's lived here all this time dresses in mouse colors. You've lived a claustrophobic life. If you'd had any friends it would be different. Besides, I can do as well as you do, unfolding boxes. I've done the same when I had jobs before I quit for this easier life. I won't be cruel. I'd never be cruel. I'll let you live in the crawl space as long as you want.

Your daydream is Willard. Or most of him, though not all. For sure his eyes. For sure his elegant slim hands and the big gold ring. You'll ask if it's a school ring.

Or one of us will.

Then I hear banging. And not long after that, the crash. They break open the door. It splinters where the deadbolt is. If I'd put it in the middle of the door instead of at the top, it might have held better.

By the time the door goes down I'm right outside it, watching. They run downstairs without seeing me.

I go and look out the window. He's leaving — hurries down the street with only one arm in his coat sleeve and it's the wrong sleeve. Other hand holds up his pants. What did you do to send him off so upset?

I open the window and call out, "Willard!" But he doesn't hear or doesn't want to. Is he trying to get away? From you or me?

What did you do to scare him so? Everything was fine when I came down to eat. But maybe getting locked in scared him. Or maybe you told him to go and never come back and you threw his coat at him as he left. Or he thinks you're me and is in love with me even though he told you he loved you. Or, like most men, he's unwilling to commit to anybody.

But here you go, out the door right behind him. You have your coat on properly and your clothes all straightened up. You're wearing your red leather pants. Now you're the one calling, "Willard."

You'd not have done that before. You've changed. You'll take back your life. Everybody will make way for you now. You'll have an evil look. You'll frown. People will step off the sidewalk to let you go by.

I want for us to live as we did but you'll set traps. I'll trip on trip wires. Fall down the stairs in the middle of the night. There won't be any more quarters lying around. You'll put a deadbolt on the crawl space door. Or better yet, you'll barricade it shut with a dresser. Nobody will even know there's a door there.

I made you what you are today, grand and real, but you'll lock me up up here with nothing but your mousey clothes. Your old trunks. Your dust and dark.

I dress in the wornout clothes I wore when I came. I pack the nightgown, the black underwear. I grab a handful of quarters. I don't touch your secret stash of twenties. I pet the cat. I leave your credit cards and keys on the hall table. I don't steal.

THE LOVELY UGLY

WE KNEW THEY WERE ON THEIR WAY LONG BEFORE THEY got here. Several years ago we saw the speck moving towards us. We said, Oh, no, not more smart people … if people they are … if smart … (but they do have to be fairly intelligent to get here in the first place) … but we're already full up. There are limits to how big a population a world can hold comfortably, and so that everybody has fun.

We were watching from the trees when they landed. They took us for creatures both ignorant and wild. We played into that role, howling and jumping up and down. Our hooting was really our laughing. They looked so funny we couldn't help it so we hooted to cover it up.

Then we glided out from the trees and moved closer to the clearing where they had set up camp. That was a clearing we had prepared for them ahead of time. Plenty long enough for their lander. From our experiences with space flight we knew the exact dimensions they would need. We also knew they'd like it near a stream. We picked a little stream, not suitable for navigation. We didn't realize until they'd landed and we saw who they were, that they'd need a path before they could reach the water.

We pretended to get tamer and tamer. We pretended to accept their gifts of beads and bracelets. Couldn't they see those would just hold us down?

And they brought what they call dogs. They use them for all sorts of things, including warning them that we're about to glide in.

We started imitating their dogs, they love them so much and we wanted to seem just a little bit more intelligent than the dogs are. The creatures began to love us, too. Pretty soon they let us lean over their shoulders and we could see how all their machines were made. We didn't disable any of those things till later.

Now we tell each other, "Bad dog, no!" Or, "Good dog," and a few pats. I saw one of us give her mate a snack saying, "Good dog." They laughed so hard they fell off their branch.

It helps that we have fur and they have none because they seem to consider furry creatures more animal. They think simply wearing clothes makes them more civilized than we are. But when have we ever needed clothes?

I don't think they have any idea … and we're glad they don't … that we already had space flight and gave it up a long time ago, since this is the best of all possible worlds. We've already checked out a lot of other planets, so we know. And after all, we were made for *this* world. And even for our anomalous moon.

On some worlds, the natives lie around and complain all day (no matter how long the day) that their world is getting more and more crowded, or hotter and hotter, or full of dust and smoke …. Those various natives kept saying, "It didn't used to be this bad," and yet they don't do a single thing about it, or not enough. Actually, there's hardly any world that couldn't be a paradise if the natives bothered to make it so.

Until now, we've never seen intelligent creatures with neither fur nor feathers nor scales. These creatures are hard to look at. It's as if they have some form of mange. At first we thought they'd infect us with hairlessness.

You can see their veins.

We're teaching these Uglys a pidgin language we invented just for them. We don't want them delving too deeply into our lives. On the other hand, we pretend to learn their language *very* slowly. I'm a trained linguist and am fluent in many alien languages, but in their presence I've limited myself to twenty-five words and a few simple phrases.

They're jealous of our gliding. They hack themselves around in the underbrush looking up at us in the canopy. They gasp, and, "Wow," and, "Oh my God." Half the time our younger ones are swooping around just for them.

They wonder that there are no paths. When have we ever needed paths?

They wonder at the length of our arms and at our arm flaps — at the skirt of skin across from knee to knee. Not just for beauty, but all the better for gliding.

The forest around them is filling up with their paths. Now, what with their little land planes disabled, they can't go far. They didn't ask *us* if we wanted paths or not. They think us too ignorant to have planted and nurtured the forest on purpose. Too ignorant to have laid out bushes with thorns and fish berry plants all over the forest floor.

●　◑　○　◐　●

As they were settling in and wondering what was safe to eat …. (They *had* to settle in. We had disabled their lander) … we pretended to eat all sorts of things we wouldn't normally touch. We didn't want them taking any of our favorite foods. We picked safe things — we didn't want to poison them. We found them food we don't bother with. Coarse things that take a long time to chew, and things full of lots of little bones so you spend more time spitting out than taking in. They were food jokes. We watched them testing and eating all those tough and gristly things. Our little ones were laughing right in front of them, but those creatures don't recognize a laugh when they see one even though our laugh is much like theirs. They probably thought the little ones had hiccups.

So we were laughing more than ever, while they, on the other hand, forced to stay on a planet full of thorns and forced to eat all those unpleasant things, were laughing less and less.

They have ears, but not to speak of, so you can't look there for signs of rage.

●   ◑   ○   ◐   ●

Just once they ate one of us. (They felt the lack of protein.) That was not so funny. Especially to my family. I was her great uncle. She was still in her baby fat. They roasted her over a fire. They'd probably still be trying to eat our young tender ones if we hadn't … well, shown them *exactly* how it feels. None of them is young and tender. Which one to pick was a hard choice. We wanted all their pilots and navigators saved in case we wanted them off our planet. We decided on one of the dog handlers since there are two. We didn't eat him, just left him where they'd find him, beside the path to the stream, spitted and roasted just as they had done to Jally.

But their eating Jally was partly our own fault because of the kind of food we'd shown them. After that we decided we had to let them have fish berries. Lots of protein and they slip down easily. We hated to see them eating up our supply after we'd spent so much time coaxing out the eggs but they did need better nourishment.

We noticed they took one of us, instead of one of their dogs. Even though we're, clearly, smarter than dogs. Of course the dogs are not easily replaceable, and I suppose they think we are.

● ◑ ○ ◐ ●

Connie? Donnie? I call her Dearie. I do like her color, though she only has that little bit of it on the top of her head. She'd look a lot better if she had fur on her chin and cheeks as the males do. I can see blue veins on her forehead. Arms! Even worse. She, and all of them, are anatomy lessons for our young ones. She's my counterpart, a linguist.

We've wondered all this time how it would be to mate with them, so I'm trying to be nice and not joke too much. Since I'm the main one chosen to study them, I'm also the logical one to study their sex tactics.

If sex doesn't work out with me, there's one of them I'd like Dearie to mate with. It would be fun and funny if she did because he's the ugliest and the oldest. He's even furless on the top of his head where most of them have, at least, some fur. Since she's pretty, according to her own kind … they all say so … that would be a good joke. He's Jake. I call him Joke. He thinks I can't say it properly. He's their captain.

My chances with Dearie are pretty good because we hear them say, about us, and over and over, how beautiful we are! How graceful. How wild and natural. How good natured. (That's because we didn't want them saying, Bad dog, to *us*.)

*   *   *   *   *

They told us, "We can help you with your enemies," as if we still had any. What kind of a world do they think this is? I mean we have space flight, we should stoop so low as to have enemies? It makes us wonder about where *they* came from. What kind of a planet is that? With space flight *and* enemies? Where were their priorities? We knew right then it wasn't *us* that wasn't civilized.

They did come with a lot of weapons. They never go anywhere without a pistol and some kind of blinding spray. And, of course, machetes to hack themselves around.

I don't know why or how they ever got started, grew up and thrived and ate and killed without good teeth. Also without fur. Makes us wonder. Without their weapons I don't think they could have survived very long on any planet.

We've been careful not to show them *our* teeth.

*   *   *   *   *

To test things out as to sex, I take Dearie out in the forest, just the two of us. She started out with her sketchbook, camera, and recorder. (I've got my chip. If I had to carry around all those things, I'd not be able to glide.) Even though she has a camera, she loves to draw: trees and bugs and especially us. I once asked, "Why, when also cameras?" Back on her planet, she's an artist. I was glad to hear they still practice ancient arts.

She brought her machete but she gets worn out trying to make herself a path. There's frustration in the set of her mouth. I tell her, "Sit." (That's what they always say to their dogs and to us, too.) I say, "Stay. Rest." I give her some fish berries. These are bigger and sweeter than the ones we usually let them have. Then, "Come," I say. "Do as if baby on back." (By now I let myself use over fifty words and several phrases.) She does, and I try to glide with her as we do with our little ones. That turns out to be impossible. I had no idea they were so heavy. Even though she's smaller and looks thinner than I, she must weigh four times as much. That changes my mind about a lot of things. Easier if I rode on *her* back. I can't help laughing at the thought.

She laughs, too. She understands how silly it all is. This is the first time I've laughed *with* one of them.

"You're made like a bird," she says. "Hollow bones, I'll bet." She pats my shoulder. Rubs the top of my head. I let her pat and stroke. It's what they do to their dogs but never to each other. A bad sign for my chances to check on their mating ploys because, much as they love them, they don't mate with their dogs.

I don't think she has any idea that I'm wooing her. So, all right then, maybe I'll talk up Captain Joke. We could learn things from those two. Still, having breasts that are large and furless is a nice idea and attracts us. We all ... . I mean all us *males* like it. Though we haven't squeezed them yet. Not even by mistake. Too bad they cover them up with clothes. Are these creatures ever naked? We haven't seen it, so maybe not. They must bathe in their lander. Perhaps they're even as ugly to each other as they are to us. Maybe that's why they love their dogs so, because they see the beauty of fur.

I didn't even squeeze her breasts when I had the chance a few minutes ago.

Maybe next time.

● ◑ ○ ◐ ●

I spend many an afternoon being interviewed by her. She, thinking she's teaching her language to me (I already know it) and me teaching her our pidgin. By now we've often laughed together. There's always lots to laugh about with so many language mistakes. She said the river ran, which is all right in her language, and I said, well cooked smells, which is all right in mine.

She likes me, but as what? Pretty smart pet?

I talk up Captain Joke but I don't need to. She's already in love with him. I can see why. He's a kind creature and, though he gives the orders, he does it with grace and good humor. He often looks worried, but he never gets angry. These people have qualities worth preserving. Serious as Joke always is, he is probably worth saving. I always say, laughing isn't everything, though some of us seem to think so.

● ◑ ○ ◐ ●

They keep saying, "What huge trees. What a dense and high canopy." And we keep saying, "There's a reason for that."

We also say, "You must do something about your lander." Still they haven't done anything. They don't think we're smart enough to say anything about such things as landers.

You'd think they'd be asking about the Eye. It isn't as if we haven't taught them the words for it: "Moon of day. Eye of Night." Our anomaly.

We laugh that they don't ask, "What Eye?" And, "What Moon of Day?" And though, to us, and we're brought up that way, everything *is* a laughing matter, this is not.

● ◑ ○ ◐ ●

Our downy underwear fur has started to grow. We puff out. Looks like their dogs are doing that, too. Just as our fur grows, little by little, the Uglies add more clothes. They've put on jackets, but I can often still see down the females' necks into the tops of their breasts.

So far they've been living in their lander. (They've piped water from the stream all the way to it). They should move it into the forest even if they have to push it. What do they think those trees are for? Instead they're building useless houses and sawing up firewood. Houses with steps up. They already have stairways everywhere, into their disabled fliers, into their disabled lander. We do see how necessary stairs are for their kind of disability.

I help build Dearie's house. I do most of the roof because I can glide, but she's up there working beside me. I'm glad to see she's not afraid of heights though some of the others are.

She may suspect we're smarter than we pretend to be. I have, on several occasions, seen what I take as admiration on her face.

Even though it's awfully hard to like the looks of hairless creatures, she's beginning to look pretty good to me: Odd and exotic, and then there's those big naked comical breasts … .

By now all our other males are paired off for the season. That leaves it up to me to find out about sex and breasts and let the others know.

They kiss their dogs so they do know about kissing. I'll start with a kiss. It will be strange what with their odd teeth. I wonder if I can lock on.

Dearie's new house is full of mating bugs. I hate to think of how it'll be after the eggs hatch, but now it's pleasant and musical. They sing to each other in perfect fifths and thirds so that everything vibrates in sync with their song.

●　◓　○　◑　◕

We're in the almost finished house. (This will just be a test. I don't know how far I'll go.) I put my arms around her. I keep my teeth covered and kiss a slow and careful kiss. It's not the kind she kisses at her dog.

She pushes back, shocked. By her forehead I see how startled she is. But she isn't angry, just puzzled. Says, "What's this about? What does it mean?"

She checks her ear to make sure her recorder is on, then looks around for her sketchbook. It's on the table. She reaches for it but I'm still holding her.

Her dog starts barking and trying to get between us.

I can't help laughing. I laugh so much I let her go. I can't go on with it.

"You can't draw it," I say. "And it's not to be listened to either."

I wish I had started with her breasts. At least I would have seen what they were like.

It takes her a little while to think about it, and then she laughs, too. Says, "Is this another joke?"

She knows us so well she knows it could be.

"I didn't want it to be, but it got to be one."

Now she she checks her ear to see that her recorder is on, but it always is. I have a feeling she's trying to avoid the whole situation. I don't think she knows what to do.

There's a gold and green beetle, big as her hand, on the wall behind her, singing. I point him out. I say, "That's his love song."

She films the bug. I can see his love song doesn't have any effect on her.

I know they can love because I see how they are with their dogs, though I don't see any of that with each other. The males tap each other now and then and the females hug sometimes, but it's the dogs that get the most loving attention. And all the time, too.

Odd, Dearie is in love with Joke and yet doesn't ever show it or say anything about it. I can smell it. Perhaps it's the wrong time of year for these creatures though some of them have paired up, but if there's ever mating, it must take place in the lander.

We've always wanted bugs around us that tweet and twitter and harmonize — that glisten and glow. They're mating this time of year so their eggs will last through the Eye though they themselves won't. We respond as if they called to us, so most of us have gone into the forest by now. But I have no mate of my own. It was my choice to stay with the Uglies and keep researching though the bugs make me yearn as they do all of us.

I spend the night alone in her almost finished house listening to the bugs. I'm more comfortable in the trees, but this is a better place to hear them singing their sex songs.

We've built a work table and shelves and she's already moved the computer in. She's left all her drawings, too. I hate to think what will happen to them. If I have a chance, I will save them.

Next morning, here she is, greeting me with her happy hello and her usual eager wave. Good signs she's not bothered by what happened yesterday. Also good that she wearing long pants today. I don't have to look at naked, blue veined legs that remind us all of grubs that have not yet seen the light of day.

She comes in, hugging her sketchbook. I take it from her. I will no longer make a pretence at not speaking their language perfectly. I say, "Today let us do as the bugs tell us to do. We have been good friends. We have laughed together."

She looks at me, shocked at my sudden perfect accent, and tries to take back her sketchbook but I don't let her. I say, "This is about to be a pleasant day."

I kiss her, gently, but this time, I kiss as we do to each other, teeth to teeth. How odd she is. I hold her with one hand and with the other pull open her sweater and shirt, stop kissing and look … and there they are … in all their exaggeration.

I feel them. What a wonder!

In my attempt to kiss them, we fall, I, on top of her.

She tries to push away and yells for help, but, since she's always the first one out of the lander, there's nobody around to hear. She surrenders. Or consents? I don't know which. It's the dog that goes crazy, grabs my ankle and pulls, but I'm as if deaf to all but the bugs' song. I'm humming in harmony with them and wishing she would hum, too.

When I get up, her face is blank. I wish there were more ways to read these people. With their dogs, the tail glued down tight between their legs, with us, the ears back against our head. No ambiguity possible. Now, with her, there's nothing at all.

Then she breathes as if she's been holding her breath and begins to shake. Is she, and finally, responding to the bugs' song?

She tries to speak but can't. She picks up her shirt (several buttons are torn out. I hadn't realized I was so violent), pulls on her pants, and runs out. Captain Joke is coming out of the lander. She runs to him. They hug and keep hugging. Perhaps I've finally brought them together.

She sits on the ground and he kneels next to her. I see him talk and talk. I move towards them and prick my ears forward.

He's saying, "It's all right." And she's saying, "No it's not."

"It *is*. It'll be all right."

"No. It won't."

"Come on inside."

I can tell by the way she clings to him that she doesn't want to let go and it looks as if he doesn't want to either.

Though most of the others are paired off, everybody seems to avoid getting close to Captain Joke as if they think his time is too important or as if they think he needs to save all his thoughts and energy for making decisions. Now they'll pair. I can smell it from here.

He helps her up the steps into the lander, but then comes right out again. She doesn't.

He runs towards me. I don't need any big ears to read that he's going to attack me.

In spite of all their problems, I've never seen him angry until now. I think he's going to take out his pistol, but he doesn't. There's no point in trying to fight somebody four, maybe five, times my weight. We do have ways to defend ourselves, but we don't want to reveal them, and I'm curious. This will all go on to my chip.

He grabs me by the wrist and easily twirls me upside down and back again. To him I weigh nothing. I hear my shoulder pop. When he lets go, my arm hangs, useless. I know what that means. If I can't glide and grab I'll be as helpless as these creatures. I'll not even be able to save myself let alone Dearie and Captain Joke.

I'm in a lot of pain, but I say, as if *for* him. "I know. Bad dog. No, no, no! But sorry dog. Sorry dog."

I'm hanging on to my arm trying to keep it from hurting. I make excuses. "It was the bugs' song." It was, but it also wasn't. (If I was with my own kind they'd be laughing at me. They'd be saying, Bad dog, no!, too.) I almost say, I'm just an animal, what do I know? But I know better than to say that though I now know I don't understand these people as well as I thought.

As if to a dog, he says, "Lie down." I wonder what other torture he has for me. But I do it. I'm resigned and perhaps I deserve whatever he'll do. But he puts his foot in my armpit, grabs my arm, twists, and pops my shoulder back into its socket. So it wasn't broken. It doesn't completely stop hurting, but it's a lot better.

"Thank you."

"Get up."

I do, this time expecting maybe even more help, but as soon as I'm up he knocks me, with one punch, several yards away. Comes and stands over me. "Get up," he says again.

This time I know better.

But he's calming down. I can see it on his face. He's not going to hit me again.

"Don't *ever*…" he says, "*Ever! …*"

He's shaking and he's gone from red to pale, but It's over. I do get up.

I'm as wobbly as he is. And my shoulder still hurts. I don't know if I can glide or not.

I had no idea something so fun and ordinary and harmless would cause so much trouble. And even the Captain gets in a rage though he never has before. But maybe he will love her now. Unless I've spoiled her some way.

But he did tell her it would be all right.

But she didn't believe him.

He sits down, for the first time looking worn out and discouraged. I'm sorry to see it. I say so.

"Get out of here and don't come back."

Instead I sit beside him. I say, "You need to know some things and there's only a few days before it happens. I can put back … I think you call it the mag-rotor? and you must fly the lander in under the trees."

"What?"

As with Dearie, I no longer pretend I'm not fluent in their language. "I can put the mag-rotor back."

This time I don't see it coming.

I try to talk as he's hitting. "The Eye," I say. "You have to know …."

I roll over, my face in the fireproof earth we had prepared for them so they wouldn't set the forest on fire. But that stuff, up my nose, is worse than facing his punches.

I sit up spitting gravel.

"I fear that I'm your only hope."

He grabs me just as he did before, lifts me and twirls me and slams me down and this time does break my arm. I hear it and then see it. The bone has broken through the skin. I'm bleeding.

I'm nobody's hope anymore. Not even my own.

I don't feel the pain right away but it doesn't take long.

He sits beside me, calming down. I'm gasping and holding on to my arm. I see he's taking in what I said a moment before.

But I'm in pain. Can't he see that? I'm sure he could set and wrap my arm as well as anyone even though he's not their doctor.

He stares at me but doesn't see me or my pain. He sees nothing but his own thoughts. "So … we're at your mercy, and have been all this time. And I suppose you could have fought back just now and didn't."

I groan. If I could get back into the trees I could get something for pain.

"Donnie doesn't want to see you anymore, ever, and I don't either."

That pains me more than I thought it would. Though right now my arm hurts more. My gentle informant is more to me than just an informant.

I say, "What can I do to make it right? I will do whatever needs to be done."

Now he finally notices the blood and my broken arm.

I say, "Do you people have anything for pain?"

"Come inside the lander."

But I still sit. "There are important things you have to know. We … they, not I … were going to let you stay right here. Your lander will be tossed away. There'll be gravity and tides from the Eye. Even your mother ship could be lost if it doesn't get out of the way."

"Come on. We do have things for pain. We'll talk inside."

I've been losing blood all this time. I'm feeling faint. I get up, but the ground seems to slant sideways towards me and hits me on the head.

● ◑ ○ ◐ ●

Somebody strokes my arm. At first I think I'm back with my mother and then I see the hand that strokes is hairless. Ugly. Blue veined. I pull away, horrified.

And then I remember.

I'm in the lander. Bandaged, sedated. Window beside me looking out at our grand great trees. I hadn't known the Uglies had such comfortable beds. They have good medical facilities. We — all of us — shouldn't have looked down on them. If we wanted to laugh, it should have been a different kind of laugh.

But there's the Eye. They have to prepare. I try to jump out of bed but the person holding my hand … she's their doctor … holds me down.

"How many days have I been out? We must prepare. You have to move the lander."

She says, "You've only been unconscious for a few hours."

"Let me speak to Captain Jo … Jake."

They decide the best thing to do is to pack up and go off-planet. My kind takes time off from sex and helps them pack. We fix all their little land planes and move them under the trees. Donnie and Captain Jake and three others will ride out the Eye in the canopy with scientific instruments, both ours and theirs. I'll stay with them. They've never seen a planet with such a strange erratic moon. Actually, in all our travels, neither have we. Perhaps it's a captured asteroid.

After they study the Eye, they'll stick around a while but more as our equals though not quite. We'll let them see how we live symbiotically with the trees, but we don't trust them with our science. There's something important lacking in their cerebrum.

It looks as if my two favorite Uglies, Captain Jake and Donnie won't be getting together as I'd hoped. Though they do feel love. There's some kind of taboo going on I don't understand. And it's the same with Donnie's relationship to me. She loves me but thinks any sex between us is forbidden, just as it is with dogs. I can live with that. Except, when the bugs sing and we vibrate with what the Uglies and we also call "the music of the spheres" (strange how both languages have the same concept though they don't have bugs that harmonize), and even though they're still the least prepossessing of any aliens we've ever seen anywhere ... I told Donnie to keep hold of that blinding eye spray because I can't vouch for what I'll do.

IF NOT FOREVER, WHEN?

In the beginning there was a goddess from whom all things flawed flowed. Pretending to be sure of herself, she made a man. She chose a turk's-head squash for the head, bamboo for arms and legs. She liked the knee joints (apples) and the belly button (a lentil). She used old gold pieces for eyes. It was a sacrifice, but she wanted him to have eyes as golden as a toad's, and she wanted to sacrifice. Into the mouth she blew her own hot breath and called "Man, man" — in a loving way, of course, for who would come to any other kind of call — but he didn't wake up.

She thought of names, then, to summon him forth by: Sir Delight or Daylight or Midnight Blue. Mister Old Gold, Mister Pleasure-in-the-Morning, Mister Radish. Nothing worked, but she did not despair. She knew that always the proper word comes first, as "meadowlark" and then the lark. (It is the word that differentiates it from some other, lesser bird.) She was not in a hurry. There were many things yet to consider, as: How instill a scorn for commerce? How instill a passion for art? She knew, as was already written, that when — or if — he did come to, he would "immediately experience, first fear, and then desire." When that desire came, she wanted to be ready to imprint him with herself. She needed for him to follow her everywhere. She wanted him to wake up and find her dancing there, with her green goddess-scarves. Unfortunately the phone rang and, at just that moment, the golden eyes opened. It was the sound that woke him. She was in the next room answering the phone.

The first thing he saw was himself in the mirror she'd brought in to check up on her own dancing. She had wanted to make sure his first sight of her would be at her most graceful. One would think, by this first view of himself, that he would be narcissistic like the rest of us, but he saw his big red head which frightened him. First fear, then, as was predicted. After that, desire; and he was attracted to the glassy surface of the mirror rather than to his image in it, and hence, to all things with sheen and sparkle and depth, including the pupils of eyes, windows, puddles, bubbles, clear soups, chrome, rhinestones, ice cubes .... It was a good thing she wore glasses.

The world had already been formed by then, the ground below and firmament above, New York on one coast, L.A. on the other, complete down to the tiniest blade of grass.

His first words were: "I want," and after that, "I go." (Inside she'd opened up *Webster's Third International* to give him ballast, and he could spell as well as speak.)

Already he'd started for a door, but it was the closet so she had time to lock the front one. "I go?" he asked, realizing his mistake and then he reached to hold her hand but missed. She had pulled back because she wasn't sure who he was yet. She knew his being cannot yet have blossomed and was still but a tiny dot (which is as we all begin). And she knew she hardly knew him (what was there to know so far?), but already she felt pain as if her lover or her youngest son was leaving. "You need guidance," she said, "even the suburbs will destroy you, not to mention the city. And you have no money and no knowledge of it. You might have to trade your eyes for nourishment and then you would lose your hope and your good red color."

He said, "I will not squander this present moment with thoughts of other moments no less nor more important than this very one."

"At least tell me your name before you go." (Perhaps with the name she would have some control.) She was thinking she wanted to kiss his imitation lips because she'd drawn them so fine and so full, but when he turned and looked straight at her, she noticed that she'd set the golden eyes much too close. Even so, his luminosity was not like any other living squash she'd ever seen.

"I am just this which I am, as you see."

Oh, my God! she thought. He has said "I am that I am," or might as well have. I have fashioned my own master. This always happens. (She had already born six chiefs of state.) She knew that were he an ordinary person, he would not be saying "I am" so soon after coming into being. She wondered if she had fallen in love with him for that reason — for that great "I am" — or if it was mainly because he wanted to leave her.

This time when he reached for the door she let him. In less than five minutes he'd figured out the locks and the doorknob and started down the stairs. She followed as she was, in her green goddess-dress, taking only time to grab her purse and running shoes. On the table in the hall she'd left the squash seeds from when she'd hollowed out his head in order to fill it with the good brown broth of thought. She had roasted them and salted and buttered them. She grabbed those also so as to have a snack for later.

Though stiff and with jerks — also a limp (she must have made one leg quite a bit too short) — he stepped out into the sunshine like a king, arms raised, fingers spread. "Look," he said, "look." His eyes just then caught the sun and she saw a spark in each one. "Look," he said, "here are the leaves of the trees as well as the branches," for there were trees there, lined up along the curb all the way to Second Avenue and it was spring. "And these are the trunks of them. How unusual."

"No," she said, "it isn't. Besides, the force that causes trees to grow is known." She was glad she had made him a head taller than most men. "I forgot to tell you," she said, "that the world is round and floats in an infinite black sky."

"How unusual," he said.

She said, "It isn't. Look at me, am I unusual?"

"I didn't choose another world than this one," he said. "I didn't choose this nor another one unlike it."

But she was thinking it was she who'd not only chosen him, but everything to make him out of — this particular squash and this particular sugar cane between his legs. And she was thinking she'd rather have lost control of the wind and the tides and the local weather (and that sometimes happened) than of him.

When she saw that he *would* leave, her hope had been that he'd head straight for the art museums, but he turned in the opposite direction. She decided, anyway, to tell him all the ways in which art is useful. "It starts conversations," she said. "It stands for other things. It tells all, and more than can be said in words. It attracts important people. It begins again and again.

Sometimes just one single sung note can be of unimaginable length and beauty."

Talking about art made her realize she had dressed him all wrong. She'd thought of dignity instead. She'd given him a navy-blue pin-striped suit with vest, a wine-red tie, white shirt, Homburg. And he did look princely, red and tall and already his beard was growing. A soft, green fuzz.

Just then a sparrow flew down and perched on his shoulder. She was thinking that this was unusual, but she didn't want to say it, and anyway, before she could, it flew off. She was pretty sure it was a sign of something.

By now they'd reached the corner. "Watch how everyone crosses when it says MILK," she said, "and how they all don't cross when it says DON'T MILK." She was thinking if she confused him he would need her more. Also, surreptitiously, she began to nibble at the squash seeds, thinking in that way to gain some power over him. "Red for go," she said, and, "There are as many mysteries as there are shades of green.

There, in the sunshine — and he having had a sparrow on his shoulder — she was thinking she was glad she had made him even though she'd always preferred manageable miracles and, if any, only tiny flaws. And she thought that though he limped, he walked and talked as if he were lord of the stuff that holds the birds up. But she wouldn't call him that, even if those were the only words there were to stop him and bring him back. Lord of Air, indeed, and he already too proud and not yet in this world half an hour! Perhaps she should trip him. Have him fall down right there in the gutter. Show him just how much the air held up a thing like him. It would be a favor to him in the long run. And she did that, catching his heel from behind with her toe in a way she knew how to do, so that his own left toe hit his own right heel and he thought he'd tripped himself. He went down but got up just as proud as ever, though limping a little more than before so that she thought maybe it would suit her purposes better if she just told him about his imperfections, from close-set eyes to naiveté. He walked as though he didn't have a single fault. It was ludicrous. Who would ever love him? But of course she did. And what she ached to say was that, and call him "Lord of the See-Through Air," and say "Glory, glory. Holiness is in you." (And, anyway, who else was there to love just then?)

But where was he off to like this? Did he believe in *do* not *be*? (One wouldn't suspect this of vegetable matter.) But better to move around and do, than be some vague hero of the contemplative life, whether artist or not.

There were shop windows now along the Avenue. Often something glittering in them made him pause: stainless steel pans, a dress all sequins, eyeglasses … . "Do you want a pair?" Eggs, she called them. "Do you want some of those eggs?" (Perhaps she could win him over with a gift.) He picked tortoise-shell frames and pinkish lenses and seemed so pleased with himself that she tripped him again and the glasses fell off and he stepped on them and they broke. "Look what you did," she said, and said that he should watch where he was milking. Here, in the shadow of a building, without the glint of the sun, his golden eyes were blank. All surface. Vegetal.

"Are you unhappy?" Searching his face in vain for signs of sadness.

But even in this light she was struck by his beauty. Perhaps it was exactly those flaws that made him so attractive, or perhaps because she'd made him *by hand*, one piece at a time (it showed), and she'd not considered the consequences (though when had she ever?). Let there be ambulatory vegetal matter, and there was, and let nothing obviate its vivid originality. Let such things shine forth (in their own natures) as pumpkin, apple, maidenhair fern.

"If you're unhappy, art can give you joy," she said. "Art laughs a lot and is full of non sequiturs. It's a chance to rise above the everyday or, on the other hand, get back down to it. A cow might moo no better than MOMA." She doubted MOMA was in *Webster's Third*. All the better then if he thought she'd said, "Mama."

He took a right and then a left and she thought maybe he was, after all, headed for the Museum of Modern Art, or maybe, though she hoped not, Macy's or Altman's. She almost praised him for, at least, a step in the right direction, but it turned out he was going to the Empire State Building. How steer him away from it?

"Did I already tell you that art is short and for our time? We must hurry. Everything changes." But he didn't hesitate.

It was her breath, damn it, the first breath in his lungs. That would be true even if it turned out he really was — and she still wasn't sure of it — was the Lord of Air, and yet now hardly a backward glance at her and not even an answer. "If you must go up, at least take the elevator. There'll be a good view all the way to Long Island, but is that art?" she said, and, "The air's no cleaner up there than down here."

She grabbed his arm, but she'd made him of strong resilient stuff. He jounced her off and started up the stairs pointing with the first fingers of each hand and saying, "Pot, pot." She had no idea what he meant and she knew it was her own fault.

"Don't you even know what an elevator is? You don't even know."

At the seventh landing she was already out of breath but she managed to grab the back of his suit jacket. "Well, what *do* you think about art then?" She was trying to slow him down with talk. "Maybe you think it's not for the masses. You think air is democratic. If you can spell at all you know there's not that much difference: art or air — air, art. Maybe all there is up there is nothing but polluted art from here to New Jersey. The sky so yellow all the eggs in the world won't help."

But he didn't slow down much even with her hanging onto the back of his coat like that, though she saw the dull gleam of his eye as he looked back. Duller than ever here on the stairs.

"Lord of Art," she said, "Art." That got to him. "Arty?" she said, thinking: airy, airborne, aerie, aeronaut, wings … . "You can't fly. I hope you know that. I hope you have that much sense."

What he answered was, "If I understand the universe, it is unusual and it is up."

"It isn't. The universe is no more there than right here." At least he wasn't climbing quite so fast. "Taken even one day at a time, you know, life is incomprehensible. We can't unravel the secrets of a single hour. Choose the happiness at hand. If not love now, then when?"

But he had pulled away from her. Well, there was an easy solution she should have thought of before. She took the elevator from the sixteenth floor and waited for him at the observation deck. By the time he came she'd eaten all the squash seeds. How many years of bad luck would that mean?

He had those same blank eyes. Had she just not noticed that in the beginning because of the sun? "Are you unhappy?"

She could have called him Lord of the Evening Air right then and there, and whether true or not, she knew it would please him. Later she always said she had the power to call him back and had always had it, and had it until the very last minute; but right then she didn't know what was important anymore, air or art, or even which was which or what could set fire to the land or move hearts the most: love or money, money or love, and what little she had of either she couldn't spare. At least not without some discussion.

"I had this dance prepared," she said, "but I never got a chance to dance it. Watch this. Watch my scarves. It's air in all its aspects. It won't take long." And she began to do that dance she'd wanted to be doing when he woke. When she caught the flashes of the sun's rays — the setting sun by now — she thought he was watching and she twirled and pirouetted faster and faster until she was too dizzy to stand up. When she stopped, though everything was turning, she could see that he was already up almost to the base of the spire, hanging on with only one hand and still pointing up, though the gesture was wavering. She had been dancing for nobody but herself.

Everything was spinning, but she had the thought that plant life turns towards the sun and heads right out for the universe as fast as it can. It always does.

"Wait," she said. You need grounding."

She thought she heard him mumble, then, "Let there be light," as though in some doubt about it. Surprising since, though evening, it was still light. And then he was off. She didn't know if on purpose or by mistake. For a moment it seemed as though he hovered in the air and she thought she saw the sun as hat or halo, just before the wind took his coat-tail and the flapping sounds began. She didn't have time to wonder whether fall or flight. There was just that split second in which to make a decision. There was just that flash and — reddish, flecked with gray, black — something flew by. Osprey, condor, or some other endangered species, rising from the navy-blue suit.

She would stay up there now and watch the sunset, and after that stare at the stars (though she knew they were nothing but other suns) wondering who, after all was said and done, brought existence into being and continued to cause things to occur, here, or anywhere else? But she would try again (as she always did). She wondered if she wanted slave or master? Son or lover? Mister Radish or Mister Ion — Mister Neutron? Or Lord of the Poisoned Lakes and Sky?

BABY

THEY CALLED HIM BABY, HE WAS SIX FEET TALL, LEAN, AND had the look of a hungry hunting animal, but the robots called him Baby.

Someone had once written in a neat script in a tome and on a white paper the carefully chosen name, Christopher John Correy, but there was no one left who could say that this particular name on this particular paper and in this particular book was the name of the man called Baby by robots.

Until a few years ago the city had had all the food it takes to make a man full grown and to keep him sleek and healthy, but now Baby's hip bones jutted forward from a concave stomach, his ribs arched above, and the strong muscles lay just beneath the skin and showed in lined bunches when he moved.

He stood naked in the dining room, damp bare feet on the smooth black tile. He shut his eyes tight and said in a whisper, "Please, please and please, be meat." Then he swallowed the saliva that came at the thought of food. He chewed on nothing and waited, hoping, but not expecting. "I said please," he whispered.

There was no one in the room but him and he watched with fox eyes on the kitchen door until it opened and a model B maid came in. The soup plates on her tray top held only brown powder. House 76 had lost its water pipes in the last freeze of the season because the heat had gone out.

But Baby hadn't come for soup. Sometimes 76 had meat and if not meat, usually an edible dessert. Baby was hungry enough for anything at all.

The model B put a soup plate in front of each empty chair around the table, and then it waited by the kitchen door, and Baby waited, and after a time the model B took the plates away. The next course was meat, or had been, but something had gone wrong and the roast was burned to a dry black lump.

The Please is fooling me, Baby thought. It wants to make me angry.

The meat was impossible to eat, but the model B cut it with knife fingers, not noticing how the black flaked off and fell to the floor. It served each plate with the dark, woody chunks and also with something unrecognizable, an overcooked or spoiled vegetable or perhaps a moldy salad. Then it waited again and after a while took the untouched plates away and came in with the dessert chocolate pie with whipped cream. A dairy still came to 76 and with milk from one of the underground farms where the robots still tended cows. And the stove had timed just right this time.

Baby glanced out the glass wall behind him. "Overseer, Rob 10, please not be there now, please." He shut his eyes and whispered it. Then he moved fast, reaching under model B's knives just before they came down to split the pie. Model B didn't even notice its knives cut nothing. It was a poor automatic thing on a track and it had no eye. The stove ran it, adjusting it for each task as it loaded the tray. But overseer Rob was like the maid. His eye flickered red, observant, and his legs telescoped at the knees and could run faster than Baby.

Baby ran across the hall balancing the pie. The walls at the end, still working smoothly, lifted to let him out into the back yard. 76's walls were not discriminating anymore. They had opencd and closed for Baby for a number of years now.

"Overseer, Rob 10, please not be there now, please."

The overseer wasn't.

Baby climbed the artificial hill at the back of the house at a crouching run, and pushed through the overgrown hedge into the neglected yard of the house that had lost its overseer six years ago. He flopped down on his stomach behind the young trees and bushes. He pushed out his lips and sucked at the whipped cream on the top of the pie, not caring about the long scratches the hedge had made across his body.

He would not have much time, here, so close to his own home, so he concentrated on eating rapidly and without relish. This was something just to fill his stomach. He was hungry now for meat or milk.

He was losing faith in Please. It didn't work as often as it used to. And he was losing faith in Nursie too, but she could still catch him when he was close to his home like this. In spite of how she was now, her arms were still long enough, and her eye still saw. She was slower, but not too slow. She was strong, broad-bottomed with a caterpillar tread and she could still lift him. He was only really safe from her a couple of miles or so from his house. And even then it was usually only a matter of time for her to find him. Now he was behind 75 and his own home was just next door.

"Baby, Baby. Come to Nursie, you scallywag."

Baby raised his head, mouth dripping chocolate, smears on nose and cheeks. He leaned over the pie like an animal over a fresh kill, wary and challenging.

"Baby, come to Nursie. It's time for your nap. Don't make Nursie hunt all over, that's a good Baby. I've milk and cookies."

I'd take a nap for milk and cookies, Baby thought, but the glass is always empty now and the cookies, when there are any, aren't fit to eat. He bent to the pie again. His teeth scraped on the pan as he bit at the crust, tearing at it dog-like.

He couldn't get away now. She would find him and catch him, and take the pie away if he didn't finish it fast. Pies are not for little babies, she would say.

There was silence while she circled, slowly scanning, and he wolfed the last of the crust. At the half circle she caught the warmth, and with a wheeze, scratch, scratch, wheeze, scratch, scratch, she came after him. She sounded slower than she was. Baby didn't try to get away. In a moment one of her long flexible arms reached out into the bushes and took him about the waist gently but firmly. He yielded to the pull, stood up and walked towards Nursie, leaning on her soft arm. He hadn't tried to fight her for a long time now. It had always been useless.

"There's a good boy. Here's milk and cookies, and then we'll pop into bed for a nap." She put the empty sip-glass into his hand. "Baby do it all by himself."

"There *is* no milk for Baby here. You never have milk for me anymore."

"Yes, it's there. I got it from the dairy box just now. The milk-robs came, early, early, while you were still asleep, and they brought this good milk just for Baby."

A feeling came over him like getting into a warm bath

only the warmth flowed inside him. For a moment he could say nothing at all, and then he said, "Where's my milk," in a whisper. His arm muscles tightened and he clenched his fists against his stomach.

There was something wrong with him lately, and it was getting worse. Something that gnawed at him and knotted his stomach like this. A great need, overpowering, for an unknown thing. It drove him to far wanderings about the city, to taking stupid risks, to fits of running after nothing in the empty streets, to staring at the sky, sometimes to a wild howling, and to climbing, climbing dizzily and trembling on narrow perches about the high buildings.

"Where's my milk?" He screamed it this time. "Ask Rob 6 if there is milk there." The overseer will tell her and then she will doubt. She will no longer believe in Please nor in Central, and because she is so sure, her doubt will be devastating. He would see her fall on the ground and scream with horror of her lost belief.

"Come, drink it up," she said.

"Central is stopped! There is no Please!" he shouted.

Both soft mother-arms came out to embrace him. There was a place, a specially built place at her breast (or what stood for breast) to cradle a baby or pillow a young head, but it was too low for him now even when he knelt. Still, she pulled him to her.

"Don't worry, Baby. Don't cry. There's always milk for Baby. As much as you want. Come along and we'll get some more."

"There isn't any milk." He was calm suddenly. "Please ask Rob 6. I said, please. Now ask Rob 6, please."

"Such a good, polite boy. All right, we'll ask Rob 6 if you want. Yes. You said please, didn't you. Yes you did."

There was a time a long time ago when Baby always answered eagerly and proudly, "Yes, I did, didn't I," but now he said nothing, his face as expressionless as Nursie's flat tray of features always was.

She took his strong hand, calloused from climbing, and led him across his own neat lawn to his home. The front wall panel rose to let them in as they neared. Nursie stopped just inside, and Baby knew she was scanning for Rob 6. Maybe she was even talking to him in the silent way they had that Baby could never hear. A long time ago he had felt for the first time the fierce frustration of not hearing. Even though the discovery of it had come gradually, the understanding came all at once. It was as if he "knew" they were doing it long before he "realized" it. That day a feeling like the one he had now had washed over him in a hot flush. They're hard and hurt-proof, and I'm soft; they're strong with long changeable arms, and I'm weak and only one shape; and now they talk together and I can't hear it. My Nursie talks silently to that Rob 6.

That day of realization he had gone down to the high buildings where the statue was, tall to the third window of one of them, and he had climbed all the way to the top of the white head for the first time. He scraped his thumb on the way up. He remembered the blood smearing the fleshy part of his hand, and the drops making three red lines down his arm.

At the top he had shouted, "I wish to be Rob 6." He sat right on the big head with a foot on each ear, drunk with height. "I don't want to be Baby anymore. I must be more than I am. Please, please, please, and please. Baby said please."

He had looked at the hot summer sun and shouted, "I say please twice to the sun in the sky," and then he turned towards

Central, "and four times to Central." He liked the sun best, but he knew Central was more powerful. He smeared the blood from his hand across the white statue head and shut his eyes tight. I am getting hard and strong, he thought. I have one eye here in the center and it flickers red. He could feel his two eyes merging slowly to just above his nose. My arms are interchangeable, and if l jump I will land on rubber feet and my knees will spring, one section up into the other, and I won't be hurt. I am Rob number one thousand and twenty-six. I am changed.

And he had jumped then.

It took Nursie almost a whole day to find him. "You naughty boy. You naughty, naughty boy, to go so far from home." She carried him back gently and called the Rob-Doc, and Baby had lain in bed a long time after that. She had been happy with him for being a good boy all that time, but he had cried each night with pain and frustration, and he had wondered, since he couldn't be Rob 6, when he would be at least a man, whatever that was. Nursie always just said, sometime.

And now he would try to hurt her as he had hurt then, inside, and as he hurt now with an unknown need.

She started off, after the few seconds' wait at the door, pulling Baby along after her. Her broad caterpillar tread easily mounted the stone steps behind the huge carefully rustic fireplace. She crossed, in rubbery silence, the metal-tiled hallway while Baby pad-padded behind her, leaving dirty damp outlines of his feet on the spotless floor. They crossed the kitchen by the center ramp and entered the door to the brain center of house 74.

The room was large and filled with wires and pipes and conveyer belts, but the main control unit was small. The thing that ran everything in the house including this maze of criss-crossing wires and pipes, was bread-box size. Rob 6 stood before it, propped back on his third leg, the one he used for balance when walking and as a prop when standing still. He wore his mechanic hands and had plugged himself into one side of the control unit by a long flexible thumb.

"There is something wrong." Rob 6 said, "but it is not here. Control is fine."

"Baby says there is no milk," Nursie said, "but I heard the milk robs come this morning. Baby is fooling Nursie again. He fools and fools. And, Rob 6, Baby is geting so big. *Such* a big boy. Too big for Nursie. Or do I need to be fixed too? Will you check, Robby 6?"

"You are thirty-eight years old. You should have been replaced."

"We make do with what we have. Yes we do." She chanted it as if she were reciting a nursery rhyme. "But *now*, Robby 6, *is* there milk in the dairy box for Baby?"

"I doubt it."

"I don't understand. I don't understand at all. There is always milk in the dairy box at seven twenty-three."

"Things are not going right and they are getting worse. There is something wrong with 74 now, but Control is fine. Library did not send a tape with motor repair information. I dialed and none came. And I asked and Central did not answer."

"That's too bad, too bad," Nursie chanted, and then she said, "But if at first you don't succeed, try, try again," and, "Things will be better tomorrow."

"Not without human beings."

"They'll come back. Mommy and Daddy will come back *later*."

"Nurse 16, you helped to bury them yourself after the enemy seeded the sickness."

"Why Rob 6! And in front of Baby too! He understands things now, you know."

Baby squatted down, flat-footed, on the metal-grilled floor of the control room. Rob 6 and Nursie never used chairs and neither did he since he'd outgrown his highchair. "He's only said it a thousand times already," he muttered, sullen faced, carefully not looking at them.

It wasn't going to happen now either, not ever. No matter what he said or did, Nursie would be the same. She would never know anything she didn't already know now. Her eye looks at me, but she doesn't really see me at all, he thought. If I were gone or even stopped like some of the robots, she would say only, "He's coming back *later*," like she says over and over about Mommy and Daddy and Jeannie. She sees my shape, but not me. I am a nothing thing to her, but *she* is less than that even.

"Baby was inside Nursie then," Nursie said. "That was a long time ago and you were just a little scallywag."

"You're just a nothing," Baby said.

"Hush, dear. That's not very polite. You know, I kept you inside me a whole extra year like your Mommy and Daddy said and when you came out you were just as safe as can be, and now you're growing up to be a little gentleman just like Mommy and Daddy wanted you to be."

Baby breathed out loudly and hunched lower over his knees. She will *not* change and she will never see me. "You're both just nothings," he said, "and there is no Central and no Please at all."

"What a thing to say," Nursie said.

"Ask, then — ask Central and Library. Ask *them* why there is no milk anymore."

Rob 6 and Nursie stood silent. They're asking, Baby thought, feeling an unbearable irritation. Rob 6, even, is asking Central and he knows it doesn't answer.

"Central doesn't answer," Rob 6 said.

Suddenly Baby found it difficult to breathe. Squatting over his knces was too cramping and he stood up. "Central never answers anymore." His voice sounded different to him, low and tense. "Yesterday and yesterday and yesterday before that, a long time before even, it didn't arnswer, but you keep asking and asking."

"It is right to ask Central first," Rob 6 said.

"Of course it is," Nursie said. "You know that, yes you do. Always ask Central *first*. It will tell you what to do *next*."

He began to tremble and he felt a hot knot swell in his stomach. Part of him seemed to stand apart atnd ask, what's wrong lately? Rob 6 and Nursie are not so different than they used to be.

He remembered a time when they had seemed enough in every way, observant enough, intelligent enough, loving enough, but that was a long time ago, and he had changed somehow and he was changing even more. Now he was full of unreasonable, uncontrollable angry feelings.

He kept his eyes carefully off Nursie. He felt he would burst if he looked at her empty, wide eye. "Rob 6," he spoke slowly, "Central will never answer ... *never answer* anymore.

What are you going to do about it?"

Rob 6 stood silent. Is he asking again, Baby wondered? Is he asking Central what will he do now that Central is out?

Suddenly it was too much. The swelling hot knot inside him burst and he was shouting. "This is the end of it. I will not listen to any one of you anymore. You don't understand anything. You have no eyes and no ears that are any more good than stopped ones."

"Let's not have a tantrum now," Nursie said, interrupting him. "Why, Baby needs his nap. My goodness, no wonder. It's way past the time." She reached out to him.

Fighing wouldn't do any good. He could never hurt her, never dent her, in her mind nor in her body. He was still nothing to her even when he fought, but now he fought. He bit at the soft arms and kicked at her treads, bruising his feet, and he began to laugh an odd, sobbing laugh. The fighting was silly and the laughter shook him so that it was only weak fighting anyway. "You can't even see me. You never have. Never, never."

She was carrying him slowly, but easily, up the wide low stairway, and she was talking, gently soothing. "You must learn to be a *good* boy, and not fight. You know, there's an enemy, a barbarous enemy, far away, and we, the robots, protect the city for all the peace-loving peoples of the world, for this city is more than just a place for people to live and work. It stands for a way of life. It is a haven of civilized living and we must keep it safe."

He'd heard all this before.

Tall wide-leaved plants, rooted at the foot of the stairs, brushed at them as they rose. Baby tore off a whole branch with one violent sweep of his arm.

"No, no," Nursie said. "Mustn't touch." This made Baby laugh louder and more, though he didn't know why, and the laughing hurt his stomach, but he couldn't stop.

They crossed the balcony, Nursie swaying a little with Baby's tossing weight. The door of the nursery slid open as it always did instantly for Nursie, but never for anyone else, not even Baby, though it would have opened for Mommy and Daddy.

They were there, in his bright special room, circular, windowed top to bottom, with a blue ceiling where stars winked on and off. A room specially planned by a loving mother and father for a son named Christopher John.

Nursie put him gently into his bed and shut the gate. "You'll feel much better after your nap," she said. "Then you'll be my good boy again and we'll play in the sandpile at the park if you like."

Baby doubled up with painful laughter. Why was everything so funny now?

She left and the gay red door slid shut after her, shut to stay, until she came back.

The bed was youth-size. Baby lay, knees drawn up. Laughing and holding his stomach. Gradually the laughter stopped and it was like after crying, leaving him empty and looking at his starred ceiling.

Later he put his feel tight against the bottom of the bed and braced his hands at the top. "This is not even my bed," he said out loud. "It's too small." And he pushed until the wood panel broke and his feet came through and he lay out straight. "I'm me," he said. "They can't see me, but I am me, and quite big."

He got up and stepped over the side of the bed. He went

to the section of the wall with movable panels. He had broken the levers long before, on that moonlit night of the first escape when he was half the size he was now. House had not registered it even then so no one came to fix it. He slid the glass panel to the side, letting the hot outside air come in. He grinned again, pulling his lips back from his teeth, a dog grin, or wolf.

He stepped out on the thin wire frame that held the patio roof. "Please," he said, but there was a downturning of his voice, half mockery, yet not quite sure. He ran out on the frame, tight-rope style, sure-footed, jumped at the end and landed rolling in the grass beyond the gray-and-orange circle of the patio. There was no one in sight.

"Good Please?" He loped across the back, leaped the dried-up stony bed where the imitation stream used to run, pumped in a rambling circle about the back yard. He climbed the carefully random rocks at the far end and jumped a retaining wall to the footwalk below.

The sub-belt entrance, a stone lean-to at the corner park, was a 200-yard sprint. Baby ran down the slow-moving ramp into the bright white-tiled tunnel and at the bottom stepped easily from the slower belts to the fastest. But even there he kept running along the moving aisle past the line of seats.

This was not a time for sitting. Now he was going farther and faster than ever before, and never coming back. He went at an easy run, hands low, relaxed, head tipped back. He looked ahead down the long bright tunnel, empty and bare as far as he could see — but then everywhere he had ever looked had been empty and bare except for occasional robots.

He ran until, even in this cool place, the sweat dripped down from under his arms. He felt the dampness between his shoulder blades and on his upper lip and he smelled himself, a sticky, unrobot smell, bitter and sweet. After a while he tired and sprawled, knees spread wide, in one of the hard molded chairs at the side.

A long time has passed, he knew. Usually he was impatient with the sub-belt. He had never been able to stay underground more than about an hour without coming up to take a look, but this time he had the patience to stay. The running had eased the turmoil but something still smoldered inside him and now he had a new kind of patience.

He lay back, eyes half shut, not moving, hypnotized by the long white way before him and the humming movement. Hours were nothing to him now.

It was hunger, finally, that woke him to reality again, but still he didn't go up outside. He began a series of belt-changings, branching off at random but staying on the fast lanes. His stomach growled and he knew that even leaving the belts was no insurance of a meal. He would have to hunt and sneak and hide from overseers or wild dogs. But if this was to be forever, a change for keeps, it had to be far and devious, and so he stayed.

Much later he took the slower lanes to the slowest and then to a rising ramp.

He came out on a wide-walled footwalk. The summer sun was low and red, and Baby stood, watching it. He could almost see it move past the tree tops. He whispered nothing, but he felt the feeling he used to feel when he said Please and it was important, the same feeling when Rob 6 asked Central and Central used to answer and was always right.

He stared at the sun, thinking, this will be the place, Sun. Here I will be me and robots will not tell me what to do and I won't belong to any house or any overseer.

He walked across the grassy tree-lined footwalk to the smooth gray wall. It was half again as tall as he was and had not the slightest hand hold. Baby bent his knees low, jumped from a stand, and grasped the top with both hands. He swung his left foot up, curled the toes over the top and then pulled himself up. Resting on elbows and one knee, he looked down into the garden, a richer, larger garden than he had ever seen before. He felt an exhilarating excitement for this looked like something really new and different.

He rolled gently over the wall and landed on hands and knees in the grass. He stood up and walked boldly down the neatly kept path that led away from the wall. He didn't hide or watch for overseers. Whatever would happen, he felt, would be different here in this different place, and he went eagerly forward to meet whatever would come.

He passed rows of thick hedges, then a group of tall, pungent-smelling pine trees. He rounded a bank of white-flowered bushes and there, before him, surrounded by cut hedges like the walls of a room, was a fountain and a statue.

The pool was edged with natural-looking rocks and on the largest rock in the center was a figure of stone about his own size.

Baby laughed out loud then, splashed through the clear cold water and climbed up the slippery rock to stand just below the figure. He had seen others, oddly shaped like this, in parks and downtown sections sometimes: the rounded body, looking strangely lumpy top and bottom, with a thin waist in the center. He knew the names that went with this shape were woman, girl, and lady.

This figure held the head of a serpent. The long snake body crossed the waist just under one of the pointed chest-lumps. The snake's mouth was wide, and inside there was the tiny pipe where the water of the fountain came flowing.

Baby stooped and drank from the serpent's mouth, and then looked up and it seemed as if the statue's bent head and half-closed eyes looked at him with a steady gaze, and there was something there that was not like a robot. Something that made him sad.

He reached up and ran his fingers down the soft curve of the cheek, so soft-looking but so hard to the touch. He touched the nose and then his own nose. This is a little baby too, he thought, smaller than I am. He went round to the back. He laughed because the hair hung down so far from the head. He ran his hand from under the arm, inward to the waist and down over the hips and he laughed again because his own shape was right and this shape was a joke.

Then he remembered how hot it was and how cool the water below felt on his legs. It was a shallow pool. The water came only just above his knees, but he climbed down and lay full length in it, splashing and blowing and putting his head in all the way.

He sat up, wiping the water from his face with the palms of his hands, and there, in the path before him, it seemed as if the statue had come to life, colored a rosy tan. It was all there, but different from the stone: damply curling tan-brown hair, the darker etched eyebrows, tan-brown eyes, lips lightly red and also the tips of the two round shapes at the chest.

Soft, it was, but it stood like the statue, and he, half rising on one knee, stood like a statue too. He stared a long time, not moving, afraid almost to breathe even, and the other stared back. Then he stood up slowly, so slowly, as if a strange mad dog or wild cat was before him. The only sound was the water dripping from his body, but that lasted only a few moments and again they stood and stared. Then Baby moved again, stepping slowly forward this time. He was not afraid. This creature was smaller than he was and looked so vulnerable.

The creature took a step back then, and Baby took a faster step forward. Then the thing turned and ran, but Baby caught it easily in two leaps and they fell together, one warm soft body against another. This contact shocked them. They drew apart quickly, stilled again like statues, and they stared silently. Then slowly Baby touched a finger to the creature's chest. The wonder of the feel made him draw his hand away again, but slowly this time. "Soft," he said in a whisper. "Soft and warm," and then he touched his own chest. "I too."

The other stared silently a moment and then asked suddenly, also in a whisper, "Are you … human?"

Baby grasped the creature's upper arm then, shaking it boldly but lightly back and forth. "You feel good," he said. "Strange, but good."

"I'm human," it said then.

"So am I. I'm Baby."

"I'm Honey."

"I came to find a new thing and I found you."

"They all say there are no humans left."

"Rob 6 and Nursie are wrong and so are all the others, and now there's you. I'm glad I ran away from them and came here. Why is your hair so long?"

"It just is."

"And you're shaped all wrong."

"It's you that's wrong. This is the way I am. Like the statue is the way to be and that's my way."

"I know. You're woman. You look funny, but you feel nice." He cupped the other's chin in his palm. He ran his fingers over the lips and then down across the neck and lower even, to the pink, soft tip of the round shape at the chest. She drew away. "You tickle," she said.

"I like human beings," Baby said, "better than Nursie or Rob 6 or dogs and cats. I didn't think I would, but I do."

"I think I do too."

They both stiffened at the sound of a distance voice. "Honey, Honey. Where are you? It's almost time for bed."

They stared at each other but they didn't move to go.

The Nursie came nearer. Baby could hear the wheeze and scratch. When she rounded the corner, finally, she looked exactly like his own Nursie, but he could tell, absolutely, it wasn't Nurse 16.

She reached quickly and drew Honey away from him. "What are you doing here?" she asked. "This is private property."

Without thinking, Baby gave the information he always gave, the way Nursie had taught him. "I'm Baby number 2, family PR1-54-238, overseer Rob 1026. I live in Forest Knolls, and I came here and found this human being."

"How did you get in?"

"I climbed the wall."

"Those wall guards, they just don't work anymore." She stood motionless and Baby knew she was calling some other rob. He looked at the human being again, fascinated with the curiously shaped body, drawn by its softness and vulnerability, and he waited, staring at it, and it stared too, back at him. He could see its eyes move, tracing the contours of his body. In a few minutes the overseer came.

"Trespasser," the Nursie said. "Male too. I do hope nothing happened. 2, PR 1-54-238, O-1025. And we must do something about the wall guards. Poor Honey must be protected from this sort of thing."

The robot made a quick examination. "Nothing happened," he said. "There's been no trespasser for eighteen years and four months now." He took Baby firmly, rounding each wrist with an all-purpose pincer hand, and led him away.

Baby went quietly, too dazed to think. He kept his head turned back, watching the creature called Honey until they rounded a corner.

The robot took him to a rambling house, all glass and vines and stone. The wall lifted on a small corner room. The overseer pushed Baby in and the wall came down again. There was a white marble table, and large plants growing beside it from a dirt section in the floor, and there were three long low green lounge chairs. Baby lay back in one. He was filled with silent wonder. Eyes wide, he watched the twilight fade outside, lights come on in other parts of the house, and curtains close.

Later the overseer brought cold unsour milk and a plate with the meat cooked just right. Baby ate and drank squatting on the floor beside the low table, spilling gravy across it as he lifted the meat in his hands, It was the best meal he'd bad in a long time, but now he didn't notice the taste or care about it.

After he ate he walked about the room like a caged animal. The lights went out in the other parts of the house. Baby pounded his fists against the glass walls and gave a shout, but the walls of the little room held the sound in tight, he knew, and he gave only one call.

He stood, nose against the glass, and after a while, in the dark, the creature came and the wall lifted for it and slid shut after it.

Baby's impatience left the moment it came in.

He touched its hand, but he did not speak and neither did the creature. Softness, warmth … there was something here that was the answer to everything.

What was the answer?

He pulled at the creature roughly then, and it sucked in its breath and pulled away, and he let go. What was the answer? It was tantalizing, close, and yet …

He touched the creature's hair gently, and it didn't move away this time. He felt full of gentleness and of violence too, and he held himself tight, tensing his muscles against themselves.

They sat down together on the edge of one of the lounge chairs. They touched each other and they watched each other smile in the dim light of the rising half-moon.

The answer was close … closer … and yet so far. Not to know and to be so close was worse than the howling and the running in moonlit streets. Much worse.

He grabbed the other, shaking it, squeezing the answer out with all his violent pent-up strength. Answer! But it only cried out in pain and then made a sobbing sound. And when he loosed his grip a bit because of the sounds it made, it pulled away and the panel was open and shut again before he realized it and the creature was gone.

When Rob 6 came in the early morning to take the lost boy home, the marble table was broken, the plants were trampled. The foam from inside the three lounges was strewn about the room. Baby had a scratch across his cheek, black-and-blue marks on his legs, and bloody knuckles, but he went quietly, wrist cuffed in Rob 6's two metal fingers.

At home Nursie bathed him and put him in his room. "I wish you would try to be good," she said. "I wish you would just try."

He slept heavily for a short while, then climbed out the window and took the same sub-belt.

He tried to remember the time it took, and the changes. Once he came out at an edge of the great city where the towers of the barrier wall stretched giant pointing fingers that sent invisible currents arcing across the city to protect it from an enemy that never came anymore.

At night he took the belt that led home to Forest Knolls. His eyes were slits now, his mouth a firm line. There would be no more fits of running in empty streets, or wild howling, or climbing. Instead, this crease between the eyes.

He searched the next day, and the next, and the next …

The important thing, the answer to everything, was somewhere there in the vast, decaying city, an answer to the robots and to the decay, to the city and the world and most of all to him, but it was … *lost*.

DESERT CHILD

An unbeliever once wrote: God is alive and well and living in the desert. She wrote, "Surely if he's anywhere at all …"
—Susan Coulson

YOU CAN SMELL HIM, STRONG AND BITTER. HE PRICKS AND bites. There's either too much of everything or not enough. When water, too much water, when dry too dry. Too cold at night, too hot in the daytime. The ground shakes. All summer long, smoke from distant fires. You hear him in the buzz of bugs, the rattle of rattlesnakes.

There's no wind now, but there has been — winds that pick up sand and swirl it into devils.

Whatever God — He, She, or It (laughing, ah *ha*! ah *ha*!) … whatever's out there — brings, it's never reasonable. As though there could ever be reasons for any of this.

You'd think we wouldn't live here. You'd think we'd let the ragged, mangy, fearsome creature slither back, fill our huts with sand, return our little oasis to the desert that It owns and won't let go.

There's this man … whatever desert thing that's out there left him to make do with what there was to make do with. Stretched him to nothing but string and bone. Dried him, scarred him, gave him a limp, took away his voice so there's nothing left but a whisper. His gray handlebar mustache is the only flourishing thing about him.

I don't think he's as old as he looks. I'm trying to build him up with oatmeal and goat cheese. That's all I have to build somebody up with.

I can count on him for help, though, even if I don't ask, and I don't. He sees a thing needs doing and does it. After, I sometimes see him lean back and stretch as if his back was sore.

We don't even know what his name really is. They call this place Archer's Corner, but there's no corner and he's not Archer, though he was here by himself before we came. First I met him, he said, "Everybody calls me Red." And I said, "They should have changed that to Gray a long time ago." At the time I thought he might have smiled, but maybe he just squinted. Now that I know him better, I know he doesn't see well.

Though he was here before we came, he always acts as if it's he who doesn't belong. I suppose he has squatter's rights. Nobody's tried to kick him out so far.

There's something about him that draws me. Not grace, but it's as if there's a special grace of the graceless.

●　◐　○　◑　●

It's not quite so desert-like here. We have our creek, coming down icy cold. We have willows along its edges. There's a wild blackberry patch. We only have to go down the path a little way for water. The creek was inclined to swish your pail away if you weren't careful, but Red (Gray) made a dam of stones and pulled over a log to still the stream in one place so the children could get water by themselves. He walked along the river a while ago and brought back two pails, mismatched socks, diapers, all hooked on branches way downstream.

He does all the work the other men either won't do or don't have time for. He put up the swing and the teeter-totter for the children. There's only five children here, and one's just a baby, but he thought it was worthwhile anyway.

It's because of him, I can sit down for a minute. The wood gathered, my goats safely in and milked, the water's brought for the men to wash up, the soup's at the back of the stove in the mess hall, there's bacon and corn bread. Red chopped the firewood and brought the water up. For now I have a minute to sit and darn a sock and think about the child.

No-see-ums, sand mites, crows, the magpie, and now this girl. They say a magpie is a bad omen. I don't see why. I always feel good when I see one, though I always salute, as they say to do, to ward off bad luck. I don't believe in bad omens, but I salute anyway.

● ◑ ○ ◐ ●

I live apart from the others (by choice) in a hut under a cottonwood, past the cook house, and the little cold cave where we keep the goats' milk and cheese, but not far from the playground.

Our village isn't much. Nine huts, some little more than tents or half-tents, some little more than doghouses for men.

We'd call our village Dog Town if there wasn't already a gold mine by that name, for the same reason. The huts are set out helter-skelter, paths between, leading to the mess hall and beyond, to the river.

No huts are far from the river except mine and Red's. Horses and carts are kept farther downstream. My goats are near me. I want to be able to hear them in case of trouble. That's another reason I live away from the others. They don't want to be near my goats. The goat pen is coyote-proof. Even mountain-lion-proof. Red built it for me

The men are here for the tungsten. There are only a few women and children, come to be with their men and help out. I've no people of my own here. I was hired to help with the cooking and the laundry.

●   ◑   ○   ◐   ●

Last night I heard the squeak, squeak of the swing and looked out the window and there was that girl.

Who ever heard of a child alone out here in our playground swinging in the moonlight? Though I expect she goes into the goat pen to be safe, maybe cuddles up with the kids to keep warm. There's no place for her to have come from. We're a long ways from anywhere. It's as if she dropped from the sky.

She must live off the smell of sage. How else could she stay alive, scrabbling about from rabbit brush to black brush? Perhaps she milks our nannies in the middle of the night.

The children saw her first several days ago, but they never said a word till Jenny told me. They knew their mothers wouldn't want her around, considering they're always talking about another mouth to feed (that's what they say about Red all the time, and he eats like a bird).They saw her in the playground swinging just as I did. She runs every time they get near, but she came out once to Jenny. Wouldn't you know ... to somebody three years old. I suppose she thought Jenny couldn't tell about it, but she could and just as clear as could be. Jenny said she was dirty and that she had funny eyes and that she'd been whipped. "Worse than any of us," she said, eyes wide with the wonder of it.

"How do you know?"

"I saw the marks."

I'm the one looks after all the orphaned and wounded creatures (including poor old Red). The mothers are right, we don't want another mouth to feed, but a child is a child, and right and wrong is right and wrong.

● ◑ ○ ◐ ●

I went out when the moon was high and put a piece of cornbread on the teeter-totter, then came back and sat in the shadow on my stoop and watched. I had a lariat looped and ready to go. Who I caught (in a manner of speaking) was old Red/Gray. I told him what I was doing and how, so far, she hadn't shown herself, though the moon was about to go down. I told him what Jenny had said.

He sat beside me and rolled himself a cigarette. It was the closest he'd gotten to me (or anybody) in all this time. Any other man would have taken the lariat from me and said he could do it better.

With the moon still up and the old man's company, I felt

as happy as I have in a long time. We didn't say a word, just looked at how everything was silvery, and listened to the creek — sounding silvery.

Finally he said, "When we get her, what will we do with her?"

I liked how he said we. "What do you think we ought to do?"

"It might be harder than you think. I'll bet she won't be anything like these children here. Jenny's right, she's been treated bad."

I had a funny feeling he was talking about himself more than about this girl. "*You!*" I said, but I stopped myself from the rest of it, though I got chills up and down my spine from thinking of it. I changed my "*You!*" (which I'd shouted out louder than I meant to) to "*You'll* help."

He looked at me as if he suspected what I was really going to say. I said, "If I could just coax her to come to me." (I was thinking, if I can coax her, maybe I can coax him, old Gray/ Red, to come out of himself a little.) "If I could just convince her we don't whip children. Anyway, *I* don't."

He looked at me. Thought. Said, "She won't come."

"How do you know?" But I knew how he knows or thinks he knows.

"You'll have to tame her first." All the time I was thinking: Well, just how tame are you, old man?

I wish I could think of things to talk about that would make him tell me about himself, but I don't ever hardly even dare say thank you for all the things he does for me.

We sat a while longer. Coyotes howled, and I started to worry about girl. I got up, thinking to go take a look in the goat pen to see if she was safe.

"Don't," Red said.

So I didn't. Then I said, "It's time we gave up for tonight."

"Leave the cornbread."

"Goodness knows what'll eat it."

We don't have that much cornmeal. You can't grow it here because some critter always gets the ears before we do. Red fenced a tiny garden for me — fenced it a foot deep under the ground and across the top, too, because of the gophers. We got some squash and green beans, but you can't grow corn that way.

● ◑ ○ ◐ ●

There are a couple of men here I stay away from. Most of the men are more bluster than bite, but there are two …. They shot my tame raven. (That raven could even say a few words: "Land's sake," and, "Oh p'shaw." Things I say to myself when I'm alone. It could bark like a dog. I'd named him Jack.) I saw one of them shoot it while the other stood by. I thought to run out and stop him, but I didn't dare. They already call me old witch and old crow. I was glad Red was off someplace that day. He'd have tried to stop them and got himself hurt.

Anyway, two nights later, somebody shoots the girl. I don't know who did it, but I suppose one of those two. I heard the bangs as if right in my ear. Two. Whoever did it must have been standing by my window. I heard the crunch-crunch of somebody running off right after. If I talk about it, next thing they'll be shooting me. They'll say they thought it was a coyote. A coyote on the swing? They wouldn't say fox. Everybody knows how much I like foxes. Or maybe they would say fox just to torment me.

I run out. Red is there already. There she is, not dead though.

She's not a cute child. Stringy. Starving. And I've never seen anybody this dirty. She's wearing a sort of sack and nothing else. Scratchy. Not burlap but might as well be. There's something odd with her eyes. The iris is striped both black and green, and there's a membrane at the corner that isn't supposed to be there. As if she were a lizard. Tied around her neck with a blue cord there's … a thing. I have no idea what it is. Smooth, gray — looks to be basalt with green streaks of copper across it. You can find rocks like that around here, but this one is polished and shaped and contains a square chunk of magnetite.

She's conscious but she doesn't make a sound. Like any wounded wild thing I'm afraid she'll bite. Red is, too. We both keep back. She looks to be shot in the side. One bullet must have missed. At least they didn't use the old buffalo rifle. Looks to be a .22. Thank goodness.

Then she reaches up to me and I know she won't bite. Besides, the way she reaches, bite or not, I don't care anymore. She says, "Ah. Bah" I take it as "Ma." I reach for her. But it's Red gathers her up first, gentle as could be, and puts her in my arms after I stand up. I take her to my cabin and put her on my table, my pillow under her head. Red boils water and sharpens a kitchen knife. While I'm waiting for him to be ready, I cut the sack she wears off with my sewing scisors. I cut away a lot of her matted hair, too. There's just not going to be the combing of any of it.

We try to give her wine to knock her out some, but she won't take it. Locks her mouth and turns her head away. Red says to leave her be, so we have to get the bullet out while shes wide awake. She doesn't make a sound. In fact, she has no expression all through it, neither when refusing the wine nor when Red is cutting into her. I wish she'd yell. I wouldn't feel quite so bad if she'd make a noise.

Getting the bullet out, Red knows what he's doing. I'm not surprised. It's as if I always knew he could do most anything.

Poor old man. Afterwards he looks older than ever, exhausted and in some sort of pain of his own. I try to get him to drink some of the wine before going off to his tent. "Elder-berry," I say. "I made it myself." But he won't.

We wrap her in the quilt and put her on my cot. After he leaves, I lie on the floor (my clothes on), but I can't sleep. I'm cold. The girl has my quilt wrapped around her.

Later I hear her crying. She does it so quietly, at first I don't know what's making that breathy, panting sound. I think: It's about time she let herself feel something. I want to touch her, but I know better than to show I heard.

●　◑　○　◐　●

At first she's in no shape to be out and about. I don't think people know we have her … except maybe the one who shot her. Or they don't care. And nobody cares much what I do as long as I keep doing my jobs, and nobody cares what Red does at all. He stays with her when I'm out busy with what I was hired for. He tells her stories. One evening I come back and sit on the stoop listening — that whispery voice of his that doesn't sound out. I can't hear much, but just the raspy, breathy sound is soothing. I hate to go in, because I'll have to make supper for the girl first thing and she won't eat it anyway. She's starved for sure, but she won't eat just anything. She sniffs, thinks, then decides. As if she's not used to our food. I try to tempt her with special things, but her taste seems hit-or-miss. I just can't tell what she'll hate next. When I finally do go in, Red has already made stew. I should have known. She's picked out all the carrots, laid them carefully on the quilt, but ate the rest.

"Well, I can tell you're not a rabbit."

She hides her head under my quilt and says her usual, "Bah. Ah."

So far that's all she's ever said. I don't think that "Bah" is "Mah." I'm beginning to wonder if she can talk at all. I think there's something wrong with her tongue. I try to look in her mouth, but she scratches me. I don't have to look all the way in. I can see her tongue when she says "Bah." It seems too short. And I think she never saw a teapot or a fork. She turns things over and wonders about them. I don't think she ever saw an oil lamp or matches.

● ◑ ○ ◐ ●

As soon as she's able to be up and around a bit, and we leave her alone now and then, she steals. Hides things in pack-rat places. Knives, scissors, food (even carrots), summer hats, winter hats, sweaters, canteens she fills with water or goats' milk (the milk sours quickly). She doesn't eat the food she hides. She wraps it carefully, as though she thinks to keep it. I have to smell it out when it gets rotten. (Mice are coming in more than ever.) There's a purpose in all this. She's getting ready to take off. Though I can't imagine how she could carry all this or where she'd go.

I give her things, but it doesn't help. I give her my warmest wool socks. First thing I know they've disappeared.

*   *   *   *   *

So far I've managed to avoid calling her anything. Odd, because I always name my wounded or orphaned creatures, my crows, my baby skunk .... (Red says it's a wonder I haven't nursed a wounded mouse.) They all had names. I think it's that I'm a little afraid of her. What does she want with knives and scissors? Then I come home one evening and hear Red calling her Sage. "Better than Snake Weed," I say, though I'm thinking she might be more like snake weed.

I've already put the rest of the sharp things up where I don't think she can reach, but I know she could get anywhere she wants. She's a lot smaller than I am, but she's a lot more spry.

Then there's the lamps. I keep them in the wall sconces all the time. I hide the oil and the matches up in the eaves with the knives, but if I can get up there, she could get up better. I think the matches are going, one by one.

*   *   *   *   *

By now everybody knows she's here with me. They're calling her the witch's child. They call her that because I'm their witch. Any woman of a certain age and even moderately ugly, one that likes to live away from others, gets to be a witch. Once everybody got sick and they blamed it on me though I got just as sick as any of them. And they're suspicious of anybody that takes in wounded wild things as I do. Of course having a raven made me all the more a witch. It's as if instead of a black cat.

Sage has mostly been quiet all this time. I always did like quiet people — like Red — but I'm thinking I should talk to Sage or she'll never speak. Maybe she could at least understand a few more words than my, "Oh p'shaw!" I start naming things. "This here's a cup. This here's a lamp. This, a blouse. This, a sweater. Feel how this is wool. And this, cotton. This here we're doing is washing our hands."

She likes my blue blouse with the lacy collar best. (On her, it's a dress.) She looks frightened whenever I take it to wash it. She actually sits under the line waiting for it to dry. Then puts it on still damp.

Now that she's been cleaned up and hair cut … . It's too short, but she doesn't look bad even so. Her nose is small and pointy, her hair is white-blond. My blue blouse suits her better than it does me. She looks not at all like a witch's child, much more fairy — more fey, though they don't stop calling her that. Knowing them, I know they never will. (I'm the one with witch-colored hair, straight, black, streaked with gray.) Her eyes make her look so odd. Even I wonder, now and then, if she really *is* a witch's child.

But then she starts being the witch's child in truth. She starts to steal knives from everybody, not just me. When the children try to get near her, she claws them. Of course she clawed me earlier on when I tried to look in her mouth. I should have cut her nails a long time ago. They look extraordinarily strong. I wonder if I could have.

● ◑ ○ ◐ ●

Then … . It's a soft, cool, moonlit evening — everybody outside to be in it. Lopsided gibbous moon. Shadows long. The shadow of the teeter-totter and the swing looking out of shape. Catty-cornered. Everything catty-cornered.

We've heard mountain lions screeching and caterwauling, sometimes right here in our little village. This is worse. I have no idea what it is or where it comes from. I think of all sorts of animals, wounded, dying, or, more like it, furious, frenzied. It seems to come from everywhere. It's like a screech owl and banshee and pack of fighting cats all at once. The whole camp stands still. All you can do is drop what you're holding and cover your ears.

Then it stops and I see her — my blue blouse — up at the top of one of the cottonwoods by the creek.

Men gather under the tree. Practically right away two of them start chopping it down, one on each side. They make the cuts, one above the other. The tree will fall exactly where they want it to.

There are several men leaning on their rifles. How can grown men, some with children of their own, even think to shoot a child? Of course they don't think she really is one. And, well, she's been making a lot of trouble.

The tree falls — exactly where they wanted it to, slanting along the river. All sorts of smaller trees come down with it. I can't believe she's not hurt. But then I see my blue blouse off towards another, smaller, tree. They shoot. At first I think at her, and I run forward to protect her, but then I see the dust fly up on the ground around her. They keep shooting. It's just for fun. As if there hasn't been any shooting fun for a long time.

I yell, "Wait! She'll come to me." I don't know why I say

that. She never has before. She's never done one single thing I said, even when I knew she understood.

Then — lucky or unlucky, I don't know which — the magpie flies out, straight up from where the tree went down. Flies off with a squawk. Everybody steps back. They all salute. They look at me as if it's my bird — the witching bird, worse than my raven — but they let me through.

I scramble over the brush towards my blue blouse. The brush grabs at me. I'll be nothing but scratches. My clothes catch on the branches, but I pull away and rip them.

I don't know how much language she's picked up. Probably more than she lets on, but I don't say much more than, "Sage," and, "Come," and, "Everything's all right," which it isn't. I say them like I talk to all my creatures. It's the tone of voice that counts.

No doubt she'd be able to get away from me if she wanted to. No doubt she knows they'd shoot her — yet again. I'll not be surprised if they shoot me. Though how are they going to run their mess hall, get all their laundry done, without me? One man has brought out a whip. I'm not sure whether that's for me or Sage.

Where is Red? My poor old man? I hope he stays hidden. He'll get himself in trouble if he tries to protect me.

I reach out to her and she to me. I grab her wrist, my hand circling around it all the way. How thin she still is.

It takes a while for us to get out from under all the branches and twigs. Both of us get more scratches and our clothes more torn than ever. Nobody moves or says a word. They just wait. A boy throws a stone. She deserves it, the way she's been treating the children. One of the men gives him a slap. There's just that one stone. It doesn't start anything. Everybody just stands and waits.

Finally we get away from all those branches. Now I'm really scared, but they move away as if they're afraid of us. I move carefully and hang on tight to Sage. I start back to my hut, but before we get there, I hear the whip. At first I just hear the crack of it, and then it lands on us. We run. Right on past my shack. We feel the whip once more before we head straight out into the desert.

This is all done in silence. Then I hear one loud, "Good riddance." Meant for both of us, I'm sure. They'll have a hard time without me, but I'm sure they think it's worth it to be rid of the girl. Then they shoot a dozen times. I look back. It's not at us. It's in the air. Just for fun again.

By now it's dark, but there's that gibbous moon. At first we go as fast as we can. We stumble and fall, but hurry on. Then I turn towards the stream. I don't want to get lost, and we'll need water. She outruns me. Out scrabbles me. Part of the time she's on all fours. Hands and feet, not knees. It's a better way in the almost-dark. Pretty soon I have to slow down.

Sage is far ahead already, but I have to stop and rest. I think, Well, there she goes. That's the last of her. I sit on a downed willow. Nothing but desert on each side of the creek. There's no place to go except along its banks. It's still warm now, but it'll be cold soon. I wonder how long we'll last. If *I'll* last? Sage has done it before. *She'll* last.

I don't wish she'd never come. Any more than I wish my wounded raven had never come, though he was a lot of extra work, too. And he did peck me, especially at the beginning. That was just in order to find out what I was made of. Could be Sage acts as she does for the same reason. Wondering what

I'm made of, same as I wonder about her.

Coyotes yip. Not far off. The breeze is picking up. Are my goats locked in? What with all these goings-on, I suppose the people forgot them. Or they remembered, and there'll be goat stew by tomorrow, poor things. When they were babies I brought them in to my hut when it was cold. We were friends. I'll miss them. But "Good riddance" cuts both ways. I haven't been happy here. Red is the only person I really like. (Not counting the children, that is.) I hope he'll be all right without me. I wonder where he was through all this. I wonder where he is. Witch! I wish I really was one.

Then I hear crunch, crunch, crunching. Uneven. Somebody with a limp. Somebody breathing hard. I don't wait to make sure. "Red?"

Of course Red. And with bundles and a full backpack. No wonder he's breathing hard. He collapses in front of me but only for a minute, then starts to unpack some of the things, sweaters, blankets, clothes, salve for scratches and whip wounds. Matches. Fishing line. I couldn't have conjured up more good things if I'd been a witch in truth.

He lights a small fire. "They may see it. For sure they'll smell it, but they won't bother with us anymore." He begins to lay out milk and cheese when … of course, though this time no crunch, crunches … here is Sage, come slently, from the other direction. Hunkering down like an animal as if to tell us, Don't hurt me, I'll not do any harm. She's never liked being hugged before, but this time she lets us. We both hug her at the same time. I get the feeling that Red's hugging me and wouldn't dare do it any other way. I'm hugging him, too, and I wouldn't dare do it any way but this.

Then we both work to soothe her scratches. Then Red puts salve on my scratches and whip marks. (Am I to be thought a witch because I have a cream that takes the pain away? I suppose so. I was the one kept the yeast for the bread alive. That's suspect, too.) My blue blouse is a rag, but Red has thought to bring another, and another for me. Two sweaters, a blue one for Sage.

We change clothes and wrap ourselves in blankets. Sage cuddles up with me. Red, discreetly, behind us. I have a funny feeling, sleeping next to a thing that can make that noise, but I guess I don't have to be afraid of mountain lions. She could out-yowl any of them. The wind picks up. The fire goes out. Rather than get up and feed it logs, I move back against Red. He turns and puts his arm around us. It feels perfectly natural.

●　○　○　○　●

At dawn we pack up and move — upstream, towards the mountains. Red insists on carrying most of the bundles. I hate to see him limping along, leaning over. I think I'm in better shape than he is. I insist on carrying one blanket and some of the food or I just won't move. I make Sage help with a small bundle of food and the smallest canteen. (Empty now. We'll need to fill them later, when the creek will be deep in a canyon and we can't climb down to it.) She doesn't object.

As we go higher, she gets more and more nervous. Or maybe excited. Even with the extra weight of the bundle, she gives a little jump every now and then, but I don't think it's out of happiness. She's starting to pant. Pretty soon she's the one leading. We don't mind until she tries to turn us away from the stream, off into the desert. I'm guessing it's a hundred in the shade. Maybe more. We try to ask her why, but she can't tell us. She says her usual "Bah'" and "Ah." She points … not as we do with a finger, but with her fist. She punches out towards the left. When we go on upstream, she doesn't follow.

Red says, "Let's let her show us what she needs to." I had hoped to get higher and cooler. We'll miss the shade. We didn't bring hats. Even Red didn't think to bring any. We can't go out there without them. Before we leave the brush and trees, we make some hats … or, rather, hattish things out of branches with leaves. We fill the canteens.

As we head out — into what looks like emptiness, but isn't — lizards scurry, a rattlesnake warns from a few yards away, but Sage hardly bothers to step aside. I wonder if she knows what it is. Stink bugs raise their hind ends to stink us, a horned toad lumbers away, lucky not to get stepped on, a road runner runs off … .

By afternoon we're all worn out. Even Sage doesn't jump anymore. Mostly it's the heat that tires us so. I take the small canteen from her. We've drunk quite a bit from all of them. I'm getting worried we may run out before we can get back to the creek. Of course we could hike back by moonlight, when its cooler. Cold, actually. We'll have the opposite problem.

But then I hear buzzing. At first I think it's the desert. It does seem a desert sound. I notice it stays with us, and then I see it comes from that stone around Sage's neck. Red and I give each other a look. Sage walks faster, but poor Red … . I take the big canteen from his shoulder. He lets me, though he insists on keeping most of the bundles.

We come to a place where rocks have been as if tossed from

above. There are more and more as we walk on. And then we come to the edge of a crater, and in it a huge, twisted, shattered thing. Big as a house and kind of like one. *Two* houses. *Three!* One side all black and the other all white. I never saw anything like it. Red and I just stand there while Sage squats down beside us and hugs herself — as if she were cold.

● ◗ ○ ◖ ●

They lived for a while. Four of them. They had barrels of things to drink, but some were broken. At any rate, they're all empty now. They're chubby, soft, with big stomachs and thin legs. I wonder if they'd have been able to climb out of the crater if they tried. They sat in the shade of the wreckage on hammock-like things of wire and cloth, their empty barrels beside them. They moved as the sun turned. You can see the back-and-forth marks in the sand. When the sun rose to noon and no shade at all, they wore bits of metal and cloth for hats. If they're anything like us, they wouldn't last long without their drinks.

What would you do if you wanted to save your child? Or what if she was the only one left who wasn't hurt? And you knew you couldn't last in this awesome and awful place. How far to water? How far to help? You'd send the only able-bodied one out, or maybe out to save herself if she could.

But, no. As Red and I walk in among the creatures, we see an entirely different story. Sage, the little slave, sent to do the hardest, most dangerous work of going for help. The others, too high-class to do it. "We'll just rest here in the shade until you bring back food and water." How could they know how long it would take? The scratches on Sage's back that looked like beatings *were* from beatings.

But then why did she come back here? Eagerly. *Maybe* eagerly. At least agitated. It's that stone she wears. Maybe she couldn't help but come. When we got close enough it started to call her.

Red and I walk in among them while Sage hunkers down hugging herself again, turned away from the wreck, shivering even in this heat but expressionless as usual.

None seem wounded. They're fine. They wear silky things, and they all wear blue — the exact blue of my blouse — while she came to us dressed in that brown, scratchy bag. One by one, Red checks them. All are dead. He also checks the mouth of one of them. "Their tongues are like ours," he says.

We put our arms around each other. I rest my head on his shoulder, and he rests his head on top of my head. We stand this way for a few minutes. Then he says, "We'll hide out for a while. Up along the stream in the mountains."

"She can't talk … ever. Did they do that to her?"

"I suppose."

"I'll teach her to read and write."

"And when she gets to be some civilized … it's the wild things will civilize her … then we'll go to town. The big town …."

" … and get her another blue silk blouse."

"Maybe two. And some for you."

Then Red goes to Sage. She flinches when she sees the knife, as though of course something bad will happen to her, but she'll bear it anyway, whatever it is. He cuts the stone off. It's not easy. It buzzes more than ever for a moment, then stops when the cord is cut though. He throws it high and away

— way over the top of the crater. A real baseball kind of pitch. He holds his shoulder afterwards. He shouldn't have done that.

It's coming on twilight. Cooling down. Our water's almost gone. We need to get back to the river before morning or we'll be in trouble. We put on sweaters, take a last drink — partly to lighten our loads — and climb the bank.

For once the desert takes us in as if we belong to it, everything luminous, numinous … . Radiant. Stars … . Turning, turning. The Big Dipper swinging around the Little Dipper. North over our right shoulders. Shooting stars as if for luck.

Whenever I sit down to write too consciously (and I do sometimes) it ends up with no resonance. It looks and feels planned. When I do that it has no … what? Underwear? Underside? This is why Kafka is my favorite writer. Kafka's stories aren't about what they're about. I like them for what they don't say …. Kafka's stories are not about their stories.

—CAROL EMSHWILLER, 2002

ALL I KNOW OF FREEDOM

I'M MAKING DO WITH LESS. AND THEN LESS AND LESS AND less. I'm even eating less. But I don't know if it's better to eat a lot so as to live off my fat later on, or eat less so as to be in practice for not having enough food. I've heard, though, that it you're fat, you stretch your stomach so you need more food to feel satisfied, so I've decided it's better to shrink mine.

I'm practicing for getting out of here.

I won't be able to take anything but the clothes I'll be wearing and what I can stuff in my pockets.

Also I'm hardening myself up for the cold. Sometimes I sleep with the window open no matter what the temperature. I live in the attic. Nobody notices what I do up here. I even have a book though I don't know how to read it.

If I keep quiet and do my jobs I'm practically invisible. Just like Mother said: "It's always good to behave yourself so as not to get noticed." She also said, "Stand up straight, say thank you and please." I don't. I keep quiet and hunch over so as not to be seen.

I was sold for quite a respectable sum. Or so Mother told me, and proudly. I don't blame her. I presume she had to do it. And these are not the worst people to be sold to. I've heard some get beaten. These people don't do that.

Trouble is, now that I'm getting breasts, I can tell that they're beginning to see me no matter how quiet I keep.

I tried to leave before but I didn't get far. I was too young. I didn't realize how hard it would be and how I'd have to be tired and hungry — how I'd have to maybe be freezing or wet. That's part of running away. This time I'll be ready. That time I came back by myself. They didn't even know I had gone.

● ◓ ○ ◑ ●

When they took me, they promised they'd let me go to school so I was glad to go with them, but they never did let me. They kept saying, "Next year," and when it was next year they still said it. Pretty soon even they stopped saying it because it was clear there wasn't going to be a "next year" for me.

There are lots of books around. More than anybody would ever need. I thought maybe I could teach myself to read. I looked at captions under pictures, but there aren't very many pictures and that hasn't helped much. If I waited till the baby was a bit older, surely there would be some simpler books, but I'm not going to wait.

● ◓ ○ ◑ ●

When they first took me, it was just great. I couldn't believe my luck. Plane rides and hotels. Wonderful food — though some of it so odd I didn't dare eat it, and I was homesick every now and then for lentils. They got me the first frilly blouse I ever had … and that was the last, too. It was tan and silky. I did all sorts of things I'd never have had a chance to do except for them — as they kept telling me. That's when I thought I really would get to go to school.

They kept telling me I should be grateful — and I was. Actually I'm still grateful, but I think I've paid them back enough by now. I don't know how long I've been here. I wish I'd had the sense to mark off the years.

The one good thing is, they never whip me. That's what they used to do back home and it's one of the reasons I wanted to get out of there. They always talk sweetly. My so-called father calls me a hundred different things. They all sound good. "Madam, if you'd be so kind … Miss, by your leave." Talking that way is his joke. Like, "My dear, clean the toilet and be quick about it. Sweetheart, change the bed and wash the sheets." (He doesn't even say "sweetheart" or "my dear" to his wife.) Now and then he says, "Miss Whatever-your-name-is … " He really does forget my name and that's why he says "madam" and "my dear." That's odd, too, because they're the ones named me what they wanted me to be. My real name was much too long and complicated for them to remember. They never even tried.

Now that I'm getting breasts my so-called father is looking at me in a different way. All that fancy language he talks, all those "madam"s and "sweetheart"s, "dear lady"s and "by your leave"s might turn into something entirely different. He pinched my breasts as though to see how much they'd grown.

My so-called mother ("Call me Mother in front of people." Though people hardly ever come here) … she was the one decided what to name me when they took me. She wanted something simple and easy to say. She calls me B. I do know that letter. She spells it B-e-e. I know A and C, and E, and some others, too. I like O.

Here, I have to do what I don't want to all the time. I mean *all* the time. Easier to list what I *don't* do than what I do. And I can't think of a thing I don't do.

They'll miss me when I'm gone. I'm going to have to be careful, though I don't think they can risk setting the cops on me since I'm here llegally. I didn't realize that until recently. I'm a secret. They bought me when I was ten. To get me in the country they pretended I was their daughter and got some sort of phony passport.

I don't want to do anything to put the baby in danger. I'll leave at night when they're home. I'm sorry for the house plants. I don't think my so-called parents will remember that they'll need to water them. Maybe they'll forget about the baby, too. At least it'll make a fuss.

There's a big wall around their place and an iron gate that's always locked. There's broken glass along the top of the wall and sharp points on top of the gate. They say to keep robbers out, but I think it's for keeping me in.

But I have the gate key now. They've turned the house upside down. They've frisked me and more than once. He did it. Looked everywhere on and *in* my body. Then, for the first time, they whipped me. I almost told them where the key was, but I managed not to. Finally they got tired and stopped. Then my so-called father scared me in another way than pinching breasts. He said I was a pretty girl but he could make it so I wasn't if I didn't behave myself.

But they're not all bad. They were kind enough to give me a day to rest up after that. I guess they knew I'd need it. "Mother" even served me supper in bed. She said, "You'll get breakfast in bed, too, if you show us where that key is." They were extra nice all day (I got dessert. I got a heating pad on my sore spots) but I said I didn't know so I didn't get breakfast in bed.

Next day I pretend I'm worse off than I am. I hobble around and sit down (sideways) whenever I get to sit. They'll never think I could go off tomorrow. Weather report says rain. Perfect.

●　◑　○　◐　◉

Middle of the night and I'm off — my pockets full of peanut butter sandwiches. Now all I have to do is find a school. I'm not sure what a school looks like even though I've seen pictures. I know sometimes it's a little school and sometimes it's a great big building school. At least it should say *school* on it. I can read that. It's got two Os.

After I let myself out, I hide the key under a big tree next to a parking lot a few blocks away. I dig it in nice and deep. That's what I did last time I ran away and how I got back in before they found out. That time they didn't even know the key was gone. They'd left it on the hall table.

It's drizzling but I have a big black garbage bag over me. I walk on down the road, turn a corner and then another corner. Walking anywhere I want. I keep turning corners just because I can.

This right now is what it's like to be free. Sometimes I run even though I have a lot of heavy stuff in my pockets. Sometimes I hop and jump. All I know about freedom is what I know right now.

I turned so many corners at first I don't suppose I get far, but now I'm getting somewhere. I've taken smaller and smaller roads and this one is the smallest of all.

Then I hear something crying. I hold still and listen. There's a big bush by the side of the road that would make a good place to hide. That's got to be where the creature is. I move closer. The crying stops.

Since I don't know what it is, I'm a little worried about reaching around in there. But I'm thinking how I know what it feels like to be wet and homeless even though I haven't been that way very long.

I crawl under the bushes and feel around until I touch wet fur. The creature cries again. It doesn't bite me. I pull it out and under the streetlight.

It's nothing but skin and bones and so dirty and matted, I hardly know what it is. But then … it's just what I've always wanted and knew I'd never get to have. I even have a name all picked out. I don't know yet if it's a boy or girl, but I'll call it Mr. O'Brien. There was once a man came to visit my so-called parents and that was his name. I was in the kitchen cleaning up and he looked in at me with curiosity and kindness. I would have said something but he took me by surprise. They usually kept me hidden when people visited. If he had come again I would have been ready to say something, or I'd have made some sort of sign, but he never came back. Usually when there were guests "Mother" locked me in the attic. I only saw that man for a few seconds, but I'll remember him forever.

This Mr. O'Brien here is some kind of puppy, I don't know what kind. It's mostly brownish unless this is dirt. I hope we get to be friends and that it grows up to be big and dangerous. I'd like to see my so-called father try to come after me then.

I put Mr. O. in with me, under my big black garbage bag.

We walk until there aren't any more street lights. I'm

looking for the real Mr. O'Brien, or a school, whichever comes first, though right now any dry warm place would do.

●   ◑   ○   ◐   ●

But no good place comes along. Then we see a big doghouse at the end of a dog run but no dog there and it's quite a ways from the house. At least it's out of the rain. We crawl in. I get stiff all curled up there and have to stretch my legs out into the rain. We don't sleep much. We leave as soon as it's even a little bit light. I share one of my peanut butter sandwiches with Mr. O'Brien.

That morning just about at dawn (we've already walked for a while) I see a school way out here in the middle of nowhere. At least it says SCHOOL on it. It's no bigger than a little house and has a big back yard with an old sand pile and a side and two swings. I know about those from a long time ago.

I push on the doors and look in the windows. It looks abandoned. But what a nice place to hide. Two rooms. A few little chairs and tables. It would be nice if some books were still there, too, but I don't see any.

Except I can't get in. I try all the windows but I don't want to break any.

We give up and go on.

I share another peanut butter sandwich with Mr. O.

At evening we come to another school. This one is entirely different. It's big and it looks scary. It says SCHOOL on it but almost all the people there are grown ups. And some look very old. They're kind of raggedy, too. The men have beards and the women wear long skirts. There's a big banner right under where it says SCHOOL but of course I can't read it.

They're all very busy, but not doing school-like things. They've rigged up all sorts of unschoolish tents, and there are canvas shades over what looks like a cooking place with lots of pots. In the big back field, they're building a huge shiny long thing with no windows at all. Hard to tell what it is because of the scaffolding around it. It takes up the whole field. People in neat while coveralls are working on it.

I'm going to ask somebody what's going on, but I'd like to ask a kid, except there aren't very many around. Odd, but all the kids I see are girls and they're all wearing skirts.

I wait and watch a long time. Good that Mr. O'Brien seems to like being with me and that he's a nice quiet dog. We're both the shy type. We share another peanut butter sandwich. We're going to run out pretty soon.

We're sitting behind some big bushes to eat and we're not paying attention. All of a sudden here's just what I wanted, a girl about my age practically right beside us. She's wearing a long torn dirty skirt.

First thing she says is — that is, after we stare at each other for a couple of minutes — "I wish I could wear blue jeans like yours, but they won't let me. Skirts are always in the way. Are you trying to hide? What's your dog's name?"

"Mr. O'Brien"

She sits down right next to us and looks as if she'd like to share our sandwich with us, but I can smell what's cooking in those pots under the canvas shades so I know she'll get food.

"Why are you hiding?"

"We're not. We're just having lunch. What does that say there, under where it says *School?*"

"Can't you read?"

I really am embarrassed. I almost say I can except I need glasses. But I decide not to lie.

"It says *Prepare, the end is nigh*."

"The end of what?"

"The world of course, silly." She looks at me as if I really am dumb. "It's in the middle of ending right now, can't you tell? Everybody knows that. All you have to do is look around. And look how hot it is already and it isn't even lunch time."

Have they kept me so isolated back home I don't even know it's the end of the world? I wouldn't be surprised, though. When I was cleaning up in the kitchen, I heard the news when they listened to it and things did sound bad. Lots of wars and earthquakes and horrible toxic spills and even right near us there was a gas truck crashed into a house and exploded and killed everybody and burned up four houses.

"You have to get ready." she says.

"How? What should I do?"

"You can join us. We're going to a better world. We need more young girls. It's going to take a long time to get somewhere and it's the young women who'll have to have a lot of babies on the way so we can start up the new population. We won't need a lot of men. I'm going to have all the babies I can. I'm precious. You would be, too, if you joined us."

I'm thinking how lucky it is that I ran into these people. "If I join can you teach me to read?"

"Sure, and I'm good at reading."

I can't believe my luck.

"You can't bring a dog, though. You'll have to get rid of him."

"Right now?"

Maybe I'm not as lucky as I thought.

"Well, pretty soon, anyway. You can find it a good home, though I don't suppose this world will last much longer what with all that's been happening, but dogs don't live a long time anyway. He might die before the world ends so that's all right."

Not so all right with me.

"Come on, they'll be glad to have you join up. I'll ask them if you can keep the dog till we leave. They'll probably say yes because, like I said, they really do want more girls like us." She says again, "We're the most important ones of all."

●　○　○　◑　●

Turns out they do want me. I make them all happy, especially when I say I'm running away and my people wouldn't dare tell the police since I was illegal in the first place. They think I've come to the exact right spot. "Sent by God," they say. But they sure don't like Mr. O'Brien. ("That's a growing dog. He'll eat a lot.") I promise I won't ever take more than my share and I'll split my food with him. I tell them I'm used to making do with less.

Turns out Eppie … the girl … (It's short for Hephzibah. Her mother has a funny name, too, Ziporah) … is a bit younger than I am, she's only eleven. Turns out she and I will share a little tent behind her family's big one. Mr. O. will sleep in there with us. (Her parents sure don't want him around. He's getting not so shy and is very bouncy. I have to keep an eye on him all the time. He likes to chew shoes.)

They take me inside their spaceship and show me where

I'll be living after we leave. The rooms for mothers are all along the side and the nursery is across from them. What looks like the walls will be the floors after we get going. There's a play room for when the babies get older. It's full of all kinds of great toys, most I never saw before in my whole life. Well, I do know my so-called parents kept me ignorant but I didn't know how much I didn't know. But now that Eppie is teaching me to read I'll be able to read all that. Books can tell you everything you need to know. I've got a really good start. Eppie says I'm going faster than she thought anybody could. I think I actually did learn something just looking at those books and thinking about the letters.

I do a lot of work here but, since I'm free, it's entirely different. They tell me I'm one of their best helpers because I know how to do a lot of things and I'm a pretty good cook, too, and getting better.

Those people in white have better tents than the rest of us do, and the head preacher even has the whole upstairs of the school just for his offices and living space. We listen to "our" radio station all day long. They … we keep asking for more money all the time though they seem to have a lot already. They keep saying, "God will reward you for your generosity."

● ◑ ○ ◐ ●

Meanwhile my breasts are getting bigger all the time. I'll have to get a bra some way. Eppie hasn't reached that stage yet so I don't think I can ask her anything. I don't feel close to Eppie's mother, but she's the one comes to me, and about another thing, too. I didn't know anything about that either, which shows how I wasn't told anything back at my so-called home. Eppie's mother keeps saying, "Isn't that nice. That means now you can have babies. We're going to need lots." She says, "I'll be taking care of you. I'm the midwife."

Things are moving right along — not only with my breasts. The scaffolding is off the spaceship and they're about to stand it up. There's a new kind of scaffolding for that. Also there's been a lot more end of the world disasters, floods and earthquakes, and right here a tornado that ruined a lot of houses in town and killed eight people including a baby, but it went right around us so everybody here knows that God is in favor of what we're doing.

● ☽ ○ ☾ ●

There are only four young men that are supposed to be our … "husbands," I guess you'd call them. They're supposed to be the fathers of all the new babies. They're only bringing a few males compared to females. They said they're the best and the healthiest. Only one looks like the sort they're talking about … sort of a hero type … curly yellow hair … . He doesn't appeal to me at all. Too good looking. I think I'm sort of in love with the real Mr. O'Brien. He's not handsome, but I could see on his face how kind he was. The other three "husbands" are young. One, like Eppie, is only eleven.

Then that oldest handsome boy Jed (for Jedediah) … grabs me and kisses me before I hardly know what's happening. I had been out throwing the garbage in the garbage bins and he followed me and pushed me down behind the bins. That boy … . He goes around grinning and looking us girls over. He knows he's one of the few fathers and he's already lording it over everybody, like he thinks he's the most important person on the trip. I suppose most everybody picked to be one of the fathers would act that way, but I sure don't like it. Eppie and I feel special, too, but we don't go around as if we were queens.

Thank goodness Mr. O'Brien is with me … as he always is. I try to fight the boy off and then Mr. O'Brien actually bites him. Grabs his wrist and pulls him away. Draws blood. The boy kicks Mr. O. hard, but Mr. O. doesn't stop. Grabs him by his pants leg and rips it.

The boy says, "Look where he bit me."

"It's just scratches."

"You have to sew these pants up," and I say, "Okay," and he says, "Not only that, but you're going to have to do this one of these days, why not now? We can get things started."

He's been boasting about exercising every day up in the ship's gym. I could feel how strong he is. He probably was chosen for his good looks, too. I don't want to ever have a stuck-up little baby that looks like him.

"You're not the only boy that's coming."

"One of these years you'll have to pick me. That's the rule. We have to mix up our genes."

"Maybe you'll be dead before it happens. Or I will be. I hope so, anyway."

He squeezed my breasts even harder than my so-called father did back there at home. This is the first I start thinking about what really is going on here.

Just as I wished him to, Mr. O protected me. Even bit hard enough to draw blood. I feel safe with him around.

Eppie and her family are going to be away for a couple of days while they go say goodbye to Eppie's grandparents. They have to leave Eppie's little brother with them. He can't come because of a heart murmur. Lots of others are off to say good-bye, too. People over forty aren't allowed to come. I can see why. They wouldn't last long enough.

I'm going out to find Mr. O'Brien a good home. ("The dog has got to go. We can't be a Noah's Ark. The lord will supply the needed animals when we get there." Actually they're bringing some cows and chickens but just so as to have eggs and milk for the trip.) They're telling us younger ones to get ready to name all the new kinds of animals we'll find when we get there. There won't be any need for meat so God will leave those animals out.

I don't ever need a leash. Mr. O. sticks right by me all the time. I think he remembers that I rescued him and warmed him with my own body. I'll bet he remembers sleeping in that doghouse.

He's gotten pretty big now, just as I wanted, and he'd willingly die defending me if he had to. He's exactly everything I wished for.

It's so hot everybody in town is just sort of waiting for it to be fall and be cooler. The town is all shut up during the heat of the day. Even lots of stores are closed from noon to three. People are at the movies or sitting next to their air conditioners. Some people spend a lot of time walking up and down in the big cool grocery store and the K-Mart. Eppie says, "Where we're going it'll be a wonderful new world like this one used to be. God will make it so."

All around town I tell people what a great dog he is and why I need to let him go. After a while I only try where they already have a dog. Nobody wants him and lots of times I wouldn't want him at some of those places either.

When people find out I'm from the end-of-the-world people, they laugh at me. Turns out they call us crazies. One lady said I looked nice and neat compared to some of them, though, she said, Mr. O'Brien looks like he belongs with them. Then she said why didn't I clip him some so he'd be more comfortable in this heat. I hadn't thought of that. She has three dogs of her own and a big fenced-in yard, and she's really nice. She said she boarded dogs and also clipped dogs for people and she knew I couldn't afford it but she'd clip Mr. O. for me anyway.

We went up on her closed-in porch where it was cool and she got water for Mr. O'Brien and ice tea for me. There was a parrot there and she told me to hold out my hand and he flew right to me. Then she got out her clippers and showed me how he should be clipped, and even let me do some of it. Mr. O. looked a lot better after we got through with him. I asked again if she wouldn't take him. She said she couldn't afford the food for such a big dog and she said she already had two cats and the parrot and her three terriers and she needed the rest of her space for boarding. Then she says, "Why don't you take him out in the country to some farm? If I was Mr. O'Brien, I'd like to live on a farm with lots of room and work to do."

That's such a good idea. I say I'll go look right away.

"But," she says, "if I were you, I'd not go with those crazies. They really are crazies you know. Why don't you come over here and work for me? You've got a knack with animals and I could use a helper."

I don't know what to say, so I say, "But they taught me to read."

She looks at me funny, then realizes she's staring, and looks down at Mr. O. instead, as if she doesn't know what to say either. Finally she says, "Great dog. If he were mine, I wouldn't get rid of him for anything."

● ◑ ○ ◐ ●

I do find a good home for Mr. O. way out on a farm. They're going to change his name to Buster. I'm thinking they'd like his name if they had ever met the real Mr. O'Brien. They're going to keep him tied up until he gets used to them and to me not being there, otherwise he'd follow me back. As I leave, I hear him barking and barking, and then it changes to crying. But they said he'd get used it. They said it always takes a while. And it was cooler out there and there were other dogs and lots of other animals. I would have liked it there myself. But now I'm thinking I gave away the only thing I ever loved, and the only thing that ever loved me.

And then I worry. It was a long hot walk out of town, are they going to give him water? He needs it right away. They seemed like nice enough people but sometimes people forget or don't notice.

As I get back to the group, here's Eppie. She can see that I've been crying. Also that Mr. O. isn't with me.

She says, "Good. You did it. That dog was just too big. I'm glad he's out of our pup tent. Can you picture him bouncing around in a spaceship!"

I have to admit he took up more than his share of the tent.

I say, "I'm worried he's thirsty and they won't give him water. Maybe I should go back and check."

"Are you going to be worrying about that dog all though the whole trip?"

She's right, I *am* going to worry. I say, "Maybe I shouldn't go with you."

But then she gets all upset. "Oh no." She practically yells it, and hugs me. "You're my best friend."

I think I'm her best friend because I'm so ignorant about the world that she can keep telling me things. I do learn a lot from her but I know some of it's wrong. Though I'm certainly grateful for those reading lessons. She wants to be a teacher and she's good at it, but I'm not really her best friend, I'm just her best and most willing pupil.

●　◓　○　◑　◉

We've already packed up most of our belongings and arranged them in our state rooms. My room is next to Eppie's, just as we wanted. The rooms are small, but they have big metal mirrors so they seem larger. We had our choice of colors. I wanted mine to be all woody colors: tans and browns. I knew it would be a long time before I saw any real wood. Eppie's is yellow and blue and white. She put her favorite pictures on the walls. They had to be glued down tight. She couldn't put up pictures in the pup tent but she had these all ready to go. Funny to think of those pictures of handsome men ... I guess they're movie stars ... going all the way off to Paradise where they'll be old men or dead before we even get there. I wonder why she even has them.

I guess I'd most want a picture of Mr. O., but then I'd never stop thinking about him. Except I don't want to ever stop. Besides, I don't know how to get a picture, anyway.

● ◑ ○ ◐ ●

There's a big rally our last night on earth. They talk about the beautiful world God will lead them to out in Proxima Centauri. They keep calling it Paradise, but the moon is out and almost full, and I don't see how any place can be more beautiful than right here. Besides, this world has Mr. O. in it. I do know my so-called father and mother would never find me on that new world, but even so, I'm not sure I want to go. Besides, Mr. O. would keep me safe. He did it before.

The preacher (dressed all raggedy like we're all supposed to be because of renouncing worldly things) … he says … shouts, "And so this evil world will soon burn as if it's hell itself. Parts that don't burn will be covered with water. Already dozens of islands have been lost to the sea. Soon every river will be poisoned. You know it. You know it. You see it already happening. Look at Godless New Orleans. Look at Voodoo-filled Haiti. How God punished them.

"I will not be among you, I'm old and I'm not the best of the best, but you are. You're the chosen."

The moon is so bright I wouldn't even need a flashlight. There's a little breeze and it's cool for a change.

" … and there will be the winds of a hundred hurricanes and they will last a hundred years, and the earth will shake … . You know it. You know it. You've seen it already."

I pretend to head to the bathrooms. Eppie says, "Wait a

minute. This is the best part. He's telling about earthquakes that never stop." But I keep going.

" … earthquakes that never stop … I say again *never*. Never! Imagine it. Imagine."

● ◑ ○ ◐ ●

I reach the farm in the middle of the night. The other dogs there bark like crazy. Luckily they still have Mr. O. tied up in the front of the house. He's almost chewed through his rope. He'd have been free in another day or so. We hug and he cries with joy and so do I. The lights go on in the house and I untie him fast and we run, but not towards the end-of-the-world people. Maybe we can spend the night back in that doghouse.

In the doghouse we find a half-dead kitten. We can't do anything about it until morning so we all just cuddle up together.

From now on I'm going to do the opposite of the end-of-the-world people. I'm going to take in animals, and Mr. O'Brien and this kitten are the first ones.

Except the kitten dies in the night. It was just too bitten up and I didn't have any way to help save it. I had thought about that woman who did grooming. She'd know how to help, but it died before I could get it to her. At least it didn't have to die alone. I told it I loved it and that it was a good kitty. I hope it understood.

● ◑ ○ ◐ ●

The end-of-the-world people leave in the morning. We hear the great roar and see the flash of their going. It lights up the whole sky. It's exciting, and for a minute I wish I was with them. I shout and Mr. O. gives a howl. Then we run, as if to follow it.

We run. And run and run and don't care where. All of a sudden here's that little two-room school that looks like a house. This time I don't think twice. I break a window and we fall inside, all worn out.

We lie there the rest of the day feeling sad … about Eppie being gone, but glad we're here together. We don't even worry about not having anything to eat. When it gets dark, we sleep.

But in the morning, we're hungry and thirsty. There's no water here that works. Everything is turned off. No electricity. I find how to turn the water on under the house. I know about that from home, but I don't know how to turn on the electricity. At least we have something to drink.

I don't know what to do or where to go or how to get food, and then I think about that lady who said I'd be a good helper.

●   ◑   ○   ◐ ●

Mrs. Sindee feeds us and I get hired and I'm going to get paid.

Things do get worse. Everybody wonders where fall got to and if it'll ever cool off. And there's earthquakes where they never had them before, even one right here, and then Mrs. Sindee gets flooded out. I help her clean up after the water goes back down. Good thing is, people go on wanting their animals clipped and boarded sometimes and it finally does cool down. In fact it gets too cold. Mr. O'Brien and I and even Mrs. Sindee … we don't even care. We wear our long underwear and Mr.

O'Brien grows a heavy coat of new fur.

Mr. O'Brien and I live in that old school and so far nobody has found out. And whenever we find a wounded bird or cat or whatever, we rescue it. And everything we rescue turns out to be the best there is just like Mr. O'Brien. We're all making do with less, but we already have seven books.

I wonder if they'll ever reach Proxima Centauri.

PUBLICATION HISTORY

"Baby", *The Magazine of Fantasy & Science Fiction*, 1958

"Pelt", *The Magazine of Fantasy & Science Fiction*, 1958

"Day at the Beach", *The Magazine of Fantasy & Science Fiction*, 1959

"Sex and/or Mr. Morrison", *Dangerous Visions* (ed. Harlan Ellison), 1967

"Al", *Orbit 10* (ed. Damon Knight), 1972

"The Start of the End of It All" (as "The Start of the End of the World"), *Universe 11* (ed. Terry Carr), 1981

"Yukon", *TriQuarterly*, 1986

"If Not Forever, When?", *Psycritic*, 1987

"Moon Songs", original to *The Start of the End of It All*, 1990

"Mrs. Jones", *Omni*, 1993

"Creature", *The Magazine of Fantasy & Science Fiction*, 2001

"Desert Child", original to *Report to the Men's Club*, 2002

"Grandma", *The Magazine of Fantasy & Science Fiction*, 2002

"Boys", *SciFiction*, 2003

"All of Us Can Almost…", *SciFiction*, 2004

"I Live with You and You Don't Know It", *The Magazine of Fantasy & Science Fiction*, 2005

"The Bird Painter in Time of War", *Asimov's Science Fiction*, 2008

"The Lovely Ugly", *Asimov's Science Fiction*, 2010

"All I Know of Freedom", *After: Nineteen Stories of Apocalypse and Dystopia* (ed. Ellen Datlow), 2012

ACKNOWLEDGMENTS

This book would not exist without the support of Carol Emshwiller's children Eve, Peter, and Susan. As literary executor for her mother's estate, Susan provided me with carte blanche to create the book I envisioned, and I hope that the results honor that great trust and leap of faith.

Over the years, I have had conversations with many friends about the work of Carol Emshwiller, and those conversations influenced this selection. When I graduated from high school, James Patrick Kelly sent me a copy of *The Norton Book of Science Fiction* signed by everyone at that year's Sycamore Hill writers conference, including Carol Emshwiller, and I remember the thrill of seeing her signature and wondering what the human being behind some of my favorite stories was like in person. Not too many years later, I had the opportunity to let Carol know that I was the strange kid whose book Jim had asked her to sign. Later, conversations with Christopher Barzak, Richard Bowes, Samuel Delany, Gregory Feeley, John Kessel, Meghan McCarron, and Ann VanderMeer stuck with me enough to affect how I chose stories for this volume. To them and every other enthusiastic Emshwillerian, I feel immense gratitude.

Kelly Link deserves thanks not only for taking the time to write an introduction for this volume, but also for her decades of championing Carol Emshwiller's work. Some of the first books Kelly published with her husband Gavin J. Grant at Small Beer Press were key works by Carol: the novel *The Mount* and the collection *Report to the Men's Club*, and they also published her stories in their zine *Lady Churchill's Rosebud Wristlet* and reprinted Carol's first novel, *Carmen Dog*. Kelly and Gavin's commitment to Carol's work in the first part of the 21st century was essential to many of us being able to appreciate the full range and magic of her writing.

Thank you, too, to Luis Ortiz and Nonstop Press for their editions of *The Collected Stories of Carol Emshwiller*, which made so many hard-to-find stories available once again. Putting *Moon Songs* together would have been vastly more difficult without those volumes. Also important for my work was Luis's important biographical art book *Emshwiller: Infinity x Two: The Art & Life of Ed & Carol Emshwiller*.

The Third Man Books and Third Man Records staff have been a delight to work with. Art director Jordan Williams and designer Amin Qutteineh make the process of design and production a joy and inspiration. Editor-in-chief Chet Weise not only supported my rather off-the-cuff idea to bring this book into the world, but also provided essential work on the manuscript as I rushed to get it finished. I am honored to be able to welcome Carol Emshwiller into the Third Man family; I hope she would like this little home we are giving to her words.

CAROL EMSHWILLER (1921-2019) published her first short story in 1955, and became a regular contributor to science fiction and fantasy magazines as well as literary journals. Her books include the World Fantasy Award-winning collection *The Start of the End of It All*, the Philip K. Dick Award-winning novel *The Mount*, and two volumes of *Collected Stories*. Her short stories won a Pushcart Prize and two Nebula Awards, and in 2005 she received the World Fantasy Award for Life Achievement.

MATTHEW CHENEY is the author of the story collections *The Last Vanishing Man* (Third Man Books) and *Blood: Stories* (Black Lawrence Press), the novella *Changes in the Land* (Lethe Press), and works of nonfiction from Bloomsbury Academic and punctum books.

KELLY LINK is the author of the collections *Stranger Things Happen, Magic for Beginners, Pretty Monsters, Get in Trouble*, and *White Cat, Black Dog* and the novel *The Book of Love*. She has won a Hugo Award, Nebula Awards, received a grant from the National Endowment for the Arts, been a finalist for the Pulitzer Prize, and was a 2018 MacArthur Fellow. She is the co-founder of Small Beer Press (who published multiple books by Carol Emshwiller) and co-edits the occasional zine *Lady Churchill's Rosebud Wristlet*. She is the owner of Book Moon, an independent bookshop in Easthampton, Massachusetts.

www.ingramcontent.com/pod-product-compliance
Lightning Source LLC
Chambersburg PA
CBHW022003310726
48972CB00006B/1495